THE PAIN RETURNS

This time it spr—
so agonizing th—
aware that Zilla—
ask her to ring—— ,out only a croak
emerged from her lips.

Then she saw that she had an audience.
The children were standing beside their Aunt
Zilla, their dark eyes seeming to glow with a
strange luminosity that accentuated the golden
flecks round their pupils. They showed no distress at her agony, in fact she saw with a feverish
horror that they were beginning to smile. The
pain eased slightly, but immediately her stomach lurched and it felt as though all her internal
organs were turning round and round, spinning
faster and faster until she was certain that she
was about to die by some ghastly, internal strangulation. As she lost consciousness she managed to cry out once, a desperate beseeching
appeal for help...

CHILDREN OF THE NIGHT

Also by Margaret Bingley

Devil's Child*
Such Good Neighbours
The Waiting Darkness

*Published by
POPULAR LIBRARY

CHILDREN OF THE NIGHT

MARGARET BINGLEY

POPULAR LIBRARY

An Imprint of Warner Books, Inc.

A Warner Communications Company

POPULAR LIBRARY EDITION

Popular Library® and the fanciful P design are registered trademarks
of Warner Books, Inc.

This Popular Library Edition is published by arrangement with
Judy Piatkus Limited of London.

Cover illustration by Lisa Falkenstern

Popular Library books are published by
Warner Books, Inc.
666 Fifth Avenue
New York, N.Y. 10103

W A Warner Communications Company

Printed in the United States of America

First Popular Library Printing: May, 1989
10 9 8 7 6 5 4 3 2 1

For my son, Alexander—
without whom
I would never have begun.

Author's Acknowledgment

I am extremely grateful to
Mr. R.E.F. Hardy LDS Sheffield
for his invaluable help

The childhood shows the man,
As morning shows the day. Be famous then
By wisdom; as thy empire must extend,
So let extend thy mind o'er all the world.

John Milton, *Paradise Regained*

Judith stood in front of the full length mirror in the narrow hallway and studied her reflection carefully. She was moderately satisfied with what she saw; the suit was well cut, the blouse an immaculate white. Why then should she feel so ridiculously nervous? Why were her hands shaking so much that it was almost impossible to find her car keys in the drawer of the bureau?

She knew why, and chided herself for ever setting out on this supposedly "sensible" course of action. It had all been Sue's idea, but Sue didn't have to go along tonight. Sue was safe at home with her husband of nine years and her two lively, boisterous small boys. It was Judith who had to face up to the result of that so casual discussion that Sue had instigated three months previously. It had seemed like a good idea then; now it didn't. Now it was making her feel physically unwell.

With a sigh of regret for her own weakness in following up Sue's suggestion, Judith closed the door of the bungalow firmly behind her, climbed into the dark blue Mini and set off. She was comforted by the thought that in five hours at the most she would be safely home again.

It took her longer to park the car than she had expected, and she was horrified to find that it was five minutes past eight when she finally reached the doors of Gregory's, a small and friendly restaurant that she herself had suggested they use. At least, always before it had seemed friendly, but tonight the butterflies in her stomach increased as she pushed on the heavy wooden door.

The *maître d'hôtel* appeared immediately, but she recognized his friendly smile for what it was, a well-practiced necessity of his trade since he couldn't possibly remember her. Not that it mattered, now was not the time to become cynical over waiters. She should save some of her analytical thinking for the meeting that lay ahead.

"Mr. Farino's table, please." Her voice, she was relieved to discover, sounded as cool and self-assured as normal. With another expansive smile he led her to the back of the room into one of the alcoves that took up the end section of the restaurant.

Judith had no clear idea of what the man she was meeting would look like, but she did have a fairly clear idea of what he wouldn't look like. All her preconceived notions died abruptly as Mr. Farino stood up to welcome her. He was tall, well over six feet she judged, and had a heavy, solid frame giving off an instant impression of great physical strength. He was dark, the thick wavy hair lightly sprinkled with gray flecks, and as he held out his hand she looked squarely into large, widely spaced soft brown eyes that hinted at depths of sensitivity unusual in a man.

"You're Miss Shaw, I assume?"

There was a trace of an accent, but Judith couldn't place it.

"That's right. I'm Judith Shaw." She sat down as she spoke, busying herself with her shoulder bag in an effort to regain composure.

"And I'm Marc Farino. Would you care for an aperitif?"

"Dry sherry please."

He turned his head slightly and the waiter reappeared.

"Two dry sherries, and the menus now, please."

For a few minutes they were both busy studying the lists before them. There was no need for conversation and Judith was grateful.

Her one consolation all day, when her nerves threatened to overcome her, had been that the man she was meeting, whatever his background, must in his own way feel as inadequate as she did. Why else would he be there? Now she could not believe that was true. He might be many things, but she doubted if inadequate was one of them. In which case perhaps he was deranged, or perverted? How could she have been so foolish, she thought.

"Have you decided?"

She dragged her wandering attention back to the menu. "Steak and salad, please. No french fries."

"You're slimming?"

"Just being careful!" She laughed, but he nodded gravely as though he understood. Perhaps I do look overweight, she thought in distress, perhaps those few extra pounds do show.

When the waiter had gone they were forced to look at one another again. Marc Farino kept his gaze on Judith but made no attempt to speak. She felt awkward, and gave a small laugh.

"This is awful, isn't it!"

"A trifle difficult," he acknowledged, but still he didn't smile.

"They told me at the bureau," continued Judith, determined to break the ice, "that you had children. Is that right?"

"Oh yes! I don't suppose they make many mistakes, they seem very thorough."

She clenched her teeth. Surely he could have taken the hint. Told her something about them.

"Boys or girls?"

"Four boys."

"Four!"

"They didn't tell you that?"

"No. Well, they might have done. I was so nervous I probably didn't take it in."

Their sherries arrived and he lifted his glass in a slight acknowledgment before drinking.

"And you? Do you have children?"

"Oh no! I've never been married."

"And that precludes children?"

She felt a blush beginning. "Well, in my case, yes!"

"But you like children?"

"Yes, very much."

He nodded thoughtfully.

Without any further leads she was forced to continue talking about the four children, much as she would have liked to change the subject. "How old are they?"

"Nine, eight, seven and five."

She swallowed too much sherry and coughed. "My, they must keep you busy!"

The steaks arrived and for a time they ate in silence. Judith cast one or two covert glances at the man opposite her. The bureau had mentioned "mixed parentage" but to her he looked like a man who spent a lot of time in warm climates. He had heavy, dark brows and a flat, broad forehead. She noticed too that his hands had incredibly long, spatulate fingers, like an artist or pianist.

"What do you do for a living?" she asked.

"I'm an actuary. That's in insurance."

"I do know what an actuary is!"

He smiled for the first time, a slow smile that greatly enhanced his charm.

"My apologies! And you?"

"I used to illustrate children's books. I still do a little of it, but I've had to work from home over the past few years, and of course you lose precious contacts. I couldn't live off what I earn at the moment, but . . ." she paused, unable to tell him about her mother. "I have a small inheritance," she concluded quietly. "I can take my time getting back into full-time work."

"You live in Bourne don't you?"

"Yes. A bungalow on the edge of an estate. It's quite private, I like it. I've lived there with my mother for sixteen years."

"Your mother?" The dark brows rose questioningly.

"She's dead now." Judith knew she sounded abrupt.

"I'm sorry. But you have brothers and sisters?"

"No. There was only me. My father died when I was six, you see."

She realized that he had finished his meal and was studying her with a detached kindness.

"I wasn't lonely," she continued hastily. "My mother and I were great friends. We shared the same sense of humor, the same interests, we never quarreled, not seriously."

"You must miss her very much."

Judith pushed the last piece of steak to one side. "I do, but I'd really rather not talk about it."

He poured the last of the wine into her half-full glass and nodded.

"That's why I went to the bureau though, because my mother was ill for years and I just lost touch with everyone. All my friends are married now, or heavily committed to careers, while I seem to be sitting on the sidelines watching everyone else live. So a friend of mine, Sue, suggested the marriage bureau. It took me ages to pluck up the courage and go, but after all if one can make friends, get out more, isn't it sensible?"

She was talking too much, the unaccustomed wine had loosened her tongue.

"Very sensible. You don't have to defend your decision to me. I went there as well!"

"Yes, but it's different for you."

"Why's that?"

"You've been married. Your wife died and you're left with four small boys; you need to meet women, but not because of any personal inadequacy. It's just your situation."

"Is that how you see yourself? Inadequate?"

She looked into the brown eyes and knew that she was inadequate, certainly not up to the standards he must expect. No wonder that she was the eighth woman the bureau had introduced to him.

"Yes," she said firmly, "I'm painfully shy and not at all exciting."

"I find you very interesting," he said softly as he clicked his fingers for the sweet trolley. "I'm thoroughly enjoying our dinner. Why not try the cheesecake? It's magnificent."

Again Judith wondered, as she nodded and started to eat, what the hidden pitfall was. There had to be one, otherwise he wouldn't need the services of the bureau. He was far too attractive to require any help in finding himself a woman.

Over coffee the conversation became less personal. Marc mentioned a liking for all sports but especially swimming and an interest in computer systems. Judith was forced to admit that she had no hobbies that truly absorbed her.

"I like reading and going to the theater, but I'm not good at physical things. Tennis, badminton, keep-fit, they hold no attraction for me. Doubtless I'll regret it when I hobble into middle-age, bones creaking!"

Marc gave a fleeting smile. "There's some truth in that too! However, you look fit enough."

"Oh yes, I'm fit. I've had to be really. By the end my mother had to be lifted every hour, to prevent bed sores, and for years before that I'd coped with all the physical things round the house. Painting, decorating, and so on."

"Probably far more strenuous than the despised keep-fit!"

Judith laughed. "Probably, but I can't see it taking off as an evening class."

"I imagine not." His voice was flat, as though he had lost interest in the joke.

As she finished her coffee Judith managed a discreet glance at her watch.

"Good heavens, it's nearly eleven! I had no idea, I thought it was nearer ten."

"Then the evening must have been a success."

"It's been very pleasant. Thank you for inviting me."

They looked at each other across the table, and Judith felt herself longing to touch him. To reach over the cloth and touch his hand. He drew her physically as no man had ever done before, and she was both shocked and surprised. Shocked, because she hardly knew him; surprised because she had begun to think that physical passion was not part of her makeup.

Confused she started to stand up, feeling that she should leave before he guessed how he was affecting her. It was too immature, too much the composition of frustrated spinsters' dreams, for her to wish him to know. She gave a friendly but not overwhelming smile and held out one hand. Marc, hands already in his pockets searching for his wallet, remained seated and looked up in surprise. Slowly he raised one eyebrow.

"You're not dashing off are you?"

"Well, I really should. Our dog—or rather my dog now—is getting old and can't be left for too long."

"I see. But I can call you?"

Immediately Judith's spirits lifted. She had been so worried that he wouldn't want to see her again.

"Of course. I'd like to hear from you."

"You drove yourself here?"

She smiled properly this time. "I had to. It's the chauffeur's night off."

He nodded, and yet again her small joke passed unnoticed. "In that case I can hardly accompany you. Good-night, Judith."

Then, at last, he reached out and touched her hand lightly with his own. Her breathing quickened and she turned away abruptly. Her skin tingled and it wasn't until she was standing on the pavement outside that she was able to regain her composure. All the way home she reminded herself about calf-love and the building up of false hopes.

It didn't help to cushion her when two weeks passed and the promised call failed to materialize.

Feeling doubly rejected because he had made such a point of feigning interest, she busied herself in a frenzy of gardening and vowed not to contact the bureau again. They were welcome to her money. It was all too degrading. She suspected that he had noticed her eagerness and had not known how to end the evening without promising further contact. Humiliated and ashamed she tried to forget all about him.

Exactly three weeks to the day after their dinner date the telephone rang shrilly at ten o'clock in the evening, just as Judith was about to go to bed.

"Judith?"

She recognized the voice immediately. The trace of accent. The habit of clipping his words. She clutched the receiver tightly. "Yes?"

"Judith, this is Marc. Marc Farino."

"Why, Marc, what a pleasant surprise."

"I'm sorry I didn't call earlier. The two younger boys have both had chicken-pox and life's been one mad dash between the office and home. My sister came over during the day, but I really prefer to look after them myself when I can."

Judith was elated. The silence had not after all been due

to any shortcoming on her part, nor negligence on his. She hoped that the relief didn't show in her voice.

"How horrible for them, and for you. Are they all right now?"

"Just about. Well enough for a babysitter to cope. I wondered if you would like to come out for a drink tomorrow night? I could pick you up, it seems silly to take two cars."

"I'd love to. About eight?"

"Fine. Where exactly do you live?"

She gave him careful instructions and then, when she had hung up, wrapped her arms around herself with pleasure. All at once there were things to be done. She wanted to look her very best for this second date. Somehow it was like passing tests at school, each one progressively more difficult until you arrived. But where? Cynically she knew the answer to that. Marriage. Why else go to a marriage bureau? Talk of companionship, shared interests, was only that; at least for women. She assumed it was true of the men too, or else why bother to join. For men like Marc Farino casual girlfriends would be only too easy to find.

The next day she rang Sue. She hadn't done so before because of the apparent failure of the exercise. Now, excited and more confident, she wanted Sue to share her pleasure. After her glowing description of Marc and her confession as to her own feelings for him she expected Sue to be thrilled and happy for her, but Sue was strangely reticent.

"Be careful, Judith. Remember, he can't be quite the dream man you describe. He went to the bureau too, you know. The way you describe him he should have a queue of women wanting to marry him!"

"I know, and it is a bit odd. Still, aren't you pleased? It was your idea you know!"

"Of course I'm pleased, but I don't want you hurt. Don't go to some out-of-the-way spot tonight, will you? After all, you don't know much about him."

Judith was annoyed. She didn't want cold water thrown over her excitement. "Of course I do. He's got four small boys . . ."

"Have you met them?" Sue interrupted.

"No! He didn't bring them to the restaurant with him!"

"Then you don't know."

"But they told me at the bureau."

"He could have lied to them."

"For crying out loud, Sue! Why should he?"

"I don't know, Judith, and probably he didn't. I'm only trying to keep your feet on the ground. Look, promise you'll ring me tomorrow. That way I won't have to worry for too long!"

"Yes, I promise. Now I'll have to go and get ready for my Jack the Ripper!"

"That's not funny." Sue sounded so worried that Judith apologized then hung up. She wished she had never called. Now there would be a niggle of doubt hanging over her all the evening.

Marc arrived five minutes early. When she answered the door to him he seemed to fill the doorway. Even inside he made the bungalow look small and cramped. He sat in her mother's chair, and Judith noticed again the very long fingers as he rested his hands on the wooden sides of the seat. All at once Sue's warning seemed more sensible and she felt nervous.

"Would you like a drink here before we go?"

"No thanks. As I'm driving I'm rather limited."

"Of course, I forgot." His warm eyes met hers, projecting kindness. The tension in her shoulders eased. "I'll get my coat then."

He had parked his red Porsche casually, so that it blocked half of her neighbor's drive. She saw the husband staring out of his kitchen window at them and she hurried down her path and climbed quickly in. Marc closed her door for her, and she remembered Henry and the way he always drove off before she was properly settled. Then she pushed the memory away. Henry was not one of her better experiences.

"How are the children?"

He glanced sideways at her. "The same as they were last night."

She felt annoyed. "It was a genuine inquiry, there's no need to be rude."

"Sorry! They're fine. A bit sulky because I'm going out,

but that's because I've been exclusively theirs for the past few weeks.''

''They must miss their mother very much.''

It was a natural enough remark but she knew at once that it would have been better unsaid. A muscle jumped below his left ear and he gripped the steering wheel a little tighter. She sought for something else she could say, but he was quicker.

''They do. As you must miss yours.''

She knew the depths of her own sorrow, and felt ashamed at prying into the minds of four small boys who must be suffering far more than she had done. She swallowed and nodded before turning to look out of her side window.

''It's all right,'' he said gently. ''It doesn't matter. I know you meant well.''

''It was a stupid remark, and I apologize.''

He lifted his left hand from the wheel and laid it fleetingly on her right knee. ''There's no need. I hope you're hungry. They do marvelous bar snacks where I'm taking you.''

They did. It was a small pub, set well away from any towns and relying upon personal recommendations to build up their custom. One minute the car was speeding along a straight, tree-lined road miles from anywhere; the next Marc had taken two sharp turns to the left and they were driving into a small cobbled courtyard with the pub forming the boundary on three sides. There were about eight other cars there, and Judith could see the gleam of copper lamps through one of the windows.

Inside it was an antique dealer's paradise. Gleaming copper table tops and heavy brass ornaments. Several ancient wooden spinning wheels stood in corners and corn dollies hung from the walls. Even the top of the bar was gleaming copper, and the round-faced publican and his wife smiled their greeting as though they were acting the part for an advertisement rather than carrying out real business.

''What will you have, Judith?'' As he spoke the eyes of the four other women in the pub turned in his direction, and Judith could see the surprise and admiration in them. She was relieved that she wasn't the only woman to find his sheer physical presence a delight.

"Dry white wine, please."

"Take a seat while I order, then."

She felt self-conscious but walked as naturally as she could towards a small round table in the darkest corner of the room. When Marc sat down on the small stool opposite her she realized that it had been a mistake. He looked like an adult taking tea in a Wendy House. The idea made her smile.

"What's the joke, Judith?"

"You look too big for the furniture! I should have chosen a different table."

"This is fine. Nice and discreet. After all, we want to talk without having a non-paying audience!"

She laughed and sipped her wine. Marc had a whiskey which he studied closely without actually tasting.

"I expect you thought I wasn't going to call," he said abruptly.

"Of course not!"

She looked up and he was staring at her. She felt as though he could see right into her head and the lie was palpably clear to him.

"Actually, yes!"

"I'm sorry about that. I kept meaning to ring, but then one of them would start crying or being sick and the moment would pass. I was afraid you would have met another man by now."

She was startled, and it showed. "Good heavens no! I don't intend to do this again."

"I'm sorry if it's so distasteful to you."

"I didn't mean that! It's just that this sort of thing isn't really me. My friend Sue . . ."

"Yes, you told me."

"Oh!"

She was shocked into silence. Even if she had it wasn't very nice to have it pointed out like that.

"I've met quite a few people," he said diffidently.

"So they told me." Judith sounded sharp, her annoyance clear, but he was unperturbed.

"They were all very pleasant. I don't regret meeting them. We had some agreeable evenings out."

Judith didn't like to ask where they had failed, or why they had been deserted.

"Somehow, though, they were none of them suitable," he continued slowly. "I knew at once, but it wouldn't have been polite to send them straight home, do you think?" This time he did laugh, softly, almost to himself.

In the dark corner his features were obscure, only his eyes were clear, and there were golden lights in the brown depths. Lights that held her gaze and drew her to him. Almost without being aware of it she leaned across the table so that their faces were closer. He put his glass down and then reached out to cover her suddenly cold fingers with his own. Judith trembled slightly and made a slight gesture of withdrawal. His fingers closed almost imperceptibly round hers and gradually she felt a warm glow spreading through her. It was comforting, reassuring; she felt protected and secure.

"You, however, are perfect, Judith. You are exactly the sort of person I had in mind when I spoke to the administrator at the bureau."

Judith came to her senses with a start. That sounded like a well-used line, the prelude to intimacy but nothing more. The flattering words that were so desperately needed by women in her position, women almost past the point of daring to hope for any grand passion. Willing, all too willing, to settle for second or even third best if it meant security. Well, she was flattered, but she was also intelligent. If this was his way of softening her up, he was in for a disappointment, however attractive she found him. She had Sue to face the next day.

"You are not in the least what I had in mind," she said clearly.

Marc released her hands and sat back, a smile lurking at the corners of his mouth.

"I'm not?"

"No. You're too polished, too charming, altogether too much of everything!"

"Let's hope you learn to put up with the disappointment. Another drink?"

Four glasses of wine and one gammon steak with all the

trimmings later Judith knew that she could easily learn to put up with it. She hoped he couldn't tell.

"Where exactly are you from?" she asked, seeing her fifth glass of wine and knowing that she shouldn't drink it.

"Stamford."

"I know that. I meant, what country?"

"England."

His face was its usual polite mask. Attentive, alert, but without emotion. She wondered what he would be like once you really got to know him. Tried to imagine his face in passion, and succeeded.

"Your parents are English?"

"No. My father was a Cape colored. He came over here when he was twenty and managed to build up a very small chain of grocery stores. Only eight and all in the Home Counties, but we did very well by them. He was of Portuguese extraction. My mother is English."

"Your father's dead?"

"He died when I was twelve and my sister eight. My mother never married again."

"Does she still live in the south?"

"Yes, she's never been out of Surrey for more than two weeks at a time!"

"I see."

Marc moved his stool nearer to hers. "Now it's my turn. You've already told me about your parents. How about boyfriends. There must have been some!"

Judith giggled and quickly stifled the sound. "One or two." She knew that she sounded horribly flirtatious, and pushed her wine glass further away.

"None of them serious?"

She had never told anyone the truth about Henry, and she didn't intend to start now. But once she began to talk it all poured out. Marc sat motionless, listening carefully; far more carefully than Judith realized. He listened to every intonation, every hesitation, and even the things that she didn't tell him he could work out for himself.

"Henry was serious. My mother liked him, which was a point in his favor, and he seemed to like her. He understood why I couldn't leave her alone, and he even hinted that perhaps she should come and live with us although I never quite believed that. Anyway, after a year or so we became engaged. It sounds old-fashioned I suppose, but then I was. Certainly I was very sheltered. Well, Henry made it clear that an engagement entitled him to more than the lingering kisses he had been used to. So, after much soul-searching on my part, we embarked on an affair! It wasn't easy, we usually had to make do with the back of his car or his home when his parents were out, that sort of thing.''

''How old were you?'' interrupted Marc.

''Twenty. Incredible isn't it, put it down to a mother complex!''

''Go on.''

''Well, there isn't much more to go on about. After six months or so Henry announced that our engagement was off.''

''Just like that?''

''Not quite. We'd had the odd argument. Well, rows really. I wasn't quite what he wanted in a woman, and so we parted. That's it. End of story.''

''There's been no one since?''

''Boyfriends yes, but no affairs. I decided after Henry's remarks—and judging by my performance with Henry his remarks were fair—that I wasn't very good at that sort of thing, so I left it alone.''

As she stopped talking Judith looked down at her glass, it was quite empty. ''I shouldn't have told you that, should I? Now you know that I'm not exactly what you had in mind after all.''

Marc stood up, bending his head slightly to avoid the dark oak beam. ''How do you know what I have in mind, Judith? It might surprise you to learn that all I've heard tonight only strengthens my original conviction. I just hope that you find me as congenial!''

During the drive home she drifted off to sleep and when they drew up outside the bungalow her head was resting on his broad shoulder. It felt comfortable there, and she was reluctant to move. He released their seat belts and leaned across in front of her. She waited for his kiss, certain that he would expect to be asked in and half-wishing she would say yes, yet knowing she would refuse. To her amazement he leaned right over her and opened her door. The cool night air hit her in the face and she tried to locate her handbag.

"I won't get out, Judith. You should be safe enough walking up your path and I'm much later than I intended. On Saturday I'd like you to come to tea and meet the boys, if you think you can stand it?"

"So they do exist," she muttered, her head swimming.

"Definitely, and you can tell your friend Sue so!"

She stumbled onto the pavement. "I never said that Sue . . ." but he was already starting the engine and driving away.

Judith didn't remember getting to bed, and awoke next morning to the worst headache of her life. She remembered one thing very clearly though, the invitation to tea. That was something to tell Sue. Difficult as it was to believe, he really must be serious about her. She only wished he would be even a fraction more demonstrative. A goodnight kiss wouldn't have been out of place. Ironically, it was the first time in her life that she had ever wanted a man to kiss her. Marc's influence was plainly disturbing the previously predictable tenor of her life.

Yet again Sue tried to pour cold water over Judith's enthusiasm.

"Now you'll find out!" she prophesied.

"Find out what?"

"Why the other women didn't suit him. It was probably the other way around. His children didn't suit them!"

"But I like children. I enjoy your boys."

"I know you do, but you don't have them all the time. Besides, that's only two. Imagine four of them at once!"

Judith allowed her annoyance to show. "I can tell you don't want this to work out so I might as well stop keeping you up-to-date."

"I'm sorry, Judith, but you sound so convinced this is Mr. Right yet you hardly know him. You're the last person I expected to . . ."

Judith hung up on her. She wouldn't listen. She would

wait and judge for herself. Probably Sue was jealous. It must be quite a few years since she had experienced any romance in her life. Marriage and children on a limited wage didn't encourage romance. That was all it was, sour grapes.

Marc collected her at three o'clock. This time he was driving the latest Volvo estate, which she realized made sense with so many children. On the drive she tried to get the boys sorted out in her mind.

"Paul is nine, Patrick eight, Philip seven and Michael five," clarified Marc.

"No six?"

He didn't even smile.

"Are they alike?"

"In looks they are, not so much in ways."

"Do they know I'm coming to tea?"

"Of course. Now stop worrying. They're only children."

"I'm sure we'll all get on. I like boys."

"That's fortunate," said Marc dryly.

The grounds of his home were surrounded by a rough stone wall over seven feet high, and the gravel drive led to a large stone house with a slate roof. The windows were leaded and the walls covered in thick creeping vines. A very large, well-established house with immaculate front lawns and a complete absence of pedal cars and push bikes, the normal outwards signs of children on a warm summer day.

Stepping out of the sun and into the porch Judith felt goosepimples rise on the tops of her arms. The house was cool, the spacious entrance hall almost cold. She heard the heels of her navy sandals clicking on the polished parquet floor and almost slipped as one of them caught in the edge of the vividly colored Persian rug that stretched across the width of the floor. Marc put out a hand and caught her elbow in a curiously detached gesture.

"I'll go and get the boys," he said and disappeared up the stairs. Judith stood and wondered what it was that felt wrong. Then she realized that it was the lack of noise. Surely four boys wouldn't be this quiet. The only sound that reached her ears was her own nervous breathing and she shivered again.

Just as her unease was deepening a boy started to descend the stairs in front of her. She felt her eyes widen in astonishment. He was the most heart-stoppingly handsome boy she had ever seen. His dark brown hair was neatly cut but fell in a cow-lick over his forehead. Everything about the face was perfectly symmetrical—the small mouth, the slightly turned up nose, and the soft curve of the cheeks. But above all it was the eyes that caught her attention. Deep brown eyes thickly lashed and regarding her with such candor and innocence that she could hardly bear it.

He walked solemnly up to her and held out his right hand. "How do you do. I'm Paul."

"Paul. Then you're the oldest one."

"I'm the eldest, yes."

"I beg your pardon, the eldest."

Judith smiled at him, but he only opened his eyes a little more and regarded her thoughtfully. She was relieved to hear more footsteps on the stairs and looked up to see the three other boys walking sedately down, one behind the other. She looked from them to Paul and back to them. It was quite incredible, but for the difference in height they could have been quads.

When the others reached her she found herself again shaking hands, like a member of the royal family being greeted on a station platform, she thought with a suppressed giggle.

"Aren't you alike! My goodness, anyone would know you for brothers!"

She laughed, but they didn't laugh with her. They formed a small semi-circle in front of her and simply watched her face.

It was horribly disconcerting. Instinctively she took a small step back, and they immediately took one forward. This is ridiculous, she chided herself, and looked at the smallest boy.

"You must be Michael. Are you at school yet, Michael?"

"Yes."

Oh God, she thought, as monosyllabic as his father and she wished that Marc would reappear.

Paul broke away from the circle first, and opened the door

on his right. "Perhaps you'd like to sit down. This is the drawing room. Where we have tea," he added, in case she hadn't understood him.

She gave him a small smile and stepped into the room. It was large and, to her relief, light. The sun streamed in through the windows, and the cream carpet and deep gold chairs added to the sense of spaciousness. She was just thinking how impractical a decor it was for a house with four children when Marc touched her lightly on the back. She gave a gasp and spun around.

"I didn't hear you coming!"

"Sorry. It's these carpets."

He looked carefully at her.

"I've met the boys," she said quickly. "They're gorgeous. Were you as devastating when you were small?"

"Undoubtedly!"

And you still are, she thought to herself. "They're very polite," she added.

"I hope so. I do my best to instill manners into them."

This is ghastly, thought Judith. We're standing here mouthing polite inanities as though I'm looking for employment, and he's anxious for me to accept the job.

"Do sit down. My sister was here this morning and she made some cakes and so forth. We'll go and get them in."

"Let me help, please."

"Not this time. You're our visitor, and it isn't often that we have visitors. That's why the boys are so quiet. Shock!"

"I did wonder. Sue's boys are never quiet!"

"I can imagine," said Marc ironically.

He was gone quite a long time. She looked more carefully around the room. The nest of tables was tucked away in one corner, and a mahogany card table gleamed in another. Apart from that, the only furniture was the chairs. Six large, wing-backed chairs. It was not a room where children could play, or where Judith would ever feel relaxed enough to kick off her shoes and tuck her legs beneath her. She wondered about the rest of the house.

The boys filed in quietly, each one carrying a plate of cakes or scones. Marc pushed a trolley in behind them, with tea pot and cups on the top, plates of sandwiches below. It looked as though the boys had reassuringly normal appetites.

In an orderly fashion they handed the things around. There was no giggling and no scuffling. It was like a scene from a film. Judith's disbelief grew the longer that she studied them. Their incredible beauty and their impeccable manners were unreal. She wondered how many times she would have to come here before they relaxed with her and she saw them as they really were, and not as they obviously thought she would like them to be.

In the middle of her second sandwich she thought she heard a noise. She tilted her head and listened. No one else in the room gave any sign of hearing it. Then it came again, clear and distinct. A child crying.

"What's that?" she asked. Everyone stopped eating and looked up at her. Their backs were straight, their expressions alert.

She glanced at Marc. "I thought I heard a child crying."

"Yes, you did. I heard it too."

She felt relieved that it wasn't her imagination. "Who is it?"

The smallest boy edged forward on his chair. "It's only Kara."

"Kara? Who is Kara?"

The boys turned their heads, looking at each other before returning to look at her.

"Our sister." It came out almost like a chorus, the youngest just a fraction of a second behind his brothers.

"Sister? I didn't know you had a sister."

Marc stood up, carefully putting his empty plate onto the trolley. "I know, and I apologize. I didn't want to put you off. She's very young, you see, we rather hoped she'd sleep through your first visit."

"But you never mentioned her." Judith was incredulous. "You told me you had four children, why not five? Did you really think one more was likely to put me off?"

"I told you I had four sons, and that's quite true! All right I apologize. I'll go and get her down."

The door swung to behind him and again the boys turned

towards each other. Only little Michael glanced shyly at
Judith and she addressed herself to him. "How old's Kara?"

"I think she's two."

"No, she's not," interrupted Paul. "She's eighteen months."

Judith frowned. She wondered how long ago their mother
had died. Perhaps the birth of the little girl had killed her
and that was why Marc didn't mention her. She could hardly
ask the boys, sitting watchfully in front of her, so she smiled
and said nothing more. They all heard the measured tread of
Marc returning and, as one, their heads swiveled to the
door. Judith turned too, unable to resist.

The little girl in Marc's arms was rubbing at her eyes with
her knuckles, the tears still smudged on her chubby cheeks.
He set her down on the floor and she began to cry again. No
one moved towards her. They all sat in silence. Her cries
increased, and instinctively Judith bent down and picked her
up. Her padded pants were soaked right through.

"She needs changing, Marc. Would you like me to do
it?"

"If you like. I'll show you where everything's kept."

She was glad to leave the room and the four boys behind
her.

"She isn't like the boys, is she?"

"Not at all. In here is where all the nappies and so on are
kept."

He stood with his back to the door while she put Kara on
the plastic changing mat and made as good a job as she
could of exchanging a dry nappy for a wet one. It seemed to
comfort Kara who stopped crying and put her thumb in her
mouth, watching Judith out of her blue eyes.

"There, that's better isn't it?"

"I ought to explain," said Marc, remaining with his back
to the door. "She's a half-sister to the boys. Her mother was
housekeeper here after my wife died. If that shocks you,
I'm sorry, but as you've met her it's best that I'm honest."

"Where's her mother now?"

"She left."

"Without her daughter?"

"Yes. One morning she simply wasn't here. She left a

note, saying that I could give Kara a better life and so on. I wasn't pleased, but what could I do?''

"She's so fair," marveled Judith, touching the golden hair. "Such a contrast to the boys."

"Yes. She isn't one bit like the boys. But then, she's a girl so what can you expect?"

"Don't you like girls?"

He looked into her troubled face and bent forward, kissing her softly on the tip of her nose. "Not little ones!"

Behind her, still on the mat, Kara gurgled happily. Judith took a step towards Marc, willing him to kiss her again, but properly this time. He put his arms around her, locking his hands behind her waist. She lifted her head and he lowered his mouth onto hers, gently at first but with increasing pressure. She felt his hands moving up and down her back. When he slipped his tongue between her lips she started to draw away, but his grip tightened and then she didn't want him to stop.

It was only when she felt his hands fumbling with her zip that she managed to bring herself back to reality, and she pushed at his massive chest. If he had wanted to retain his hold she knew only too well that he could have done, but he released her with almost insulting speed. She felt flushed and curiously weak, and ran her fingers through her hair in an attempt to tidy herself.

"Hadn't we better get back to the boys?"

Marc nodded. "I suppose so. I'll put Kara back in her cot."

"But she's only just come down! You don't keep her locked away, I hope?"

The golden flecks in his eyes glittered for a moment but he continued to smile pleasantly. "Of course not. Keep her if you want to."

With Kara snuggled happily into her neck Judith followed Marc back into the drawing room.

The shock of the four perfect faces staring at her as soon as she walked through the door startled her. They had such adult composure.

"I've just been kissing Daddy," she said lightly, and clapped her free hand to her mouth in horror. She wondered what on earth had possessed her to say such a thing. She had intended to say that she'd been changing Kara. Marc spun around staring at her in disbelief, and then the boys started to giggle. Once they had begun they were unable to stop. Michael and Philip fell off their chairs and rolled around on the carpet while tears of laughter streamed down the faces of Paul and Patrick.

Shocked and ashamed, Judith had to bite on her bottom lip to stop herself from crying. She hung her head, unable to bear the look of censure that must be in Marc's eyes.

"Boys!" His voice was quiet, but their laughter began to die away. "Go to your rooms please. Tea is over for the afternoon."

All sounds of merriment ceased. One by one they stood up, shot quick glances at their father and then walked solemn-faced from the room. Only Michael couldn't suppress a final snort of mirth as he walked past Judith.

When they had gone she found herself clutching Kara close for solace. "Marc, I don't know what to say. I never meant . . . I can't think why I . . ." She looked at him at last and to her amazement he was smiling.

"Don't worry. It was a wonderful way to break the ice! I'm sure they consider you a great success! Now come on, let's finish off these scones."

She put Kara carefully in one of the chairs before returning to her own seat. She was grateful for his kindness, but she still couldn't understand what had happened. If this was how nerves affected her she had better get herself some tranquilizers before she visited the house again. Always supposing that she was asked.

At six o'clock Marc drove her home. The boys had remained out of sight for the last half hour and she felt thoroughly miserable and disconcerted. It had been such a strange afternoon, even now it was hard to believe that the boys were real flesh and blood, and that the whole ordeal hadn't been a long, nerve-wracking dream.

When the car stopped Marc turned off the engine. "I'm sorry about Kara, Judith. I should have told you and I apologize."

"It's all right. I understand."

"May I see you again?"

She turned towards him. "If you really want to."

"Of course I want to. I thought we might go to the pictures next week. They're showing *An Officer and a Gentleman*, I hear it's very good."

She looked at his strong face, his sensitive features, felt his sheer animal magnetism, and she knew that she wanted him. She wanted to be completely his, with or without marriage. The desire was like a physical pain and it dried her mouth. She licked her lips. "That would be very nice. What time?"

"It starts at eight, so I'd better pick you up at seven-fifteen."

"Fine. I look forward to it."

She waited a moment in case he wanted to kiss her, but when he made no move she reluctantly started to open her door. Instantly he was out and around to her side, and as she straightened up she deliberately brushed against his solid chest. He put out an arm and caught hold of her, pulling her towards him for a second and then releasing her so abruptly that she almost fell. She walked self-consciously up to her front door and when she turned to wave he was still standing watching her, his features as impassive as those of his sons.

All night the dark, haunting beauty of the boys troubled her dreams and when she awoke in the morning she felt exhausted and drained. The visit seemed to have taken far more out of her than she had realized and it wasn't until the following day, after a really good night's sleep, that she felt anything like her normal self.

She didn't ring Sue. There was something about her visit that troubled her and she didn't want Sue to sense this. After all, apart from her own incongruous remark, nothing untoward had happened. They were simply four handsome, well-behaved children. A pleasant change in these days of unchecked hooliganism that passed for play.

Judith found sitting next to Marc in the darkened cinema a disturbing experience. They were so close and yet not really touching, except by accident. The pressure of his knee against her leg when he tried to make himself more comfortable; the touching of hands when he passed her a sweet; insignificant gestures, and yet they left her incredibly aware of him. She felt as though all her senses were heightened, every nerve ending exposed. The explicit sex scene part way through the film didn't help. It concentrated on the faces of the lovers, and Judith found herself replacing the faces she could see with her own and Marc's. Except that she would never be as forthright as the heroine. Sex with Henry had always been a silent business completed as quickly as possible. Impossible to imagine herself verbalizing her desires. Even the thought of it made her blush.

On the way out Marc apologized. "I'm sorry about the language. I had no idea it would be as bad. I hope it didn't spoil the film for you."

"Of course not. I didn't mind at all."

"You liked it then?"

Judith hesitated.

"You didn't like it?"

"Yes. Yes, I did. Very much."

"That's good. As you'd never mentioned films I really didn't know what your taste was, but my sister enjoyed this so I thought it should be suitable."

"Do you see a lot of your sister?" she asked as they made their way to the car park.

"No more than I can help. She's a great manager, and inclined to take over the house whenever she calls."

"Is she married?"

"No. Even as a girl she never wanted to marry."

"I wonder why?" mused Judith.

Marc swung the car out of the car park and onto the road. "I think it's a question of color. Zilla looks completely white, unlike me, but she knows that doesn't mean she'd necessarily have white children. I think this has always bothered her. Perhaps she's ashamed, I really don't know. We never went in for meaningful conversations in our home."

Judith laughed. "That's ridiculous. Why, your children are the most attractive I've ever seen. Any parent would be proud to have them."

Marc laid a hand over hers. "Not everyone is as unbiased

as you. Mixed blood is a very mixed blessing! We don't belong anywhere.''

"Surely that isn't true? Not in England!''

"Good Lord no! Not in England!''

She knew that he was mocking her, however gently, and she resented it. The common sense prevailed. He must know far more about it than she did. Perhaps his children had suffered at school. Or even his wife, possibly her family hadn't approved of the marriage. How could she presume to know anything about a situation that, until she met Marc, she had never considered.

They seemed to get back to the bungalow very quickly. She looked at her watch.

"It's only eleven. Would you like to come in for a coffee?''

"I'd love to.''

It was a pity, she thought, that coming in for coffee had such unfortunate undertones these days. Once upon a time a coffee was a coffee, but not any more. Well, too bad. She only meant a coffee.

As soon as they were inside Judith hurried to let the dog into the garden. Sam was eleven, and once or twice there had been accidents in the kitchen, so now she left paper down just in case. However, tonight all was well. She bundled the paper up and put the kettle on. By the time Sam was scratching to come in she had filtered the coffee and put some chocolate biscuits on a plate. With the dog at her heels she went into the front room.

As Marc stood up to take the tray from her Sam gave a low growl, and the hackles started to rise on the back of his neck. Judith was amazed, and put her hand down to reassure him.

"Good dog, it's a friend. Good boy, Sam.''

The old spaniel continued to growl, flattening himself onto the carpet and showing his teeth. Marc remained standing, never taking his eyes off the dog.

"I don't understand it,'' said Judith as she tried to coax Sam forward. "He's never done this before. It must be because he isn't used to having men around the house.''

"Or he doesn't like me.''

"Of course he does. He's a proper soft thing. Come on Sam." Sam looked up at her for a moment and then back at Marc. He continued to growl warningly, but his fur went back into place and he slunk behind Judith's chair. There he remained, even refusing her offer of a chocolate biscuit to tempt him out.

"Do you like dogs, Marc?"

"Not very much. I'm not a great animal lover."

"Do the boys have any pets?"

He laughed. "Now you're doing it."

"What?"

"Ignoring Kara!"

Judith had forgotten the toddler, but she refused to admit it. "Nonsense. She isn't old enough to have a pet, that's why I didn't mention her."

"Of course! Well, we haven't been too successful with pets. Our gerbils and budgies die off at alarming speed and at present we only have empty cages littered around the garden!"

There was silence for a time as they drank their coffee, but it was a companionable silence. Then Marc put his cup down and moved forward in his chair.

"Judith, I know this is rather quick but I want you to know how I feel. If you could see your way clear to marrying me I'd be very honored, and I'd do everything in my power to make sure that you never regretted it."

She stared at him, grateful for the dim light from the standard lamp which she hoped concealed her incredulity. Her initial feeling of delight she instantly rejected. He was moving far too fast, and common sense told her that he probably had a reason. She had to refuse, but without offending him.

"Marc, I hardly know what to say. After all, we've only met a few times. We don't know each other very well, do we?"

He gave one of his enchanting but infrequent smiles. "I know all that I need to know, although I appreciate that you might want more time."

"It isn't that I don't like you, I do. It's just too quick, and in any case I'm not sure we're suited. I don't know anything about sports or computers, and you've never once asked to see any of my illustrations. Surely finding each other pleasant company isn't enough?''

"It's a great deal more than many people have."

"Your children might not like me. I might not be able to cope with them. I've lived very quietly until now. I don't know if I could adapt to a ready-made family."

"Of course you could. You're highly efficient, I know that already."

Judith flicked her fingers nervously through her light brown hair. He was proving difficult.

"What about love, Marc?"

"I didn't think that when two adults went to a marriage bureau they were necessarily looking for three-star passion."

His words shocked her. He could at least have pretended, but then he would have been cheating her. This way he was paying her the compliment of being honest.

She knew that she was physically attracted to him, but she couldn't picture herself as his wife. She needed much more time to get used to his family. Time to try and draw him out. She wanted to discover what really amused him, what his true temperament was.

She had never been an impetuous person and marriage was such a total commitment that she would need to be absolutely certain, and that would take many, many months.

She could tell that he was waiting to hear what she had to say, and sought to phrase it as tactfully as she could. She didn't want him to take her words as a complete rejection.

"Well?" He sounded anxious.

"Marc." She hesitated.

"Yes?"

"Take me to bed."

It was the worst moment of her life. She had never had any intention of going to bed with him that night. The last thing that she wanted was to have a man stay overnight in a home that was still full of memories of her mother. The words had come from nowhere, but once uttered she could not take them back. Shocked she remained sitting in her chair, completely unable to move. She wondered if she was going out of her mind.

Her feelings were obviously not apparent to Marc. As though expecting her words he quickly rose and picked her up as easily as he would one of his children. She was quite a tall woman and had never envisaged being physically swept off her feet by any man, but once he had her held against his massive chest she was lost. He seemed to embody all the security and protection she had yearned for during the past few years. For too long she had been playing the part of a strong, devoted daughter, able to cope with any crisis. Marc took her over. All at once she realized how tired and lonely she was. Her usually strong principles vanished; her mind was strangely blank, only physical feeling existed now.

He seemed to know which was her bedroom, and she was grateful that she had a double bed. He drew the curtains and then turned on the light. It was too bright, she didn't want to see him so clearly, or to have him see her. She preferred a sense of unreality and turned her head away from the glare, but felt his fingers under her chin, turning her face towards it.

"Don't be shy. You're beautiful, Judith. I like looking at you."

He was undressing swiftly and without embarrassment, but she was still in her light summer frock. She felt curiously weary and incapable of getting up and removing anything. Even through the fog that was clouding her mind she was aware of her lack of experience. Dim memories of Henry's contempt returned and she feared that this too was going to be a disaster.

Marc behaved as though he had expected to undress her himself. As he did so he talked softly to her, pausing from time to time and kissing her lightly on her forehead and cheeks. There was no sense of urgency, no sign that she was not responding as he might have expected after her startlingly frank invitation. When she was finally naked he put his arms around her and drew her to him so that they both lay on their sides with their bodies touching from shoulder to ankle. Then, very slowly, he began to caress her.

All at once she caught his hands between her own.

"Marc, I'm not on the pill."

"Don't worry, I'll see to all that," he soothed her.

For the rest of the night time had no meaning for Judith. She had no idea how long it was before he first entered her, or how great the interval before he took her again. She only knew that while it was pleasant and soothing and comforting the earth didn't move. He never hurt her, as Henry sometimes had when he was in too much of a hurry, but neither did he strike any firm response from her.

When he finally fell asleep her mind became sharper. She felt ashamed, not only ashamed of her behavior but also of her lack of passion. When she had failed to enjoy sex with Henry she had privately blamed his poor technique, with Marc that wasn't possible. The blame lay squarely on her shoulders, and she assumed that his previous offer of marriage would not be repeated in the cold light of day.

Marc awoke to see Judith lying on her back staring at the ceiling. He put out a hand and touched her lips.

"Didn't you sleep?"

She looked at him out of her candid gray eyes. "A little. Marc, I'm sorry."

"Why? Because I accepted your offer?"

"No. Because I was so . . ."

"It will improve. These things take time. Now that you've been compromised in full view of your neighbors I trust that my offer of marriage will be accepted?" He laughed, but his eyes were watchful.

Judith suddenly realized how much her acceptance mattered to him; she wondered why. He continued to watch her, the golden flecks in his pupils almost hypnotic. She searched for a way to explain why she couldn't accept yet. He kept his gaze on her. She felt strangely tired. Suddenly her doubts appeared ridiculous, childish fears.

"If you really want to marry me, even after last night, then yes. I'd love to marry you." It was done. She was committed. There was a brief flash of triumph in his eyes, and then they were tranquil again, soft and innocent.

He left before eight, promising to call her during the day. Alone she wandered around the bungalow in a dream. He seemed to take a part of her with him, for she felt disproportionately bereft.

All at once she remembered that Sam hadn't been let out. There was a large puddle on the back-door mat and he looked thoroughly dejected.

"Poor Sam, it wasn't your fault. Let's give you some food."

Unusually for him he left half of it, and then returned to his large wicker basket, rolling his eyes at her when she tried to stroke him. Judith remembered how he had growled at Marc.

"There's no one else here Sam. Come and see for yourself!"

Eventually he was persuaded to follow her, and after a tour of inspection his tail lifted and he became altogether more sprightly. She wondered how Sam would cope with a change of home. Perhaps he would like the children. Children and animals were supposed to have an affinity.

The trouble was that when she remembered the four boys it was hard to think of them as children. But they *were* only children, and Sam would have a wonderfully large garden to roam in. It would work out in the end. There were going to have to be adjustments made by everyone from Marc down to Sam, but it would work out. She was unable to think about details; if she tried too many doubts arose, doubts that only Marc's presence could erase. It had all seemed far simpler when he was with her.

When he called at lunch-time he sounded in such good spirits that her fears vanished again. He would pick her up at six and they would go to his house for their evening meal.

"That way you'll see the children as they really are. They've no idea you're coming. Don't you think that's a good idea?"

She agreed that it was. She only hoped that events wouldn't prove her wrong.

Judith found it difficult to know what to wear for her second visit to Marc's home. She didn't want to look too formal, but neither did she like to wear slacks. In the end she settled for a pleated skirt in green and yellow with a matching yellow sleeveless cotton top. She had only just finished doing her hair when the doorbell rang and she asked Marc to wait while she shut Sam in the kitchen.

The dog had run to the door at the sound of the bell, but when he saw who it was he put his tail between his legs and slunk away, casting one reproachful glance at her as he went. She made a fuss of him, then gave him a new bone for the evening before leaving him alone with his sulks.

"He'll get used to you," she assured Marc as she locked the door behind them.

"And the boys?"

"Of course."

"I hope you're right."

"He's a nice dog, Marc. I couldn't get rid of him."

"I wasn't suggesting you did. Never mind the dog, how are you?"

Judith turned her face to his. "Fine, thanks. Are you sure the boys will be pleased to see me?"

"As sure as you are that Sam will like them!"

"I'm nervous enough without your sarcastic remarks."

Marc glanced at her set profile. "Sorry! It was meant to be a joke."

Even as he apologized there was a note of amusement in his voice, and Judith wished that he didn't seem so detached. His attitude towards her didn't tie in with his pressing desire for an early marriage.

Except for last night there had been few gestures of simple affection. Even last night might not have contained affection, sex could be quite a long way removed from the more tender emotions, and she had been so immersed in her own self-consciousness she hadn't studied every nuance of Marc's behavior. Certainly there had been no affectionate words spoken after their lovemaking, but perhaps he hadn't considered them necessary. Or perhaps, she cautioned herself, it wasn't an emotion with which he was familiar.

"You're quiet," he said suddenly. "Something wrong?"

"I was thinking about last night."

"Good thoughts?"

"What do you think?" She made her query sound light and teasing.

"I've no idea. I found you very remote."

He looked solemn, and she wondered if he was beginning to have misgivings about his proposal.

"Marc, we don't have to commit ourselves to anything permanent yet."

He swung the car off the road. "Here we are. I expect the boys will be outside."

Realizing that he didn't intend to answer her she climbed out and looked around. Just as on her previous visit the front lawns were immaculate, not even a ball lying in the grass. Marc began to walk around the side of the house and she followed him.

At the back the ground fell away quickly and apart from one or two small rose beds all the garden was lawn and shrubs. At the very bottom she could see a vegetable plot and some climbing apparatus, but the boys weren't there.

"They must have gone in to get ready for tea. I suppose I'm a bit later than usual, we wasted a few minutes at the bungalow."

Before she could protest that it had scarcely taken more than four minutes to shut Sam up Marc had walked in through the French windows and she had no choice but to follow him.

This time they were in a small shelf-lined room strewn with paper and what she at first took to be a small television.

"My computer room. The children aren't allowed in here."

"Do you spent a lot of time using it?"

"Hours and hours. Where the hell are they?" he queried as he opened the door into the hall.

A door on Judith's left swung noiselessly open, and she jumped in surprise. An elderly lady appeared, looking pointedly at her watch.

"It's nearly a quarter to seven, Mr. Farino. I'm meant to leave at six-thirty."

He gave her a warm smile, then shrugged as though the time had nothing to do with him. The woman glanced at Judith in annoyance.

"My husband expects his dinner by seven." Her tone was accusing.

Judith flushed. "Look, I'm sorry, but . . ."

"That's all right. As long as it doesn't happen too often. The meal's all ready, it only needs dishing up."

"Where are the boys?"

"In their rooms."

"And Kara?" asked Judith. The other two looked at her in surprise.

"Surely she doesn't stay on her own in her room? Not at her age?"

"She's in bed," explained Marc patiently. "Mrs. Watson always puts her to bed by six."

"If there's nothing else, sir?"

"No, nothing. I'm sorry we kept you. Would you like a lift home?"

"Goodness no! It's only a few minutes down the road. Goodnight."

She went back into the kitchen and then they heard the back door close behind her. Judith was annoyed. Somehow she had been made to feel in the wrong, and yet she didn't know what she had done.

"Aren't I supposed to talk about Kara, Marc?"

He had been looking up the hall, apparently lost in thought, and he turned sharply towards her. For a moment there was a look of annoyance on his handsome features, but almost at once it vanished and he put out a hand and touched her on her face.

"Silly girl! Why on earth not?"

"You both looked put out, and I wondered if I wasn't meant to know about her yet."

"Put out? You're imagining things. Mrs. Watson is never put out!"

"Well, she was tonight, and incidentally it wasn't my fault we were late."

He walked to the foot of the stairs and called the boys. Judith was beginning to realize that this was a habit of his. If he didn't want to continue a discussion or answer a question he simply ignored it. She found it extremely aggravating.

In answer to his shout there was a thunderous pounding of feet above their heads, then four small figures were hurling themselves down the stairs in riotous confusion. Judith was standing out of their line of vision, and she was highly relieved to see them behaving so normally with their father. They were all talking at once, but she could only catch snatches of their conversations.

"Dad, it was really funny today, we were . . ."

"Dad, guess what we got Mrs. Watson to do."

"Dad, you know those empty hutches outside, well . . ."

"Boys, I've brought Judith home to supper."

Instantly their voices were stilled. Before he spoke they had all been gathered around him, tugging at his arms for attention, pulling at his jacket impatiently when he didn't answer. Now they moved away and formed a line on his right-hand side. Their faces were expressionless, their eyes clear and completely blank.

Judith felt excluded. An outsider spoiling their evening ritual. She looked at Marc, but his face was as expressionless as theirs. She looked from the boys to their father, and a chill ran over her. She wasn't needed here. What on earth had made her even consider marrying Marc? The boys didn't need a mother, and she wasn't sure that their father needed a wife. All at once she wanted to go. To walk away from them all and never return. Then Marc smiled at her and held out his hands. "Don't stay hidden, darling. Come and say hello."

She walked slowly forward, and as he took hold of her right hand she realized that it was the first time he had done so. Until now he had never once held her hand, or even given her an embrace. When he arrived at the bungalow tonight there had been no sign of affection, no indication that their intimacy of the night before meant anything to him.

She let her hand rest passively in his. "Why, you're frozen, darling. Let's go into the dining room. You'll warm up there, it gets most of the sun."

"I do feel a bit cold. This is rather a cold house, isn't it?"

"I suppose it is. We don't feel the cold much, do we, boys?"

Four "no's" endorsed his statement.

The children slipped straight into their seats, then sat with their hands in their laps staring at Judith and Marc.

"I'll help you get the meal," she said nervously.

"Thanks. Paul, will you lay an extra place, please?"

The oldest boy left his chair and walked across the room to the trolley that had been left against the wall. He took extra cutlery from a box and carefully laid a place at one end of the table.

Judith wanted to greet them all, but now it was far too late and she would only sound ridiculous. Instead she turned her back and went out into the kitchen.

Marc was busy spooning out stew from a large casserole dish. "The vegetables are in the pressure cooker. Would you do them for me?"

She felt helpless again. "How much do they eat?"

"Give everyone the same, just make sure the portions are equal or they'll create merry hell!"

"The same as for us?"

"If you would. They all eat very well."

They certainly must, thought Judith, remembering how Sue's boys picked at all their meals unless it was fish fingers and chips. She wished that Marc would try to make her feel more at ease. She watched his broad back as he deftly finished with the casserole and took jacket potatoes out of the bottom of the oven. It was strange to see such a big man so at home in a kitchen.

"How long have you been doing all the household things?" she asked. He turned around. "Elizabeth has been dead for four years, if that's what you mean."

All at once she felt desperately homesick. She wanted to go back to her own bungalow, get away from Marc's quick tongue and his children's blank indifference. He seemed to sense what she was feeling for he moved over to her, wrapping his arms around her. She rested her chin against his chest and felt his hands smoothing her hair.

"I'm sorry, this is horrible for you, isn't it? You were right, I should have warned the boys. Look, as soon as the meal's over, I'll get them off to bed. Then we can have a long chat over a couple of drinks. How does that sound?"

It sounded quite pleasant, but she was more cheered by

his affection than his words. She was beginning to suspect that he was a shy man, who found his feelings difficult to demonstrate. That would excuse quite a lot of his apparently abrupt behavior.

"Lovely! Now, hadn't we better feed your boys?"

They all ate in silence. Only Michael was willing to talk, and most of what he said was directed at his father. Now and again he would glance at Judith from beneath his long lashes, and each time she found herself smiling automatically. He had such charm that she knew she would find disciplining him impossible. She wondered if Marc appreciated how good-looking all the boys were.

As she studied them more she realized that their looks improved with the passage of time. Paul, at nine, was outstandingly handsome and Patrick nearly his equal. Philip and Michael both had traces of chubby small-boy attractiveness, but they were obviously developing along the same lines. She wished that she could see a photograph of their mother. She must have been a natural beauty, for if not, surely some imperfection would have been passed on to at least one of the children. It would be statistically impossible for all the boys to be clones of their father.

There was a bowl of fresh fruit for dessert, and then the children excused themselves from the table.

"You can all have an early night tonight," said Marc before they could leave the room. "I don't mind you reading in bed, or even playing with your toys, but I do not want any of you coming down again. Do you understand?"

All four glanced at each other and then back at their father.

"Yes, Dad." Again only Michael lagged behind them. The other three were in perfect unison. Judith found their way of talking disturbing, but suspected that this was their intention.

"Goodnight, boys," she said as they turned to go. "I hope to see you again soon."

Michael's eyes widened. "Are you the one?" He stared at her in awe.

Paul stepped forward and took hold of his youngest brother roughly by the arm, but Michael pulled away and ran up to Judith, staring at her face.

"I didn't know that! You're very nice, but I thought you'd be prettier!"

Judith looked to Marc for guidance, and was startled to see the naked rage on his face. Michael followed her glance, and gave a small cry. Slowly he backed away from her chair, keeping his eyes fixed on his father. When he got within arm's reach Paul took his chance and pulled Michael bodily out of the room. She heard him start howling as soon as the door closed behind them. When she looked back at Marc he was frowning, but the rage had dissipated.

"What was all that about, Marc?"

"Take no notice. He can be very immature."

"He's entitled to be, he is only five!"

"He's very anxious to have a new mother, that's what he meant by you being the one. You see I've never brought any women home more than once before, because I didn't want to raise false hopes in any of them. They're all lonely, they just don't show it."

Judith looked down the table at him. "Is that why you're so anxious for us to get married?"

"No! I want to marry you for purely selfish reasons. No doubt I ought to say that it's as much for them as for me, but that wouldn't be true. However, I am certain that you'll get on well with them, otherwise I wouldn't consider it." He moved across the room. "Let's go into the study, it's more intimate there."

He held the dining room door open for her and looked down with an affectionate smile.

"You haven't got a very high opinion of yourself, Judith, have you? Is it so hard to believe that a man would want you for a wife?"

"It's hard to believe that you can be so sure after such a short time, yes."

"I'm very quick at making up my mind, and I'm never wrong. I'm very grateful to the bureau for introducing us, and I hope they make all their clients as happy. Now come on, let's have that drink."

The study was larger than she had imagined, and obviously not used as a study any longer. There was no sign of a desk, papers or even books. Instead there was an open fireplace, unlit on this summer evening, and two large armchairs set on opposite sides of the dark red hearth. There was a drinks cabinet and a small oval table with three tapestry-covered chairs around it, but that was all. A window seat that was beneath the deep bay window opposite the fireplace was uncushioned, and it looked to Judith as though the room was rarely used, and certainly never by the children.

She accepted the glass of brandy from Marc gratefully. "Do the children spend a lot of time in their own rooms?"

"Quite a lot. I find it cuts down on the general mess in the rest of the house. I'll show you their rooms some time. They've all been fitted out with plenty of work tops and shelves, and they're all in complete confusion!"

"Well, they have to have somewhere they can do normal childish things."

He looked quizzically at her. "How would you define childish things?"

"Making model planes, cutting out, pasting in, things like that."

"It's obvious you're artistic. No mention of jigsaw puzzles, toy cars, Star Wars figures. All good creative play!"

Judith blushed. "I'm afraid I don't know that much about small boys. I was simply remembering the things that I enjoyed doing when I was young."

"You'll be good for them, Judith. None of them show any interest in art or craft. It's a side of their development that's been neglected."

She felt a stab of fear. "I don't know if I *will* be good for them. To tell the truth, I find them a little intimidating."

"Don't worry, you'll manage very well. I'll give you plenty of support. You won't be alone."

She looked around the room. There were no pictures anywhere. In fact she realized that so far she hadn't seen a single photograph in any of the downstairs rooms.

"Don't you take photographs, Marc?"

He seemed surprised by the question. "What sort of photographs?"

"Family ones. Surely you take pictures of the boys?"

"We used to, Elizabeth kept an album showing Paul's progress from one day to five years."

"Why five? Because he started school then?"

"No. Because then she died."

Judith felt hot with embarrassment. "I'm sorry, I should have remembered."

"Please don't worry. I'm over it now, as much as one ever gets over that sort of thing."

She tried to study his expression, but he had his back to the window and his face was in shadow.

"Was her death sudden?" she asked, feeling that this was something she ought to know about.

"Quite sudden. She was never strong; nothing specific, but a lot of minor ailments. Then one day she went to bed with what we thought was summer 'flu and never got up again. The doctors said it was a virus. All the strength seemed to drain out of her and she literally wasted away. She was down to five stone at the end, it was pretty harrowing to watch."

Judith shivered. "How old was she?"

"Twenty-four. I married her when she was eighteen, and Paul was born ten months later. She was never really well again."

"Why did you have so many children then? Surely that couldn't have helped her?"

"She wanted a big family. We both did. That was one of the reasons we got married while she was so young. We'd hoped to have six, and it gave us plenty of time."

Judith still felt that they had been foolish to press ahead so hastily, but it was hardly her place to say so. Marc sounded quite matter-of-fact about it all, but she realized how painful it must still be. "Was she very pretty?"

"Why do you want to know?"

"I suppose because of what Michael said. I thought perhaps he'd seen pictures of his mother, and that I compared unfavorably!"

Marc stood slowly up. "I'll show you a portrait of her. It was done when we got engaged. Wait there, it won't take me long to find it." Once she was alone Judith felt guilty for her prying. If Marc had wanted to tell her about

Elizabeth then presumably he would have done so. On the other hand he found it easy enough to ignore any questions he didn't choose to answer, so presumably he genuinely didn't mind talking to her about his wife.

Within a few minutes he was back, carrying a silver frame in his hands. "Here you are. It's a good likeness."

Judith stared in disbelief. She had expected to see a very fair, delicate young girl with an ethereal type of beauty. The face that looked laughingly out at her was far from ethereal. Dark wavy hair, bright hazel eyes and a square, determined looking face with just a trace of adolescent plumpness remaining. Elizabeth looked a fit, energetic, and radiantly happy young girl.

Marc put out a hand and prised the frame out of Judith's tight grip. "Not what you expected?"

"No. I don't know why, but I imagined that she was fair."

"I never much cared for dizzy blondes."

"She doesn't look at all sickly."

"I told you, that only started after Paul was born."

Judith took another swallow of her brandy. "I'd like to see Paul's album some time."

"So you shall, but not tonight. I've told you all about Elizabeth, now may I ask you something?"

"Of course."

"Tell me about your mother."

She looked away from him, staring into the empty fireplace. He sat on the arm of her chair and rested his hand on her shoulder, but she didn't notice.

"My mother had multiple sclerosis for twenty years. So, from the age of ten, I always knew that she shouldn't get over-tired. At first the attacks were infrequent, and not too debilitating. Then, as the disease progressed, it changed her. When I was sixteen she lost the use of her legs. I think that was what changed her the most. She was bitter, and difficult to please.

"We had some good times, but her moods could alter so abruptly that I learned never to rely on her good humor, even when we were out somewhere. By the end of course it was quite unpleasant. A nurse used to call in most days, but it still left me with a lot of nursing. I used to wish, on the worst days, that she would hurry up and die. I know that sounds dreadful, but it's true. Then, when she did, I felt the most appalling guilt.

"I remembered, and I still do, the times when I lost my patience with her. The times when I resented how she tried me, and I wished more than anything in the world for a chance to apologize. An opportunity to explain that it wasn't really her I was annoyed with, it was the disease.

"She's been dead six months now, but I still find myself looking at my watch to see if it's time for her medicine. It's things like that I find hardest to cope with."

Judith stopped, unable to say any more because of the lump of distress in her throat. Marc's hand moved slowly over the back of her neck.

"You've been on your own too long. Wasn't there anyone you could have gone to for a time?"

She shook her head.

"Then it's a good thing we met up. You won't have to cope with anything on your own any more. From now on I shall take care of you."

He put his other hand beneath her chin and turned her face towards him. "You've nothing to reproach yourself with," he said gently. "You did far more than most daughters would have done, and I'm sure she appreciated that."

His eyes were so kind and caring that for the first time since her mother's funeral Judith felt tears welling in her eyes. She tried to wipe them away unobtrusively but Marc pulled her to him and as she settled against him she finally shed all the tears that had been bottled up for so long. His hands continued to move soothingly over her shoulders and head, and from time to time he murmured words of comfort.

She felt so relieved at his acceptance of her tears, and so safe held against the solid bulk of him, that all her doubts about the wisdom of marriage and its responsibilities were washed away with her grief. As her sobs diminished and she allowed herself simply to rest against him he sat cradling her close, staring with expressionless eyes over her head.

When Judith finally sat up and searched in her handbag

for a handkerchief and comb he looked at her attentively, and she was again touched at his unusual tenderness. It was all the more strange coming from such a big and reticent man, but it had a devastating effect on her. At this moment a lifetime of such consideration was an attraction beyond price, and she was thankful that she had agreed to marry him.

"I'd better go and tidy myself up," she said shakily. "Where's the bathroom?"

"The best mirror is in the upstairs one. Top of the stairs and it's first door on your right. I'll go and make some coffee."

Judith expected the stair carpet to be serviceable rather than luxurious, but her feet sank into the deep pile. The same carpet covered the long length of landing that she could see by the soft glow from the night light. She opened the first door on her right and stopped abruptly. She must have missed a door, for this was Kara's room.

The little girl was standing up in her cot and when she saw Judith she held out her arms.

"Wet!"

"You poor thing. Have you been crying?"

Kara didn't reply, but her tear-stained face told its own story.

Judith looked around the room. It was spotlessly clean, but there were no toys on display. The white wooden chest of drawers had a changing mat and baby basket on it. There was a baby bouncer, plainly outgrown, in a corner of the room. Apart from that there was nothing at all. A bleak room for a little girl.

She opened the drawers, hoping to find a clean nappy. Sure enough there was a pile of soft, snowy white nappies in the second one. Taking one out she laid it on the mat and walked towards the cot. The sound of the door opening caused her to turn, and there in the doorway stood Marc.

"What are you doing here, Judith?"

"You said the first door on the right, but I must have missed one. I came in here by mistake, and the poor thing's wet."

"That's her normal condition!"

"I didn't hear her crying, did you?"

"No, but sounds don't travel well in this house. Probably the boys heard her. Sometimes one of them will see to her. I always change her when I go to bed."

"She'll get sore. Come on, sweetheart, let me get you out of there." Judith reached forward, but to her dismay Kara flinched and swayed out of reach.

She turned to Marc. "Did you see that?"

"Give her time to get used to you!"

"But she actually flinched. Marc, do you hit her when she's wet?"

He looked genuinely annoyed. "Do I look as though I'd go around hitting small children? Is that the sort of man you think I am?"

How should I know, thought Judith. You could be anything at all. Then she remembered his compassion towards her and was ashamed of her thoughts. "Of course not, but she does look scared."

Marc reached out and swung his daughter clear of the cot rails. She gave a gurgle and let him put her on the changing mat. He was so expert at handling her that Judith let him do it, feeling more and more foolish about her accusation when it was patently obvious that Kara had no fear of her father.

"I'm sorry," she said at last. "It was a silly thing to say."

"That's all right. Actually, I think the boys tease her a lot. She's always crying when they're around. I don't get the time to see what's going on, but no doubt you'll be able to put a stop to their little games."

Judging by Kara's reaction Judith felt that it must be something rather stronger than little games that went on, but she held her peace.

When Kara was settled again Marc showed Judith the bathroom. "My mistake. I forgot Kara's room, I should have said second door on the right. Coffee will be ready when you are."

As she peered in the mirror at her red-rimmed eyes and tangled hair Judith realized that Marc forgot Kara rather too easily, but this was something that she could rectify once

she was living there. She could easily become fond of Kara,
who was a nice, normal toddler in need of a lot of love.

"Will you stay over?" asked Marc as they drank their
coffee.

"I wish I could, but there's Sam."

He smiled. "You really care about that dog, don't you?"

"He's my responsibility, I can't let him down."

"If you take all your responsibilities as seriously, I can
see we're going to be very spoiled!"

"I'll do my best!"

He leaned forward in his chair. "How soon can we be
married?"

Judith didn't know what to say. "What date did you have
in mind? Next spring?"

"Next spring! Good God, no! I thought in a month or so,
about the end of August, just before the boys go back to
school after this summer holiday."

She felt a thrill of excitement that he should have such
urgent need of her, but it gave her very little time to get to
know them all properly. "Don't you think we should wait,
Marc?"

"Why? I've been a widower for four years, and you're
not getting any younger. If we're going to have a family of
our own then the sooner we get married the better."

Judith stared at him. "A family of our own?"

His normally wide-open eyes narrowed and he looked
closely at her. "Is there any reason why we can't have a
family?"

She was surprised at the coldness of his tone. He had
never sounded so remote before, and his South African
accent became more noticeable under stress. It was a harsh
accent, and intensified the sense of annoyance that his voice
conveyed.

"No, Marc. There's no reason as far as I'm concerned.
It's only that as you already have five children I hadn't
expected you to want more."

"Five?"

"The boys and Kara."

"Oh yes, five."

"I'd like to have children of my own, but as I'd reached

thirty without a steady relationship I'd rather given up the idea. It's foolish to long for things that are out of your reach.''

"How sensible you are, Judith. But now that it's possible you would like children?"

She smiled shyly at him. "Well, one will do for a start!"

"I don't expect you to produce them two at a time. Singles will be acceptable!"

"What about your other children? Wouldn't they be jealous?"

"Not at all. The boys can't wait for another brother."

"Or sister."

"Don't make jokes like that, darling. I don't want any more girls."

He laughed, but suddenly Judith noticed afresh the chill that seemed part of this house. She shivered and reached for her cardigan. "I must be going, Marc. Shall I take a taxi? You really shouldn't leave the children alone."

"Nonsense! It's no distance and Paul's very capable."

As the red Porsche ate up the miles Marc returned to the subject of children.

"Judith, I realize I seem to be laboring the point a bit, but you are sure you can have children, aren't you?"

She frowned. "Yes, of course. As a matter of fact I had a complete medical checkup soon after my mother died. I'd got rather run-down and wanted to be certain there was nothing seriously wrong. Everything was fine; I'm in full working order!"

Although she laughed, Marc could tell that he had hurt her feelings. As the car drew up outside the bungalow he put a hand on her knee. "I'm sorry, I didn't mean to sound so clinical. The trouble is that I'm already picturing us with our own children and I suddenly realized I could be taking too much for granted."

"I think you're very brave to want to increase your family. Most men spend their time complaining about their children, who they usually claim were wanted by their wife in the first place."

"I take great pride in my children," he said softly, and then glanced out of the window at the bungalow.

"You'll have to put this up for sale," he pointed out, abruptly changing the subject. "It doesn't matter if you can't sell for months, although I suppose you'd like some money of your own.

Judith put her hand on his arm. "I'll go and see the estate agent tomorrow. Marc, would you do something for me?"

His eyes were wary, but he smiled. "Of course, if I can."

"Would you mind spending an evening with Sue and Dave? They're the only friends I've got, and if it wasn't for Sue I'd never have gone to the bureau. I'd like the two of you to meet."

"Is that all! Go ahead and arrange it, any Saturday or Sunday evening. My sister will always babysit. Now, before you go . . ."

His kiss was more passionate than usual, and she knew that he wanted her to invite him in again, but remembering the children she managed to draw reluctantly away.

The bungalow was small after Marc's house, small and lonely; she wished that she had let him come in with her. However, there was Sam to see to and milk bottles to put out, and by the time she got into bed she was so tired that she decided it was fortunate she was alone. All that she wanted to do was sleep.

She didn't wake for ten hours, and even then she felt heavy headed. After so many years of uneventful routine, the strain of an emotional involvement and suppressed doubts must be taking their toll on her nerves. She decided that on the days when she didn't see Marc she would have early nights in order to compensate for all the excitement. She was pleased that he had agreed to meet Sue. It would be nice to show him off to her friend. With that unworthy thought she decided to telephone her.

Sue was plainly as delighted as Judith at the prospect of a meeting.

"I can't wait to see him. You're the last person I'd expect to be bowled over like this. He must be quite a man!"

"He is. There is one thing, Sue."

"I guessed it. He's got a wooden leg?"

Judith giggled. "No! He's colored."

Sue was silent. "When I say colored," continued Judith quickly, "I don't mean black. He's a sort of coffee shade."

"What about the children?"

"They're the same." She remembered Kara, but didn't want to bring up the subject of an illegitimate daughter yet.

"Well, if you're willing to marry him, we can scarcely object to meeting him."

Judith was shocked. "You can't mean that! You sound as though you actually mind!"

"Of course I mind. Mixed marriages hardly ever work out."

"But he only looks as though he's got a good tan!"

"Look, you don't have to convince me. I'm sure he's the perfect color and the perfect mate. If he's got a sense of humor and plenty of money then go ahead. What else counts?"

"Don't make a joke of it, Sue. I want you to be pleased for me."

There was the sound of angry yells on Sue's end of the line.

"I'm sorry, Judith, I'll have to go. Martin and Geoff are fighting. Come around this Sunday about eight and we'll all have a good natter. See you then, love."

The line clicked and Judith slowly put her receiver back. Now she understood what Marc meant about prejudice. It was the first time she had encountered it and she found it highly offensive. Sue never knew, but quite unwittingly she had helped Marc achieve his aim of marrying Judith. After her friend's display of bias she decided that Sue's judgment was not to be trusted and so alienated herself from the only person who might have succeeded in stopping the hasty union.

Despite Judith's misgivings their Sunday evening visit went off very well. The only surprise as far as she was concerned was how shy Marc became in her friends' company. He smiled a lot and spoke pleasantly when addressed, but made no attempt to either prolong or instigate conversations.

When it was coffee time Judith went out into the kitchen with Sue.

"Well, what do you think of him, Sue?"

"You were right about one thing, he's certainly handsome. I thought you were exaggerating, but he really is fantastic."

"Then you like him?"

"There isn't anything to dislike, is there? He's a bit quiet, but that's probably a good thing. No doubt his boys will be noisy enough!"

"He isn't always this quiet."

"How often have you been out visiting together?"

Judith sighed. "Never. I haven't got any family, and he doesn't seem in any hurry for me to meet his."

Sue put chocolate biscuits onto a plate. "Surely you'll have to meet them soon if you intend to marry quickly. Unless he doesn't think his family will approve of you."

Judith took the tray off the work top. "Somehow I don't think that's the reason. He doesn't give the impression that he's in the least bothered what his mother or sister think about anything. To be honest I don't think women count for much in his opinion."

Sue paused in the doorway. "Be careful, Judith. I know he's rich, and handsome, and anxious to marry you, but you're a woman. If he doesn't care for women very much, where will that put you in a year's time?"

Judith laughed. "Don't be silly. I'll be his wife. That's an entirely different matter."

Behind her friend's back Sue shook her head slowly. There was something about Marc that she couldn't take to, but she didn't know what it was. Certainly it wasn't anything obvious, and Dave was managing to talk to him quite easily. It was just that she found him a shade too reserved.

She had the impression that it wasn't shyness that made him quiet, but indifference. He didn't think very much of her and Dave and so he wasn't putting himself out to charm them in the same way he had charmed Judith. This evening was a gesture of goodwill; a sign that he understood Judith's need to introduce him to her friends. But there would be no further visits, and no invitation to his house once he had married, of that Sue was quite certain.

At eleven o'clock Marc looked at his watch and caught

Judith's eye. "We ought to be going, darling. I don't like to leave my sister there too late."

Judith stood up quickly. "I hadn't realized the time! Thanks for a lovely evening both of you, we've really enjoyed ourselves."

"You must come again," said Sue. Marc smiled vaguely and started checking his pockets for his car keys.

"You'll have to come to us, after the wedding," said Judith.

"I hope we're invited to that," put in Dave.

Marc turned around again. "We're not planning on anything elaborate. Just immediate family."

Sue was annoyed. "Judith doesn't have any family."

For the first time Marc ceased to smile. She was surprised at how penetrating his gaze was. "Well, she soon will have, won't she?"

Judith looked from Sue to Marc and back to Sue. "Of course you're invited." She laughed. "I'll need some moral support, Marc."

He shrugged and looked pointedly at his watch again.

Judith flushed. "Look, we must go. I'll ring you, Sue. Goodnight."

As the car drove away Sue turned to her husband. "What did you think?"

Dave yawned. "He seems a nice sort of bloke. Not my type, but very nice. I think Judith's lucky."

"Do you?" Sue stared out of the glass panel in their front door. "I wish I did. She deserves some luck at last."

Judith kept silent as they drove away from Sue's. She was more annoyed with Marc than she had ever been before, but he appeared quite oblivious to her silence.

"I'll drop you off, Judith, if you don't mind. As soon as I get back I'll have to take Zilla home so there's not much point in you coming too."

"That suits me," said Judith icily.

She didn't speak again, merely wished that he wouldn't drive the Porsche quite so fast as her head was beginning to ache.

"Here we are, then. I'll come straight around to you after work tomorrow and we can discuss a wedding date."

"Are you sure you need to consult me about it? You seem quite capable of drawing up the guest list on your own."

There was a long silence. Marc tapped his fingers on the steering wheel but didn't reply.

"Well?"

He turned towards her. "I didn't realize you wanted an answer."

"Of course I want an answer. You were very rude to Sue and Dave, who just happen to be the only friends I've got. I want them to come to our wedding."

"Then naturally we'll invite them."

"I doubt if they'll come after your behavior tonight."

He gave a low laugh. "If we invite them it's hardly my fault should they choose to stay away."

By now Judith's temper, which was seldom aroused, was beginning to surface. "I don't think it's anything for you to laugh about. How will you feel if I behave like that when you finally deign to introduce me to your mother and sister?"

"You can behave how you like when you meet them. And if you wanted me to drive you down to Surrey before this then I apologize. I didn't realize you were so keen to become one of the family."

"The trouble with you," shouted Judith, "is that you don't care about other people's feelings. As long as you get what you want that's all that matters.

"You don't like daughters, so you ignore Kara. You don't like my friends, so you decide to ignore them as well. You don't like animals, so Sam's an inconvenience. I suppose I'm extraordinarily lucky that you like me, considering eight other women failed to meet with your approval. You're thoroughly selfish and ill-mannered, and I don't think that I do want to marry you after all."

With that she wrenched the door open and ran up her front path. Half-blinded by her tears she fumbled to open the front door, hearing Sam's barking getting more frantic every second. Finally she managed it and stumbled inside. She let Sam into the garden, sat down at the kitchen table and sobbed to herself. Marc wasn't the kind of man to consider whether or not there was any truth in what she had said, he already knew that. No doubt by now he had already gone, and probably she wouldn't hear from him again. She laid her head on the table and wept.

"Judith?"

She snuffled and lifted her head.

"Judith, I'm sorry."

Then he was behind her, wrapping his arms around her and explaining. "I don't want to share you, I want you to myself. I know it's selfish, you're quite right about that, but it's because I care so much. I'm no good with words. I know I haven't said enough of the right things to you, but that isn't because I don't think them. I do. I love you, Judith. I want you for my wife. Of course your friends can come to the wedding. Invite anyone you want, but please, forgive me for tonight."

He was saying all the things that she wanted to hear, and because they were what she wanted to hear she chose to believe them. She could understand his inability to say the right things, she was self-conscious about expressions of affection herself. She could understand too his desire to have her all to himself. She knew that she found his children difficult to accept because she could see how they would come between her and Marc. Everything that he said made sense, and she desperately needed to be desired.

They kissed and embraced and she was even oblivious to Sam's mournful cries outside the back door. Hand-in-hand they walked to her front door, and she stood there waving when he finally drove away. That night she dreamed about her wedding, and the next day could hardly pass quickly enough for her until six o'clock came, and he was with her once more.

Again Sam had to be put in the kitchen. His animosity towards Marc was hardly conducive to marriage plans. Eventually they decided on the last Saturday in July, which left her under three weeks to get herself ready.

"We can have a honeymoon if you like," said Marc. "But really and truly I think it will be better if we go straight home, and then have a holiday alone together once the boys are back at school. That should avoid any immediate jealousy. Would you mind?''

She did mind a little, but she smiled and said, ''No, not at all,'' because she could see the sense of the arrangement. He held her hand for a moment.

''Good girl, I knew you'd understand.''

''There is one thing, Marc.''

''Yes?''

''Our bedroom. I'd rather it wasn't the same as when you were first married.''

''I'm not that insensitive. I've ordered a new king-size bed and I'm having it completely re-decorated. There won't be any ghosts, Judith. You don't have to worry about that.''

The next three weeks passed quickly. Judith shopped for new clothes, put the bungalow on the market and herself on a strict health and beauty regime in order to look her very best for the big day. To her surprise she still didn't meet Marc's sister or mother, and neither did he suggest that they sleep together again. She went to his house once or twice, but the boys were always in bed.

It was as though now she would soon be living there he wanted her to stay away until that time came. She suspected that he was afraid too much contact with the children might put her off, and she was touched by this sign of insecurity.

Then, very quickly it seemed to her, the weeks had passed and it was her wedding day. Marc had taken a reluctant Sam over to his house the night before, and so she awoke alone to a glorious warm day without a cloud in the sky. Marc had arranged for a car to take her to the church, and it was arriving at ten-forty. The wedding was at eleven and then everyone was going back to the house for a buffet lunch laid on by a catering firm. Again Marc had made all the arrangements.

''All you have to do, darling, is look lovely and arrive on time,'' he'd told her the previous evening. It was pleasant to be looked after so thoroughly, and she enjoyed a lazy soak in the bath and a last look around the bungalow that had been her home for so long. She only wished that she liked

Marc's house better, but on every visit she had felt thoroughly chilled, and she wondered what it would be like in winter.

Finally, putting such a silly worry out of her mind, she dressed carefully in her cream linen suit with dove gray blouse, shoes and gloves, and picked up her spray of red silk roses that she and Marc had chosen from a shop in Bourne.

One or two neighbors watched when the car arrived for her and she walked out of the bungalow for the last time, but no one spoke. She and her mother had always kept to themselves, and she had no idea what her neighbors were like. She had always greeted them when necessary, but that was all. Now they watched silently as she drove out of their lives, and not one of them even wondered where she would be living from now on. Within a few weeks she would be forgotten by them all.

At the church a shorter, slighter version of Marc stood waiting for the Daimler to draw to a halt. This was Craig, Marc's cousin, who was to give Judith away. She smiled shyly at him. He had Marc's wide, innocent eyes, but he lacked his physical presence. Also he smiled even less than his cousin, and seemed quite overawed by his small part in the ceremony.

As she walked down the aisle to the strains of the Wedding March, Judith's heart was fluttering wildly. She wished that she had more people there that she knew. Somehow the sight of Sue and Dave and their boys alone on her side of the church, only emphasized the loneliness of her life so far. She tried to see what Marc's mother and sister looked like, but they both had on large picture hats and she only glimpsed the backs of them before her eyes were drawn to Marc.

He was wearing a pale fawn suit and a light beige shirt with a deep brown tie. His hair was swept back more tidily than usual and it was impossible to believe that he was actually going to marry her. He looked far too remote and glamorous to be her husband, and she gripped her spray of roses so tightly that her knuckles gleamed white. Then, as she drew level with him, he smiled at her and immediately she was calm. Her stage fright disappeared, she felt composed and confident. Everything was going to be all right.

When the short service was over and they went out of the church doors Judith was surprised that there was no photographer waiting. Instead Craig took some snaps, the best man—a colleague from Marc's office—took some more, and finally Dave snapped away with his cine camera. Marc made it plain that he didn't like having his photo taken, and within fifteen minutes they were climbing into the Daimler and on their way to their home. They were now man and wife.

Judith leaned back on the seat and gave a small sigh. Marc took hold of her right hand. "Tired, darling? Never mind, it's over now. Incidentally you look very attractive. I like your outfit, it's most sophisticated."

She could hear the underlying note of laughter. "Does that surprise you, Marc?"

"It's certainly a new facet of your character. Don't get me wrong, I like the idea of several women in one. At least I won't get bored!"

She felt a flicker of worry. "I hope you won't. I hope I never bore you, Marc."

"And I hope I make you happy. There, now we've made our good resolutions we can enjoy the rest of the day."

Mrs. Watson was waiting at the front door to greet them. She had undertaken to supervise the caterers and was plainly enjoying the job.

"Welcome home sir, and madam."

Marc nodded gravely. "Thank you, Mrs. Watson." He grinned at Judith as they made their way into the drawing room. "She's one person who's having a perfect day!"

A few minutes later the next car arrived and Marc's mother and sister came into the drawing room together. Judith was astounded at how similar the two women were. They were both blonde; small, neat women with deep blue eyes and wonderful complexions. The only difference was that whereas Zilla looked full of energy her mother looked tired. Her shoulders drooped slightly as though the heat had drained her of sufficient energy to hold herself upright.

She was quite a bit shorter than Judith, who bent down to

receive her new mother-in-law's kiss. "I wish you well my dear," she said in a low, gentle voice. "At least you look a strong girl." Judith gave a puzzled glance at Marc, who shrugged and put a glass of champagne in his mother's hand.

Then it was Zilla's turn to place a restrained kiss on Judith's left cheek. "I hope you'll be very happy," she said quietly. "Don't let the boys exhaust you too soon."

Judith laughed. "I don't think they'll exhaust me, they seem very well-behaved children."

The two women glanced at each other before smiling identical, meaningless smiles, and moving away towards the table of food.

For the next hour Judith and Marc chatted to everyone who was there, and Judith noticed how well her stepsons conducted themselves, even little Michael, whereas Sue and Dave had great difficulty in preventing their two from creating mayhem after their initial shyness wore off. Once or twice Marc glanced at the two boys as they chased each other around the room, their voices rising with their self-confidence.

Finally Sue came over to Judith. "We'd better go, you can see how our two are ruining everything. Marc's boys are incredible. Are they drugged or something?"

Judith giggled. "Just in awe of their father, I think. I'll ring you soon, Sue. Thanks for coming."

Sue hugged her. "Be happy, love. Remember, we're always there."

Judith watched them go with a pang of regret. She too doubted if they would be frequent visitors to her new home.

After all the toasts and good wishes Marc's mother began to round up the boys. Judith was surprised.

"It's a surprise, for them and for you," explained Marc. "They're all going to spend the night at Zilla's, and they'll watch a film on her video as a treat. Zilla thought you'd appreciate just one night without them."

"What about Kara?"

"She's at the Watsons. Mrs. Watson will bring her back on Monday."

"I suppose she's too young to go with the boys,"

surmised Judith, but Marc had turned away to speak to Paul and didn't answer.

When everyone had finally gone the big house was strangely silent. The large room looked stark without people milling around in it, and Judith went over to the windows to catch the last of the sun's warmth. She felt shy and awkward now that she and Marc were alone.

He stood in the doorway watching her.

"How many rooms are there, Marc? I couldn't remember when I was describing the house to Sue." It wasn't that she needed to know, but she had a compulsion to talk about generalities.

"Six rooms downstairs, plus downstairs cloakroom. Six bedrooms and two bathrooms upstairs and one attic room, unused except for the boys' train sets. Do you want to see our room?" He held out a hand.

Judith walked over to him. "How big's the garden?"

"We've got an acre of ground. I'll take you around it tomorrow. There's a swimming pool and a grass court down the far side of the house. All the boys swim well, but only Philip can play tennis as yet."

They began to walk upstairs together. "You're very isolated here."

"Not really, it's an illusion. The wall all around helps to keep the rest of the world away."

"But it's very quiet."

"Not once the children get going!"

"I suppose not. It's only that once you come up the drive the rest of the world somehow ceases to exist. It's as though you've created your own little world here."

Marc stared at her.

"Don't you think so, Marc?"

"Not at all. It's probably because you're used to town streets."

Judith nodded. "Probably." She knew that wasn't the reason, but if Marc didn't feel the same then there was no point in trying to explain.

At the top of the stairs he turned left and they went along to the end of the landing. He pushed open the heavy wood-paneled door. "Here we are, our bedroom."

It was an enormous double room, and even the king size bed made little impression on it. A green and white duvet covered the bed and at the window matching green and white striped curtains hung, blowing gently in the light evening breeze. Fitted closets went the length of one wall, and a vanity unit and stool were beneath the windows where the light was best. The carpet was white shag-pile, and a white rocking chair stood in one corner of the room, its cushion covered in the same material as the curtains.

Judith looked around for a long time. "It's lovely, Marc. So light and relaxing."

"I hoped you'd like it. All this half of the closet is yours, will that be enough?"

She glanced at her cases which he had brought over the night before.

"Heavens yes! I haven't got nearly enough clothes to fill even that."

"Well, that's something you can soon remedy. We've got our own shower unit through this door here, and toilet too. It saves wandering around at night and waking the children."

She wished that she felt more relaxed, but despite the champagne and Marc's calm, quiet manner, her nerves were still jangling. It wasn't even as if this was their first night together, yet now that they were married she felt that it was a beginning, and she wanted things to go well.

Marc put his hands on her shoulders. "Don't look so worried. Marriage is meant to bring untold joys, not all the cares in the world!"

Despite his words his eyes weren't laughing, they were watchful, strangely speculative. She put her arms around his waist and hugged him. "I know. I'll feel better if I have a shower and freshen up a bit."

When she emerged from the shower she did feel better.

"I think I'll do the same," said Marc. "Incidentally," he added casually, "we're not going to take any precautions from now on, are we? I mean, we did agree we wanted a family."

"I'm still not on the pill, if that's what you mean."

"Fine. I won't be long."

Judith put on a new silk nightgown, a luxury she hadn't

been able to resist, and pondered again on Marc's love of
children. It seemed strange to her, but then what did she
really know of his deepest thoughts and desires? From her
own point of view it was nice to be able to think in terms of
having a child, and she only hoped that when she did he or
she would be as attractive as her stepchildren.

When Marc returned he was quite naked, and completely
unself-conscious. She watched him move around the room,
and he reminded her of some graceful animal. He seemed to
glide rather than walk, and his dark skin and very white
teeth reminded her of some jungle predator. Fear touched
her and she sat up straighter in the bed. This was Marc, her
husband, a man she already knew. She could not understand
the fear.

He turned out the light, then only the gleam of remaining
daylight through the curtains lit the room. It was impossible
to see him clearly and her fear intensified. She felt his hand
touch her bare shoulder, and she jumped.

"What's the matter?" Even his voice sounded different;
sharper, more harsh.

"I can't see. Why don't you put the lamp on, Marc?"

He remained silent, but his hands were wandering all over
her. He pulled her nearer to him, his movement abrupt, even
rough. She struggled slightly. "Marc, you're hurting me."

Her resistance increased the power of his grip. His breathing was quickening and he pushed impatiently at her shoulder straps. She tried to free herself and help him, but he
pinned her to the bed with his body and wrenched fiercely at
the silk. She heard it tear and gave a small cry.

"Marc, for God's sake, what's the matter? Let me take it
off."

Her fear was now turning into terror. She could just make
out the shape of his face as he lowered his mouth to hers,
and then he was kissing her savagely, drawing blood from
her lower lip. She protested briefly, but then he lowered his
mouth and teeth to her unprotected breasts and this time she
cried out in earnest.

After that it turned into a nightmare. She would not have
believed that he could so abuse her, but the more she cried
and struggled the greater his savagery became. She was

grateful at first when he finally penetrated her, but even that was primitive and brutal and seemed to go on for an eternity. She knew that she was sobbing, pleading with him to release her from the pain and horror, but he appeared deaf to everything.

Then, when she felt that she could not possibly take any more, he gave an animal howl of pleasure and collapsed against her, his weight stunning all the breath from her bruised body.

She lay quite still, not daring to move in case she instigated some fresh assault, but then she realized that it was over, at least for tonight. She pushed feebly at him, knowing full well that she couldn't move him, wanting only to show him that he was crushing her. He gave a small murmur and rolled off.

Judith waited for him to speak. Surely he would say something. Offer some words of apology or explanation. Then she heard it; the slow, regular breathing that told her he was already asleep. Now, free of him, she allowed herself the tears that she had previously held back for fear of somehow enraging him further. She hugged her arms around her aching body and prayed for deliverance from another night like this. Eventually, in the early hours of the morning, she fell into a fitful doze.

She awoke to the smell of coffee and opened her eyes to see Marc putting a cup carefully on the table beside her.

"Good morning, darling. I thought you'd like a lie-in, but it is nine and the boys will be back by ten."

Her terrified eyes stared into his warm, brown, compassionate ones.

"Did you sleep well?" he continued smoothly. "I must say I did. Probably all the champagne."

She wondered if it had been a nightmare. An overstimulated brain causing a vivid dream. Then, as she sat up, she saw livid marks over her breasts and upper arms. She moistened her lips with the coffee. Marc too was looking at her body. He reached out one hand and she flinched away from him.

"I'm sorry, Judith; it looks as though I got a bit carried

away. You shouldn't be so desirable. Now, shall I get some breakfast while you're dressing?''

She wanted to speak, to protest, to ask him why it had happened, but before she could find the right words he had gone, leaving her alone in the giant bedroom. Now it would be much harder to bring the subject up again. She knew that, and knew that he knew it too. As she painfully dragged herself from the bed she wondered with horror how she was going to find the courage to face another night with him in this room, a room that had already lost its previous charm for her.

By the time that she had showered, dried her hair and put on a coral-pink shirtwaister dress the smell of a cooked breakfast was making its way up the wide stairs and she realized that she was very hungry. Marc was standing by the stove with his back towards her when she entered the kitchen, but he seemed to know instinctively that she was there, for even as she opened her mouth to speak he called out for her to sit down, everything was ready.

The long pine table with its high stools was not the most comfortable place to eat. Judith kept wanting to lean back and only just stopping herself in time. Her plate of eggs, bacon, sausage and tomatoes looked so appetizing that she forgot her physical and mental discomfort and concentrated upon the food

"That was delicious, Marc."

He glanced down the table at her empty plate. "How about some toast and marmalade to follow?"

She was tempted, but shook her head. "I mustn't. I don't want to put on too much weight, none of my clothes will fit!''

"Don't worry. The boys will soon run any surplus flesh off you.''

"People keep implying that the boys are full of energy, yet they seem very restrained to me.''

"You'll realize what people mean once you're with them all day, every day. We can stack the dishes in the dishwasher. I usually fill it up all day and then switch it on in the evening. By the way, did I tell you that I've taken three days holiday, so you won't be left alone with the children just yet?''

Judith felt immeasurably relieved.

"I hope the good weather holds," continued Marc, "and then we can get outside with them. I thought we might take a trip to Twycross Zoo tomorrow. Would you like that?"

"I'd love it. It's years since I went to a zoo. I could take my sketchpad and do a few drawings."

"Great idea."

He smiled at her, but she quickly looked away. The memory of last night overshadowed everything. She could not bear to see a return of the expression that had so terrified her last night, and the only way to be sure of keeping it away was to avoid eye-to-eye contact. He watched her flick her gaze nervously away from him and he frowned.

In the awkward silence that followed Judith suddenly became aware of a whining noise, faint but unmistakable. She jumped to her feet.

"Sam! I'd forgotten Sam. Did you put him out this morning, Marc?"

He picked up their plates and wandered across the kitchen with them.

"No. I put him out last night. Since he's virtually incontinent I didn't want him sleeping in the study, and kitchens should never house animals. He's all right. I made him up a bed in an outbuilding. I gave him plenty of newspaper, and his basket from the bungalow."

"You had no right to do that," flared Judith. "He's never slept anywhere but indoors. He's too old to be pushed outside now."

"Nonsense. Dogs were never intended to exist as pampered toys. He's got a good warm coat on him, and as it's midsummer, I hardly think he's likely to go down with pneumonia."

Judith opened the back door and ran out onto the small patio. Over to her right she could see one end of the swimming pool, and at the edge of the house a small stone building which she assumed was used for changing. Then she heard Sam bark, and realized this was the outbuilding Marc had mentioned.

When she opened the wooden door Sam leaped out at her, putting his front paws on her chest and covering her with hysterical licks of relief and possession.

"Good boy, Sam! Good dog. Don't worry, you won't sleep out here again."

Suddenly Sam started running around Judith's ankles in frantic circles, brushing against her legs as though for reassurance. She looked back to the house. Marc was standing in the doorway watching them, but running towards him from the far side of the house came the boys, and it was the boys who were causing Sam's distress. She crouched down and tried unsuccessfully to soothe him, but as the shouts from the children grew louder, Sam slunk away from her, retreating to his stone kennel which he apparently liked more than Judith would have expected.

With one last glance back at the dog she retraced her steps to the house. The boys were gathered around Marc, all chattering loudly. When she reached them they moved back a little, giving her space to walk into the house. Instead she smiled at them.

"Hello! Did you have a good time at your aunt's?"

Four dark heads turned towards her. "Yes, thank you," they chorused.

"What film did you watch?"

"*Superman II*," said Paul politely. "It was great."

"Did you have a nice evening?" queried Patrick, his hazel eyes fixed unblinkingly on her face.

Judith felt herself blush and she was sure that one of the boys sniggered. "Yes, thank you."

"Oh good!" said Patrick, and this time they all started to giggle.

Marc cuffed Paul good-naturedly around the ears. "Get inside and change into your swimming things. It's perfect weather for the pool."

"Swimming, smashing!" They all ran inside, jostling and laughing as they went.

"I don't have a swimming costume," said Judith stiffly.

"We'll get you one tomorrow then. Perhaps you wouldn't mind watching this morning?"

"I'd prefer that, under the circumstances."

He frowned.

"I don't particularly want to display my bruises."

"Do you bruise easily? That's unfortunate. I'll go and make sure they're not leaving their clothes in a trail around the house. Won't be long."

Left alone, Judith glanced around her. The sloping lawn was in perfect condition, the rose bushes were flowering profusely, and the miniature conifers inside the stone wall were all dark green, forming a thick hedge that would one day be higher than the seven-foot barrier provided by the stones. A perfect garden, yet somehow it was too perfect, too lush. The scent from the roses was too sweet, almost overpowering, and the grass was unnaturally smooth.

It looked, she thought, as though overnight everything could easily turn rotten. Like the choicest peach that within hours begins to discolor and turns soft, the garden seemed fixed at a point in time when perfection had been reached. It was even possible that beneath the surface the process of decay had already begun, as yet invisible to human eyes, but slowly, inexorably, beginning to spread.

With a start she realized that the boys were coming out, and she tried to put the unhealthy picture of decaying vegetation out of her mind. It was a ridiculous flight of fancy, and she had no idea what had caused it. The truth was that she felt uncomfortable in the garden, and she was seeking a reason. Even so her imagination had certainly got the better of her.

They ran past her, their bare feet slapping on the patio before they found the grass and raced faster towards the pool. Michael lagged a little behind the older three, and he cast a shy glance at her from beneath his long, dark lashes. He was the only one of the children that she could feel any affinity for as yet, and so she tried to engage him in conversation.

"Don't you need arm bands, Michael?"

"Of course not. Arm bands are for babies! We all learned to swim before we could walk."

"I wish I'd done that. I didn't learn until I was twelve, and I found it quite difficult."

"Twelve!" He looked astonished. Then he gave her a

friendly grin. "You couldn't help it," he assured her. "You were a girl, weren't you?"

"That's true!"

He ran after his brothers and she followed slowly, calling for Sam as she passed his kennel. Sam ignored her, lying with his head on his front paws he followed her with his eyes, his expression mournful.

Judith sat on the garden hammock that was placed beside the pool and swung gently to and fro as she watched the boys swimming around, ducking each other a great deal but all swimming fast and well. She noticed that Philip—who, if she remembered correctly, was seven—was almost more at home in the water than he was on land. He was so far the most self-effacing of the brothers; whenever she noticed him he was behind one of the older two, but in the pool he was plainly the leader.

Unlike most children they didn't appear to be showing off for her benefit, indeed they seemed oblivious to her. Watching them jumping in and out she realized that it was possible to see that they were not white—the rays of the sun could never have achieved such a uniform shade of light coffee— but she couldn't believe that it would ever arouse any prejudice. If Sue could see them now, Judith thought, then she would be completely won over.

"You don't mind if I go in?"

"Marc! I didn't hear you."

"You were miles away."

"I was admiring the way they swim. Philip's exceptionally good, isn't he?"

"Yes. He's going to be a fine all-around athlete if he works at it."

Seeing Marc stripped down to trunks in broad daylight brought back memories of the previous night, and Judith averted her gaze from his body.

"Go in then," she said lightly. "Show me how good you are!"

He dived cleanly in at the deep end, and the water parted so smoothly there was scarcely a ripple. Then he remained beneath the surface until he popped up in the middle of the boys, who all leaped on top of him trying to push him down again. Paul climbed out and fetched a large beach ball from the edge of the grass, and Judith closed her eyes as they all began a noisy and complicated version of pig-in-the-middle.

When she opened them again they were still playing, but more quietly now. All their faces bore expressions of intense concentration, and some of the leaps that Philip made in order to secure the ball were unbelievable to Judith. He reminded her of a salmon leaping upstream, and he continued to jump lithely and effortlessly into the air without any sign of tiring.

Michael, not yet as accomplished as his brothers, began to lose interest and looked over at Judith. She waved at him. He glanced quickly around, saw that his brothers were occupied, and waved back. He gave a conspiratorial grin as he did so, and she felt a rush of affection for him. As he turned back to the game Paul's head twisted around sharply, but Judith was now sitting with her hands in her lap and she saw him shrug and look away.

It grew very warm in the hammock. She let her head rest on the back and half-closed her eyes. Marc and the boys were in a circle now, moving around and around and singing some rhyme completely unknown to Judith. She wondered what came next, whether one of them had to dive and stay immersed for a set time or something similar, but the chanting went on and still they continued to circle.

A plane flew overhead and Judith glanced up to watch its smoke trail in the sky. When she looked back at the pool Marc was in the middle of the circle, at least she thought at first it was Marc, but then she realized it couldn't be, for Marc was still in the circle, his hands linked to Paul and Michael.

The figure in the middle was faint, shimmering, but unmistakably adult. The hair was dark, dark and wavy. The face was indistinct, averted from the hammock. Judith leaned forward. The face turned towards her, and she saw the eyes. Dark eyes, full of sorrow. The lips were drawn back from the teeth in an expression of agony, and even as Judith watched she saw tears form in the eyes and roll down the pallid, translucent skin.

Remorselessly the figures in the water continued to encir-

cle this pathetic figure, who finally turned fully to Judith
with such an expression of pleading that she found herself
on her feet and running to the edge of the water.

"Stop it! Let her go! Let her go!"

Her voice rang out harshly in the warm summer air. She
heard one of the boys cry out in alarm, and heard too Sam's
frantic barking as he raced out of his kennel towards her.
Immediately Marc was at her side, water dripping from his
huge arms and shoulders.

"What is it? What's wrong?"

She looked at the boys, all standing silent now, their faces
shocked. The game was over. The woman had gone. At
least she had accomplished that by her shout. All the boys
stared at her, and the amazement in their eyes was so
obviously genuine that she suddenly wondered if the appari-
tion had only been visible to her.

Marc was frowning heavily at her, waiting for an
explanation.

"What were you doing?" she whispered.

"Doing? We were strengthening our leg muscles by
treading water. What made you cry out?"

"I saw . . ." She looked up at her husband. He too looked
shocked, shocked and yet in a strange way excited. As soon
as he realized she was looking at him his expression
changed, became bland again.

"Judith, what frightened you?" Instinctively she sensed
she should lie.

"I must have dozed off. Just for a moment, when I woke
up, I thought you had Kara in with you."

"Kara? Poor Judith, you really worry about Kara, don't
you? Rest assured, I don't throw her around like a ball even
when she is here, but right now she's still with Mrs.
Watson."

"I'm sorry. It was the dream. I'm overtired, I think I'll
go inside and make some squash for us all."

"Good idea. It's time they came out now, anyway. Come
on boys, time's up."

With a determined effort Judith managed to walk away at
a normal, steady pace. She didn't glance back to see how
the boys were taking her explanation, and she didn't run

away, much as she wanted to. Halfway to the house she realized that Sam was at her heels, slinking along beside her, belly almost on the ground. His fur stood up around his collar and saliva spattered his nose and chin. All in all he gave the impression of a very disturbed dog. He stopped at the back door, lying in the shade and refusing to enter the house.

Systematically, Judith searched the kitchen for glasses, cordial and a tray. She concentrated on the ordinary, every-day task, refusing to allow herself to dwell on what she had seen. Perhaps Marc and the children hadn't seen it; perhaps it had only been visible to her because she was the interloper. It made more sense if that was so. The distress was unlikely to have been caused by the swimmers in the pool, who should have been regarded as friends. But there was no way that Judith could be regarded as a friend, not by Elizabeth.

And it was definitely Elizabeth that she had seen in the pool. A shadow of the girl in the photograph, but unmistakably Elizabeth.

All at once her calm reasoning, her attempt at a logical explanation for such a manifestation, broke down. With a sob Judith ran out of the cool mosaic-tiled kitchen and up the stairs. Up into the bedroom, where she flung herself down on the king-size bed and continued crying. The shock combined with the terror of her wedding night had proved too much for her to cope with.

Eventually Marc came quietly into the room. He sat down next to his wife and laid a hand on the small of her back.

"Don't cry, Judith. Please don't cry like that. Tell me what you really saw. Perhaps I can help."

She bit on the knuckles of her left hand. "You can't. You'll think I'm mad."

He stroked her light brown hair soothingly. "You're the most balanced woman I've ever met. Tell me, Judith."

"I saw Elizabeth." Her voice was muffled by the duvet but he understood.

"Elizabeth? In the pool?"

"Yes."

"I suppose that's possible. She loved playing around with Paul and Patrick in the hot weather. I personally believe that when people experience strong emotions in one particular place then they leave something of themselves behind there when they die. I don't think it's anything to be upset about. After all, it's nice to think that she lives in that way. It makes death less final, don't you think?''

Judith sat up and stared at him. "You believe me then?"

"Naturally. I didn't believe your story about Kara though!"

"But she didn't look happy."

He frowned. "In what way?"

"She was crying. She looked trapped. Yes, that's it. Trapped."

"Now there I must doubt you. Why should she look trapped?"

"I don't know! I'm only telling you what I saw."

He looked away from Judith, out of the bedroom window. "I wish I'd seen her." He sounded so forlorn that she drew away from him, feeling that her presence could only emphasize his loss.

Outside the boys were playing tag on the lawn and their voices echoed in through the open window.

"Marc?"

He looked surprised to see her sitting there next to him.

"Marc, couldn't we move?"

"Move? Because you think you saw a ghost? No, we couldn't. This is my home. The boys have grown up here. It won't happen again, Judith. It was probably a combination of excitement and over-tiredness. You must be sensitive to that sort of thing."

"I'm sure I'm not."

"Then why didn't anyone else see her?"

"Perhaps they did."

He stood up. "Now you're being bloody ridiculous. Do you honestly think the children wouldn't have been distressed if they'd seen their mother materialize in front of their eyes four years after her death?" His voice was growing harsher. "Do you think that children of their age wouldn't show some emotion if that happened?"

Judith shook her head. "I'm sorry. I don't know why I said that."

"Nor do I. I accept that you've had a nasty fright. Either

you dreamed about Elizabeth or you did see her, and it's shocked you. Let's leave it at that, shall we?"

No, a voice screamed in her head. Ask him about last night. But she couldn't find the words. He studied her carefully, then came and sat next to her again.

"This is really all about last night, isn't it? I frightened you, and now you don't know what to expect from our marriage. That's why you thought you saw Elizabeth. You're probably wondering if that's how it was with her."

"I'm not. Not consciously."

"But I did frighten you?"

The screams from outside intensified. There was the sound of a slap, followed by a shriek of pain or outrage. Marc closed the window.

"Never mind them. They're always murdering each other."

Judith kept her head lowered and nodded. "You did frighten me. You hurt me too."

He put his hands over hers. "I should have warned you. The truth is, I forgot that I hadn't. I mean, I didn't forget, but I half-thought you'd understand."

"How could I? You didn't behave like that when you stayed at the bungalow."

"Last night was different. Last night I was making sure that you conceived a son."

Judith couldn't believe her ears. She quite forgot her embarrassment and lifted her eyes to his. "You don't honestly believe that what happened last night will make me give birth to a son? Marc, that's ridiculous!"

"It happens to be true. I don't know why, but that's the way it is."

"Marc, if it's true why don't other people know? You could make a fortune, there are always people desperate to have sons."

"It doesn't work for everyone, but it always works for me."

"You mean, that's how your boys were conceived? All four of them?"

He nodded.

"Didn't Elizabeth mind?"

"She understood, eventually."

"And Kara?"

He smiled. "Always back to Kara! As I explained, Kara was a mistake. A routine coupling that was intended purely for pleasure. I won't make such a mistake again."

Judith shook her head. "I can't believe it! You're an intelligent man, surely you must realize what complete nonsense you're talking."

"My intelligence doesn't come into this. I can't explain it to you; you must just take my word for it."

There was a long silence while Judith absorbed the fact that no matter what she said to Marc he wouldn't listen. He believed every word that he was saying and considered this justified his savage assault on her.

"I really don't know you at all, do I," she said at last. He smiled at her.

"Don't be silly, of course you do! I'm the same as you, a mixture of good and bad! It's over now. It won't happen again, not for a long time."

"It won't ever happen again," she said firmly; and because he smiled with his mouth and then embraced her she failed to see the look of annoyance that crossed his handsome features.

Still holding her in his arms he moved her back towards the bed, laid her down on it and unbuttoned her dress. She was rigid with fear, all her trust in him completely destroyed, but slowly, carefully and with great skill he made extensive love to her. Gradually she found herself responding; anxiously moving her hips in search of something that remained tantalizingly out of her reach, but which she desperately wanted to ease the ache in her. With a groan Marc fell against her while she was still searching, and he apologized and whispered promises and words of love until she forgot the final disappointment and remembered only the new sensations she had experienced.

Regretfully Marc left her and began to dress.

"I'll go and play cricket with the boys. Come down when you're ready."

Sleepily she watched him go, and she even managed a slight smile when she recalled his explanation for the nightmare that had been their wedding night. She found it faintly touching that an intelligent man could retain such a superstition, but it no longer worried her as much. It would only take the birth of a daughter in nine months' time to prove his theory a fallacy, and everyone knew there was a fifty/fifty chance of that happening. That was supposing that she even became pregnant this month. If she didn't his theory was still nullified.

Changing into shorts and top she went over to the window. The garden was quiet now and no game of cricket was in progress. Instead the boys were sitting in a circle on the grass, their heads together in the middle. There was no sign of Marc. In the distance, through a break in the pine trees right at the bottom of the garden, Judith saw Mrs. Watson with Kara in her arms.

The bowed, chestnut heads of the boys lifted slowly and turned as one in the direction of the newcomer. They sat, backs straight, heads unmoving, and watched the woman advance. Kara began to struggle to be put down, and as soon as her feet touched the grass she trotted as fast as her chubby legs would go in the opposite direction from the boys. Around to the front of the house, where as far as Judith knew there was no way she could enter the house. Mrs. Watson wagged a finger in the direction of the boys and then set off in pursuit of Kara. When she was out of sight the four small boys started to laugh, rolling around clutching their stomachs, their earlier discussion forgotten.

It was a strange little scene, but Judith was still wrapped in the warmth of Marc's lovemaking and so she dismissed her unease and put it down as childish mischief, made strange only because she was unable to hear what had been said. With a lighter heart she went downstairs.

Once in the hall she could hear a faint thudding on the front door. Smiling to herself she opened it and as she expected Kara was standing in the porch.

"Hello! Why didn't you come in the back way, Kara?"

"Carry!" In a gesture that was already becoming pleasantly familiar, Kara stretched out her arms, waiting patiently for Judith to lift her up.

"Come on then, lazybones!"

Leaving the door open for Mrs. Watson, Judith went

through into the kitchen, enjoying the feel of small hands clasped firmly around her neck. Marc was sitting at the table and looked quizzically at his new wife.

"Has she lost the use of her legs?"

"I found her at the front door."

"Don't sound so accusing. This isn't a home for foundlings. She does live here, and was expected!"

Judith put Kara down, and the little girl clung on to her legs.

"I saw Mrs. Watson carrying her across the lawn, but when Kara caught sight of the boys she ran away from them. I'm sure they tease her too much."

"I hope Mrs. Watson put her down first."

"I'm sorry?" Judith wasn't sure what he meant.

"Before she ran off. Otherwise it must have been a sight worth seeing."

She giggled. "Silly! Of course she did. I thought you were going to play cricket with the boys."

"They were rather more interested in their own games. I did think we might all go to Peakirk this afternoon. It's only twenty minutes in the car, and with two adults the children should remain under control!"

Judith was delighted. "I've always wanted to go there. I'll take some charcoal and a sketchpad. Are most of the birds tame?"

"Haven't you ever been there?"

Judith shook her head.

"We used to go a lot, before Elizabeth died. The birds are fairly tame, you can feed them from your hand if you like although some of the geese peck quite hard."

Judith went to move over to the fridge, but nearly fell as Kara's grip tightened.

Marc quickly stood up and put a steadying hand beneath her elbow.

"Let go, Kara! Go outside and play, we've got to get lunch."

Kara looked rebelliously at her father. "No go!"

"Well, at least sit on a chair, darling. I nearly fell then." Judith tried to sound conciliating to make up for the sharpness of Marc's tone.

"Judith, kindly don't contradict me. Kara, go outside at once."

The toddler looked from one adult to the other. Her eyes filled with tears and her bottom lip began to tremble.

"Don't start crying, it's the oldest female trick in the book and I'm not impressed. Get out of this kitchen."

He didn't raise his voice on his last sentence, in fact if anything he dropped it, but Kara gave a loud wail and then hurried out of the back door. A few seconds later there came shouts of laughter from the boys and her wails turned into prolonged sobbing.

"Marc, what are they doing to her?"

"Nothing! She's just a cry-baby."

"Of course she is, because that's exactly what she is. A baby."

"And likely to stay that way now you're around."

Judith frowned. "What does that mean?"

He put out a hand and ruffled her hair. "It means I can see I'm going to have my work cut out to stop you spoiling the children. Now, don't let's argue over Kara of all people."

"What are we doing about lunch. I mean, what is there for us to eat?"

"Mrs. Watson's back. She'll see to that. Come on, let's tell the boys about Peakirk."

Out in the garden all was relatively quiet again. Paul and Philip were playing badminton on the grass, Michael was barely visible down on the climbing frame and Patrick was sitting in the middle of the lawn reading. Of Kara there was no sign.

"Boys!"

At the sound of their father's voice they all stopped what they were doing and turned their faces towards him.

"We thought you might like to go to the wildfowl park after lunch."

"Yes, please!" they chorused.

Patrick stood up and sauntered towards them. "May I take your binoculars, Dad?"

"If you're careful. Judith is going to take her pad and do some drawings."

Instantly they all turned their attention on her. She looked around at their faces; attentive, interested, there was no suggestion that they might find her hobby boring.

"Are you good at drawing?" asked Paul.

"Quite good. I enjoy doing it too."

"Judith has done some book illustrations," said Marc.

"Then you must be good. None of us are any good at drawing."

"We'll have to learn from Judith," said Philip firmly.

She smiled. "I think being artistic is a gift rather than something you can be taught, Philip."

Philip turned away from her, not bothering to reply. How like his father he was, reflected Judith. More like him than any of the other boys. She remembered that like his father he didn't care for animals. Recalling this, she automatically looked over to Sam's kennel.

"I'm just going to make sure Sam has plenty of water, it's so hot," she explained as she walked away from them all.

"Come in and get washed," ordered Marc. "Mrs. Watson will have lunch ready soon."

The boys went inside, leaving him watching Judith through eyes that were thoughtful.

Crouching down at the entrance Judith peered inside Sam's retreat. He was curled up happily in the straw, and Kara was lying against him, her fingers clutching his soft coat. At first she seemed frightened, but as she made out Judith's features she cheered up.

"Nice dog."

"Yes he is a nice dog, Kara. It's time for lunch now, and then we're going to see some birds. Would you like that?"

Kara scrambled out onto the grass on all fours. "Pretty lady," she gurgled, catching hold of the hem of Judith's dress.

"And I think you're very pretty too. Was there a bowl of water for the dog, Kara?"

But Kara was on her way back to the house. Judith peered in at Sam again. "At least you've got one new friend, old boy! Where's your bowl? Oh yes, that's good. Well, if you want to stay here I can't force you to come out."

She gave him one final pat and then left him, his tail thumping the ground, but his ears laid back.

As soon as lunch was eaten the boys rushed off to change into trainers and collect their pocket money for bags of seed and ice creams.

Judith picked Kara out of her high chair. "Come on, I'll get you changed."

"Come off it Judith. You don't want to cart her all around with us. She'll be bored to tears."

Judith tightened her grip on Kara. She was determined to put an end to his relentless exclusion of his daughter from family matters. "I'm sure some of the boys went when they were her age."

"That was quite different."

"In what way?"

They stared at each other for a moment, and finally Marc shrugged. "Never mind. Take her if you like. There's a pushchair somewhere, I'll put that in as well. Don't expect me to push her though."

"I wouldn't dream of it."

He sighed. "I'm sorry, I don't know why I'm being so difficult. It's nice for Kara to have another female around the house, and you're quite right to stand up for her. After all, if you don't, who will?"

"Exactly! Come on, Kara, we mustn't keep the men waiting!"

The twenty-minute drive would have been completed in absolute silence if Kara hadn't been with them. The boys were all absorbed in writing things in notebooks, car numbers Judith assumed, and never spoke a word. Kara on the other hand, obviously over-excited by the unaccustomed outing, never stopped her childish babbling. Very few of the words were recognizable to Judith, but now and again she put in a "yes" or a "really" and that was enough to satisfy the little girl.

When they pulled into the gravel car park Marc's expression was thunderous.

"If she's going to come out with us regularly, she'd better learn to behave," he snapped as he assembled the pushchair.

Judith ignored him and strapped Kara in carefully. The

boys were already heading for the entrance, and several people turned to look at them as they walked past. They all stood very straight, and their distinctive coloring and striking similarity to each other made them impossible to overlook.

Despite their scuffed trainers, their faded denims and their ordinary T-shirts they all looked incredibly neat and clean. Their hair was tidy, their manners perfect, and they were a credit to their upbringing. And yet, despite her pride in their appearance, Judith felt uncomfortable. There was something abnormal in such neatness. They should feel free to be more boisterous, more rowdy. She decided that Marc had been over-strict with them since their mother died.

Once inside she was grateful for their self-control. While other adults had to keep chasing off after their children, chiding them for chasing birds or frightening nesting ones, she and Marc strolled hand in hand while the boys went ahead, pointing out different things to each other and talking excitedly, but causing no trouble at all.

Paul was the most knowledgeable. "Those are golden-eyed diving ducks," he said politely when she watched in amazement as they disappeared beneath the water, only to bob up on the other side of the lake. Then she heard a strange sound. "It's the trumpeting swans," he reassured her. "They're fenced off, because they're quite spiteful."

"You know a lot about them all, Paul. How's that?"

"I remember Mummy bringing me here. She had a book and read bits out."

"But you must have been very young."

He opened his eyes wide and gave a small, beguiling smile. "I've got a good memory."

"You must have. I expect that helps you at school too."

"Yep! Why don't you let go of Daddy's hand and do some drawing?"

Judith flushed and drew a pad and charcoal out of her large shoulder bag.

"Come into the flamingo park, there's a bench there for you to sit on," suggested Marc.

There was also a large pond with a fat, lazy carp swimming idly around. While Judith sketched the delicate, pink and white birds, Paul, Patrick and Michael sat by the pond watching the fish. Philip came and sat on the arm of the seat, his breath warm on her ear as she drew.

She was soon immersed in her subject, only vaguely aware of her silent watcher. Marc had joined the other boys, and when she had finished the birds she turned over a page and quickly did a sketch of the four of them by the water. As she drew she realized that Marc and his children had perfectly shaped heads, and she turned to see if Philip's was the same.

She took him by surprise, and caught him staring at her with such intensity that she was alarmed. His eyes, dark brown like his brothers', had the same gold flecks in them as Marc. These flecks seemed more obvious suddenly, particularly as every vestige of color had drained from his face, leaving it with a faintly muddy look. He wasn't blinking; he could almost have been in a trance.

Judith could feel his eyes boring into her, but she didn't know why. There was no sign of emotion in them; it was impossible to tell if he was angry with her or anxious to be near her.

"Philip?" Her voice came out abruptly and he jumped, his eyes flicking at once towards the rest of his family. "Did you want something, Philip?"

"No. I just liked watching you. You didn't mind, did you?"

"Of course not. Would you like to try?"

"No thank you. Not yet." He climbed down off the seat and ran over to his brother. Judith closed the pad and stood up. She no longer wanted to continue drawing. She wanted a cup of tea.

Kara had kept herself occupied all the afternoon and it was only now that she started to grizzle a little.

"You'd better get in the pushchair," said Marc. She quickly did as he suggested, then beamed up at him, all feminine charm.

He laughed. "Amazing isn't it! And they pretend it's the way we bring them up that teaches children sexism!"

Judith tried to push, but Marc wouldn't let her. "I'll do it. My penance for being so grumpy earlier. Am I forgiven?"

"Of course you are. Can we get tea here?"

"In that hut there. It's quite small; as it's fine I think we'd better bring our drinks outside. If we sit at one of the tables we can watch the ducks on the lake."

She waited with Kara while Marc and the boys went in and collected an assortment of cans and crisp packets. Finally they were all busy with their drinks, and as soon as Kara had finished her orange she fell heavily asleep.

The boys sat on the grass at the water's edge. Philip was staring over the lake, his mind obviously on other things, but Paul and Patrick were eagerly spotting different species of birds. Only Michael seemed at a loss for entertainment. Judith watched as he wandered around for a time, before smacking Paul on the back and running away. Paul turned around, saw who had done it and returned unperturbed to his birdwatching.

"He's very grown-up isn't he?" Judith remarked. "I would have expected him to hit Michael back."

"They all realize Michael is on the slow side. They make allowances."

"Slow? He seems quite quick for a five year old."

"Perhaps I should have said immature. He hasn't had much opportunity to develop properly, he never really knew his mother."

Judith would have expected the lack of a mother to have forced him to mature more quickly, but as Marc obviously knew more about children than she did she kept her thoughts to herself.

Michael circled around behind the tables for a time and then, without any warning, launched himself at Paul and Patrick with loud, aggressive shrieks. Judith watched incredulously as Paul struggled with the spitting, shouting figure who was attacking him. The contrast between Michael's normal shy politeness and this outburst of senseless fury astounded her. She glanced at Marc, who was getting to his feet and looking very angry indeed.

"Get off! Stop it, Michael!" Paul was shouting at his small brother, but whilst he was defending himself he made no move to counter-attack. Marc began to run towards the boys. There was a flash of movement, and Philip was suddenly standing over his brothers, his hands held above them. Judith's mouth went dry and her throat tightened, for in Philip's hands was a large stone and even as she watched his hands started their forceful descent.

She was never sure what happened next. Certainly Marc moved with incredible speed. One hand swung out sending Philip spinning away, the stone falling from his grasp as he fell; with the other hand he grasped the back of Michael's jeans and hoisted him into the air, leaving Paul free to run back to Judith. Michael continued to scream and struggle, even turning his head in an attempt to bite his father's hand.

Paul touched Judith on the shoulder. "I think we ought to go back to the car," he said solemnly. She looked around. Everyone was watching them, their faces frozen in disbelief.

"Good idea, Paul. I'll bring Kara. Would you open the gate?"

When they were back at the car they all stood silently, the sound of Michael's yells preceding his arrival in Marc's arms. Upon reaching the car Marc stopped, then literally threw Michael away from him. Judith screamed as she watched him fly through the air, landing on the gravel with a sickening thud.

"Get in!" snapped Marc, unlocking all the doors. The three older boys got in silently. Judith put Kara carefully between Paul and Patrick. She didn't want her next to Philip, not after what she had just witnessed. Marc slid in behind the wheel, staring stonily ahead. Judith sat trembling beside him. The complete disintegration of the children's polite veneer had shattered her. She knew now why Marc's mother and sister had cautioned her about coping.

Michael continued to lie in the car park. He had stopped screaming but he was crying and his face was scratched and bleeding down one side. He looked towards the car, but only Judith was watching him. Eventually he stood up and limped slowly back to them. Marc got out and opened one of the back doors without speaking. Michael continued to snuffle and sob, but quietly now. Marc swung the car angrily out of the car park, narrowly missing an oncoming vehicle. The journey home was completely silent.

Once they were indoors the boys all vanished with alacri-
ty. Mrs. Watson took the sleeping Kara from Judith's arms

and carried her upstairs. The house was silent. Silent, and
very cold. Ignoring Judith, Marc went into his study and
shut the door behind him. Uncertain as to what she should
do Judith remained in the hall. Presently Paul came downstairs. He looked at her in surprise.

"Where's Dad?"

"In his study. I wonder if I should go in with your
father."

Paul shook his head. "Better not. He gets furious when
one of us loses our temper like that, let alone two."

"But you didn't lose your temper, Paul. I thought you
behaved very well."

"Not me, Philip."

She remembered the stone. "Of course, Philip."

She looked down into the dark, serious little face. "Do
you know, Paul, I feel very tired. I think I'll go and rest on
the bed for a bit. Will you all be all right?"

His eyes were worried. "Naturally; we're quite used to
being on our own. Do you need an aspirin? My mummy
often used to take an aspirin after . . ."

"After?"

"After fights."

"Don't worry, Paul. I don't need an aspirin, I'm just
tired."

His liquid eyes scanned her features carefully. "We're
very glad that Daddy married you. It's nice to have someone
to teach us again."

"I'm afraid I can't teach you very much, except boring
things like table manners!"

He moved towards the kitchen, as capable of ignoring her
remarks as his father and Philip. "We all hope you'll have
some babies," he called back over his shoulder. "Some
new brothers would be nice."

As she moved slowly upstairs Judith thought that she
couldn't possibly face outings with more children than they
had already. Before sleeping she realized with a sense of
satisfaction that Kara had behaved perfectly the entire time,
which was more than could be said for the boys. Perhaps in
future Marc wouldn't be so quick to criticize her.

* * *

She slept heavily, and when she awoke she could not make out where she was. For a few minutes she looked sleepily around her, and then she remembered. She was a married woman now; she had a husband and stepchildren, and this was her home.

"Did you have a good sleep?"

"Marc!" She could just see his shape outlined in the doorway. "How long have you been standing there?"

"Not long. You looked very peaceful, I didn't like to disturb you. It's been a difficult day for you one way and another."

Judith rubbed at her eyes and sat on the edge of the bed, her feet touching the floor. "What's the time?"

"Nine-thirty. The boys are all in bed; Mrs. Watson saw to that before she left."

She searched for her shoes. "Have you eaten?"

"I wasn't hungry. I could eat now though."

"So could I. I hope there's some salad left in the fridge. It's very kind of Mrs. Watson to give up a Sunday to help out."

"She's so pleased to see me married she's only too anxious to make life smooth for you. I think she envisaged a future where all she did from nine to five, week in and week out, was run around after my children!"

It was cooler now, Judith opened her wardrobe and pulled out a long, belted cardigan. Marc remained in the doorway.

"I'm really sorry about the afternoon, Judith."

"Don't be silly, I had to see them at their worst some time."

"Rather a baptism by fire!"

She linked her arm with his and opened the door. "I was surprised at Michael. He's such a sweet little boy normally."

"He needs you, Judith. Spend as much time with him as you can."

Judith tightened her arm around his. "Of course I will, but to be honest none of them seem to need me. They're all very self-contained."

"It's a pretense. They all need you, Michael and Philip even more than Paul and Patrick."

"And you?" she teased lightly.

He released his arm and put both hands on her shoulders, then looked down at her with great tenderness. "I need you most of all, Judith. You'll never know how much finding you has meant to me, never."

"I love you too," said Judith, for surely his words were a declaration of love?

Once in the kitchen she made them chicken sandwiches and a salad which they ate from the pine table. She remembered to put their plates into the dishwasher, but Marc had to show her how to work it.

"I like these labor-saving gadgets. What am I supposed to do with all the extra time they give me?"

"Look after your new family. Believe me that will take all the time you have."

Before they went to bed Judith made one more attempt to persuade Marc to let Sam sleep in the house, but he was adamantly against it, and she had to admit that the dog was already attached to his new home. She still felt guilty as she patted him goodnight and then walked away back to the house, but Sam seemed ready to sleep and gave her no real reason to continue pleading for his re-admittance to the kitchen.

Once in bed Marc made it plain that he was ready for sleep. "That's the trouble with making love in the middle of the morning, it spoils the night! Sleep well, darling." He gave her a cool, unexpectedly passionless kiss and turned away on his side.

Judith could tell by his slow, regular breathing that he was soon asleep, but she found it more difficult. Probably because of her long evening sleep her mind was now fully alert. She tried picturing soothing country scenes and even counting sheep, but it didn't work. The bedroom was very hot, and eventually she slipped out of bed and went over to the open window.

There was a pleasantly cool breeze coming in, and she wondered why the air in the room remained so stifling. How hard I am to please, she thought, usually I find the house too cold. Now, at night, it's too hot. Quietly she went out onto the landing, hoping to find the air cooler there.

It wasn't. Even at the top of the wide staircase the atmosphere was heavy. Everywhere was silent. Not a sound came from the children's room; she couldn't even hear the ticking of any clocks. Perhaps there was a storm brewing she thought, at least that would clear the air.

All at once she heard a sharp click. She turned towards the sound, and realized that a light had come on in one of the children's bedrooms. She tiptoed towards it, unsure who slept there but hoping that no one was unwell. Outside the door she stopped, not liking to intrude until further sounds gave her cause.

There was a soft rustling noise, as though sheets had been thrown back, and then the definite padding of feet across the carpet. She expected the door to open, but it remained closed. A slight scraping sound followed, then a heavier noise and finally a light squeaking that set her teeth on edge.

Judith waited, and the squeaking continued. It sounded like chalk being dragged across a blackboard. For some reason she remained silent, not wishing to draw attention to her presence. As she waited the heat of the house intensified, and the small amount of air that came from beneath the bedroom door was so hot that she found it uncomfortable when it touched her feet. She frowned. Surely one of the boys wasn't boiling a kettle for a midnight drink, but the escaping air could have been steam so hot did it seem to her.

The relentless scratching continued; it grew faster and faster and finally she could not bear to stand there any longer. She put out her hand and grasped the door knob. Immediately the scratching ceased. She knew that one of the children was on the other side of the door, listening to her, perhaps frightened by her presence.

"It's only me, Judith. Are you all right?"

There was a pause.

"Who is that? Is it you, Paul?"

Another pause. Then the sound of feet padding towards her and slowly the door opened. A small, composed face looked out at her.

"Philip! What's the matter? Can't you sleep? It is hot, isn't it?" As she spoke Judith advanced into his room.

"Goodness, it's like an oven in here. Why don't you open a window?"

"I like it hot," he said quickly. "Please don't open the window. I can only sleep when I'm nice and warm."

"Nice and warm! You must be roasting!"

He stood by a desk and chair, his body tensed. "That's really my business, don't you think?"

His tone was so polite that it took her a moment or two to realize he was being rude. Then she rationalized that it was a long time since he had been accountable to any woman, he was bound to resent unnecessary interference.

"Of course it is. This is a strange house. It's so cold during the day."

His sharp eyes were almost insolent now. "That's how we like it to be, in the daytime."

"All of you?"

"All of us."

He looked so solemn that she had to smile. "How fortunate that the house obliges you then."

Something flickered at the back of his eyes, some moment of amusement or even condescension, but it was quickly gone. Even so Judith resented it.

"You'd better get back to bed. Boys of seven need plenty of sleep."

"I will."

She waited, but he remained like a soldier at his post.

"Go on then, get in."

He set his mouth in a mutinous line. "You're not my mummy, you can't order me about."

"I'm going to be looking after you from now on, so I think it would be nice if you learned to do as I asked."

Her pleasant tone didn't mollify him in the least. He darted a look of pure malice at her before wandering over to his bed and climbing in.

"I'm in my bed. Now you can go back to Daddy's bed."

"I will. I hope you get off to sleep soon. Goodnight, Philip."

"Goodnight." He kept his eyes on her face, and she turned towards the door.

As she was about to walk out her glance fell on the top of

his desk. She stopped and went back for a second look. There was a piece of charcoal lying beside sheets of paper. The top sheet was blank, but it didn't conceal the piece beneath it on which she could clearly see black lines. She moved the plain sheet, and caught her breath in surprise.

There, on the second sheet, was a perfect portrait of Marc. Philip had managed to catch the sheer magnetism of the face, the strength of the jaw and the contrasting gentleness of the eyes. She moved the picture and found one of Michael chasing after a goose. That too was very good, stark but effective.

Judith turned to the boy crouching watchfully on his bed. "These are excellent, Philip. Why didn't you tell me you could draw like this?"

He shrugged. "I didn't know I could. I just watched you this afternoon and then tried it out when I couldn't sleep."

"Well, they're superb. Far better than mine when I was your age. Are there any more?"

"No!"

Her hand was already moving the picture of Michael aside. Before she heard Philip properly another picture was revealed. It was of Judith, but not a true sketch, a caricature. She was standing in a garden, probably the back garden she realized, surrounded by foliage and she looked pathetically small and feeble. The scale was wrong, so that even the shrubs towered over her, and her face was turned towards the house with a look of such helpless misery that she automatically closed her eyes and piled the other pictures on top of his final one.

"Why did you do that, Philip?" she asked softly.

"You weren't meant to look, it's private."

"But why have you made me so small?"

For a moment he stared aggressively at her, and then, slowly, he smiled. He smiled at her as his father did. A gentle, charming, smile.

"Because that's how I see you. I'm tired now. Goodnight."

There was nothing she could do but leave him. She didn't know whether he slept well, she only knew that she did not.

* * *

At eight o'clock exactly Marc opened his eyes and turned his head towards Judith.

"Good morning, darling. Did you sleep well?"

Judith felt heavy-headed and lethargic, and her tone was peevish.

"No, I didn't. I was much too hot."

"I'm afraid I like a warm bedroom, sorry. You should have pushed the duvet over to my side."

"The whole house was hot. I went along the landing for some air and it was absolutely stifling. I can't think why. It's always cold in the daytime."

He smiled lazily. "You sound thoroughly irritable. Stay where you are and I'll bring your breakfast up. If it looks like being fine again I thought we'd go to Mablethorpe. It's ages since the boys, sorry the children, had a day at the sea."

Judith watched him put put on a short-sleeved shirt and light blue denims. Even this morning, cross and exhausted, she could still be stirred physically by the sight of him. She reflected that he was the most magnetically attractive man she had ever met. Perhaps it was the contrast between his powerful sixteen stone frame and his predominantly gentle personality that attracted her. She didn't know.

It puzzled and disturbed her to realize just how great a spell this sexual attraction cast over her. He could dispel all rational doubts and fears by his presence, releasing in her a physical craving that banished every other emotion. She found it both shaming and a little frightening, particularly as he himself showed no awareness of his effect upon her.

"Judith? What do you say?"

She jumped. "I was miles away! Say about what?"

"A day at the coast."

"Lovely. I'll get myself a swimming costume. Then I can join in the water sports!"

Ten minutes later Marc was back with tea and toast. "Here you are. The boys are all wildly excited, and I'm sure Kara would be if she knew what we were talking about."

He plugged his shaver into the point over the small basin in the corner of their room and started to shave.

"Did Philip mention last night?" asked Judith casually.

"No. What happened?"

"Nothing much, but when I was walking about trying to get cool I saw that his light was on. I went in to see if he was all right."

Marc turned off his shaver and turned towards her.

"You don't need to fuss over them. They're quite capable of coming to us if they're unwell. In fact, they prefer to be left alone at night."

"Well, I wasn't to know that. You'll never guess what I found him doing."

"What?" His tone was cautious.

"Drawing! What's more, he was drawing exceptionally well. You were quite wrong inferring they didn't have any artistic talent."

He switched his shaver back on. "Fancy that! As I said, you're good for them. But don't go into their rooms again at night. None of them sleep that well and they like their privacy if they get up and play. It's a golden rule in this house, never interfere unless they're making a nuisance of themselves!"

Judith felt upset. "You make it sound as though I was spying on him. It wasn't like that at all. I just wanted to make sure he was all right. You said that Philip and Michael needed the most attention, now you say leave them alone."

"Don't make a big drama out of it. I'm only saying leave them alone at night unless they call for you. Now, take that hurt look off your face. I appreciate your good intentions, and in the day time you can give them as much of your time as you like."

She sighed. "I'll get up now. Perhaps my headache will go after a shower."

"You didn't tell me you had a headache." He sounded shocked out of all proportion by her statement.

"Don't make a big drama out of it," she teased. "This honeymoon is hard work, you know!"

"Take an aspirin and stay out of the sun," he cautioned. "I'll keep the boys away more, give you a break."

"There's no need," she called as she disappeared into the

shower, but Marc remained frowning after her, a look of annoyance mixed with distress on his face.

When she came back, naked and smelling of Miss Dior, she did indeed feel better. Marc was still standing by the basin, and his gaze slid over her. She halted by the side of the bed, her gray eyes wide as he moved towards her. When he reached her he ran his large, long-fingered hands down from her shoulders to her waist, causing a tremor of pleasure to pass through her.

"I need you, Judith. You must take care of your health."

She remembered Elizabeth and thought that she understood the reason for his fear.

"Don't worry, I'm far stronger than I look!"

He covered her mouth with his, his tongue darting between her parted lips, his hands tangling themselves in her wavy hair as he tilted her head back beneath his.

Quickly he lowered her onto the bed, moving his mouth from her lips to her breasts and stabbing at first one nipple and then the other with his tongue. She could feel them hardening, and her head moved restlessly from side to side on the pillow as her excitement mounted. This time Marc made no mistakes and her pleasure rose steadily until it peaked in one glorious climax that caused her to scream aloud with the overwhelming sensation of sensuous gratification.

He kept his arms around her for a moment or two and then moved gently away. "I'd better go down and see what they're all up to. We'll set off when you're ready."

Judith smiled at him. "That was wonderful, Marc."

"For me too. See you in the kitchen!"

She lay staring thoughtfully into space. He had satisfied her physically but not emotionally. It was as though at moments of greatest intimacy, he drew back from complete commitment. She sensed that for some reason known only to himself he was reluctant to acknowledge his deepest feelings. Pushing to one side the fear that it was Elizabeth who was the barrier between them she sat up, relieved to find that her lethargy had vanished. Humming cheerfully she began to dress.

In the kitchen the boys were all busy. Paul and Patrick

were buttering rolls, Philip was mixing squash for the flasks and even Michael was occupied, half-heartedly washing lettuce in a plastic bowl at the sink.

"Good morning, boys."

As one, they turned their heads towards her, their dark eyes fixed on hers for a moment, but she was getting used to them now and it no longer disconcerted her.

"Hi!" said Paul as the others glanced away again. "We're going to the seaside."

"I know. Where's Kara?"

"She's feeding Sam," said Michael. He sounded sulky and tired.

"Michael wanted to feed him but Daddy wouldn't let him," explained Patrick.

"Can Kara manage?"

"Dad prepared the food and carried the bowl out, all she's doing is watching him eat it! Then she's going to run around the garden with him, he likes playing with her."

Marc, busy at the table, looked over his childrens' heads at Judith and smiled. "You see, I don't forget poor Sam."

"I want a pet," interrupted Michael.

"No, you don't."

"I do. I want a gerbil, like Paul and Patrick had."

"I'm sorry, Michael, I don't think you're old enough to look after a pet yet."

"Then let Philip help me."

Paul and Patrick turned towards Philip, their eyes gleaming with interest and something else, something to which Judith couldn't quite put a name.

Philip stared defiantly at them and looked at his younger brother. "I don't mind helping you with a hamster or some mice."

Paul and Patrick looked at each other, and now it was plain that it was excitement Judith had seen in their eyes, excitement that had intensified. Marc had gone very quiet and even Michael seemed taken aback. Philip continued to look around at everyone with a challenging air.

"That's kind of you," said Judith quickly. "I remember your father telling me you didn't like animals very much."

"I don't, but I'll help Michael if he wants one so badly."

"We'll talk about it later," said Marc abruptly.

"Why can't I?" wailed Michael. "It's my birthday next week, I want a hamster for my birthday."

"Then of course you can have one," said Judith. "I'll make sure it's looked after properly, Marc."

Marc shrugged, his resistance gone. "If you like. I'm sure Philip is quite capable of seeing to it if he doesn't mind. Now then, where are those rolls?"

It was half-past ten by the time they left.

"How long will it take?" inquired Judith.

"A couple of hours. I hope Kara doesn't talk all the way."

Fortunately, still worn out by her exercise at Peakirk, Kara slept the entire journey, and the boys were as silent as they had been the previous day.

The beach was crowded, but by walking along it away from the town they managed to find an area where they could set down their folding chairs and groundsheet without too many people near them.

"Did you bring your drawing things?" asked Philip eagerly.

"No, she didn't," said Marc abruptly. "She's got a headache today and I don't want you bothering her."

Before Judith could remonstrate, explain that Philip hadn't been a nuisance at Peakirk, father and son had exchanged a long glance of understanding that completely excluded Judith, and caused an inexplicable chill to run down her back.

"OK," said Philip easily, "I'll go and paddle then."

Marc watched him run athletically down the beach.

"He's a very self-contained boy," said Judith as the other children wandered off. "I think he's exactly like you."

"Yes, he is like me. I suppose they all are, but Phillip is so much like me that I feel his emotions with him. When he hurts I hurt too, it's quite painful."

"I don't suppose he hurts too often, he's very well adjusted."

"I'm glad he gives that impression."

Paul had walked back to them and stood by his father, waiting his turn to speak. Judith felt drowsy and comfortable, and decided to have a rest.

"I think I'll . . ." in mid-sentence she changed her mind, "take Kara for a walk," she finished and immediately wished that she hadn't. It was too late.

"Great idea," enthused Marc. "I'll go in the sea with the boys while you're gone. Kara, come here. Judith's going to look for some pretty shells with you."

Reluctantly Judith stood up, and as she walked away Paul watched her go, an amused smile on his face. Then he turned to his father. "Judith went in to Philip last night. She disturbed him while he was working."

"I know. I've spoken to her. It won't happen again."

"She's nice. It's a pity that she . . ."

"Don't say it. Put it out of your mind. There's no other way."

Paul slipped his small, brown hand into his father's. "She will give us brothers, won't she?"

Marc looked down into the eager eyes. "Oh yes, don't worry about that. She's going to give you some brothers. That's why she's here."

"And she'll be able to help Michael and Philip?"

"I think so. I chose her very carefully, Paul. If she can't help them no one can."

"Michael isn't so bad, it's Philip. Why is it so difficult for Philip?"

Marc looked out towards the sea where Philip was jumping through the waves and throwing the beachball with Patrick. Bright, handsome, athletic Philip.

"After the accident your mother found it very hard to accept Philip. He never really had the benefits from her that you others did."

"Nor did Michael. He was only a baby when she died, but he's not like Philip."

Marc put a hand casually on Paul's shoulders. "Philip's different."

Paul looked up at his father, his eyes shadowed. "Even more different than the rest of us?"

With a small, regretful sigh Marc nodded. "Even more different."

"He doesn't like to talk about it. He says he isn't a mutation."

Marc glanced again at his favorite son, still playing in the water. "That isn't a word I've ever cared for either. We're certainly different, but I prefer to think ahead. We are the future, Paul. Eventually, perhaps in your grandchildren's lifetime, we will be the normal ones and those people who haven't managed to progress and develop as we have, will be the outcasts."

"But until then we have to keep it secret?"

"I'm afraid we do. Try and help Philip understand." Paul nodded. "I expect Philip will be our leader when you die," he commented as he started to run towards the sea. "Oh yes," said Marc to himself, "he'll definitely be the leader."

The hot sun had made Judith's head begin to ache again, and her limbs felt heavy.

"Look Kara, there's a pretty one." She pointed to a small, pink and cream shell half-buried in the sand.

"Pretty," echoed Kara, picking it up carefully. Then she sat down heavily on the sand.

"Carry!"

"I'm tired," protested Judith. "Come on, you can walk back."

"Kara tired."

Judith looked wearily around her. Everywhere children and dogs were running over the sand, full of high spirits and boundless energy. How she envied them. Now she understood the drained look on the faces of so many young mothers. Before her marriage she had blamed women for letting themselves go, now she knew better. You had no choice, children took all your energy without your consent.

"Don't be stupid," she murmured to herself as she reluctantly picked Kara up. "You've only been married three days, you can't possibly be worn out already!"

Once she found their chairs again she deposited Kara on the groundsheet and sat down thankfully. Her legs ached and so did her back. Kara looked dainty, but she felt quite substantial when she was in Judith's arms. She closed her eyes, the sound of the gulls providing a background as she drifted off to sleep.

When she started to wake the sun was shining directly onto her face and she kept her eyes closed. She could hear two of the boys talking on the ground near her.

"You mustn't, Philip. Daddy says she's tired."

"Only for a minute. I won't hurt her. I want to try something out. It won't tire her. I'm not stupid, I know we've got to take care of her; otherwise she won't last very long."

Judith wondered what on earth they were talking about. What wouldn't last very long she thought? They made it sound like Judith herself, and she gave a small smile.

"Quickly then." That was Paul's voice she decided.

Whatever Philip wanted to do it was blessedly silent. She continued to keep her eyes closed, the sun and sea air relaxing her aching body. She let her thoughts turn to Sue. As soon as Marc went back to work she would give Sue a ring, invite her over for a morning. It would be nice to talk to Sue again.

All at once, her thoughts changed direction. She found herself visualizing the garden; the lush vegetation that still had the power to repulse her, and the clear blue swimming pool. Idly she pictured the boys in the pool, the four of them splashing around. In her half-dream they climbed out of the water and stood around the edge, in a straight line. Then another boy appeared and took his place next to Michael; exactly like the other boys, but smaller. Then another boy stood next to him; dark and handsome he still had the chubby legs of a toddler. Finally a small brown baby crawled from the bushes and joined the line. There they remained, seven identical boys in varying stages of development, all looking straight ahead of them with that impassive expression on their faces that Judith knew so well. Such handsome, terrifying children.

Unexpected fear swept over. Her heart began to thump erratically and with a suppressed scream she opened her eyes. Philip was standing in front of her and he glanced at her in surprise.

"What's wrong, Judith?"

"Nothing. I had a bad dream, that's all."

"Kara's gone down to the sea, is that allowed?"

"What?" She jumped out of the chair, scanning the edge of the water for a glimpse of the familiar fair hair.

"May I have an apple?"

"No, you may not. Come down to the sea with me, we've got to find Kara."

Philip sat down in her chair. "I've just been swimming, I'm not going all the way back."

"She can't swim like you boys, you should have stopped her," shouted Judith as she started running.

"You were the one who fell asleep," he pointed out implacably.

At the water's edge there were so many toddlers it was impossible at first to know for certain whether Kara was there or not. But the longer she looked the more frightened Judith became. She wished that she could find Marc, get him to help her, but he and the other boys had vanished too.

She spent nearly half an hour searching for Kara, asking people if they had seen the little blonde girl in her pink and white sunsuit, but no one had. Near to tears she made her way back to Philip.

"Where's your father?"

"I don't know. May I have an apple now?"

"No!" She didn't realize that she had shouted until people turned to look at her.

"I can't find her anywhere," she said in explanation of her anger, but Philip didn't look at her.

With her mind now full of strange men luring Kara away with the promise of ice cream and sweets, Judith felt frantic with fear.

"Judith? What's wrong?"

At the sound of Marc's voice she burst into tears. He walked up behind her and put his arms around her.

"What is it? Are you ill?"

"It's Kara. I've lost her."

"Silly girl," he said affectionately. "I took her with me. We went to get ice creams. Here, I brought you one back. It's melted a bit but still edible. Did you have a good sleep?"

"You should have told me," said Judith, mopping at her eyes.

"You were asleep."

"Well, Philip then."

"Philip saw us go, didn't you, Philip?"

He met Judith's incredulous stare blandly. "Yes. I saw you take her down to the sea. I told Judith Kara had gone down to the sea."

"You didn't tell me your father was with her. You let me think she was on her own!"

"Keep your voice down," said Marc. "People are staring."

"He deliberately frightened me. He wanted me to think something had happened to her."

Philip stood up, brushing sand from his long, lean legs. "I was only showing you how easy it would be to lose her. It was a joke. Can't you take a joke?"

"A joke? It was a cruel thing to do, Philip, surely you can see that."

"It wasn't cruel. It didn't hurt anyone."

"It did. It hurt my feelings. You scared me."

He looked at his father and back to Judith. "Sorry. I only meant it as a joke."

"But . . ."

"Let's forget it," said Marc impatiently. "Kara's still with us and when we've eaten these you boys can go on some amusements if you like."

"Yes, please!" they chorused, but Judith's resentment at Marc's dismissal of Philip's behavior simmered inside her, despite the perfunctory apology.

When the boys finally ran off to the amusements Marc moved his chair closer to Judith's.

"I'm sorry about that, darling. I know Philip frightened you, but I'm anxious that you and he should get on well so I didn't make too much of it."

"He doesn't like me," said Judith positively.

"He needs you. Look, I'll be perfectly frank with you. Elizabeth had difficulty in getting on with Philip, and I think that subconsciously he remembers that. He's afraid that you will reject him too, and so he's testing you out. Trying to prove to himself that what he fears is true."

"Which is?"

"That he's unlovable."

"Do you really think Philip believes that?"

Marc nodded.

"But that's terrible. You love him, and so do his brothers. How can he possibly think such a thing."

"We're not enough. He's never yet been accepted by an outsider."

Judith frowned. "Elizabeth wasn't an outsider, she was his mother."

"She was white, and . . ."

"White? You mean he feels that white people don't accept him? That's ridiculous. What about your mother, and your sister?"

"They're not very keen on Philip. They try and hide it, but he isn't stupid, he knows how they feel."

Judith sighed. It was all far more complicated than she had anticipated. "I don't understand, but I'll try and make allowances. I do realize that it will take time for all of them to accept me. After all, it's a big change in their lives. They've had you to themselves for several years."

Marc bent across and kissed her forehead. "You're so understanding, Judith. So civilized. I find that a great comfort."

At their feet Kara played contentedly with her shells.

"I had such a strange dream," said Judith conversationally, and told Marc about it.

"Perhaps it's an omen. Perhaps we're going to have three sons of our own!"

" I hope not. I don't think I could cope with eight children!"

Marc rested his head against the back of the chair and closed his eyes. "Of course you could," he said with a laugh. "At least, I hope you could. I want us to have three or even four more."

Judith too closed her eyes and smiled. "You have to be joking!"

He didn't reply, but there was no answering smile on his face. While his wife slept his mind leaped forward and charted the years ahead. It was only then that his lips curved into a smile. A smile of keen anticipation.

* * *

They left Mablethorpe at five, when Kara was no longer able to keep her eyes open, and even Michael was becoming irritable. Judith, despite her cat-naps, was still exhausted. Over the past few weeks, ever since first meeting Marc, all her energy seemed to be gradually deserting her. Every morning, especially since the wedding, the simple act of getting out of bed was an effort, and she was perpetually tired.

When they got back to the house and the boys ran off to shower the sand from their bodies Judith handed Kara thankfully over to Mrs. Watson and went slowly up to the bedroom. When she looked in the mirror she was horrified to see how pale and drawn she looked. Despite two days out in the sunshine her skin had a most unhealthy pallor. The nervous excitement and stress engendered by her marriage were taking their toll, she reflected wryly, and resolved to take things more easily, emotionally if not physically.

After splashing cold water on her face and wrists and changing into a loose cotton dress she went along to check on the boys. There were a lot of giggles coming from one room and she tapped on the door.

"It's Judith. Are you getting changed, boys?"

"Yes." It was Paul who answered her, and one of the others who smothered another giggle.

"Your father said that Michael was to put on his pajamas so that he could go straight to bed after supper."

There was a pause, and then Paul opened the door with Patrick peering out behind him.

"Michael's room is that one there," he said pointing. "Shall I tell him for you?"

"If you would."

"My pleasure." Patrick gave a muffled snort and turned his back on Judith. Paul smiled politely at her. "Anything else?"

She felt awkward, but it was impossible to complain in the face of Paul's politeness.

"Nothing else. Is Philip there with you?"

"No, he's busy in his room."

The door was closed gently in her face and she turned away, wishing she didn't feel so much of an outsider.

At Philip's door she hesitated, remembering the night. He was singing quietly to himself, and she recognized the tune, "Here we go gathering nuts in May." She was humming it to herself as she joined Marc in the study where he had poured her a drink. At the sound of the tune he looked up quickly.

"Why are you humming that tune?"

She smiled. "Why not?"

There was no answering smile from her husband. "I asked you a civil question, Judith."

Her own smile faded. "I gave you a civil answer. Why shouldn't I hum it, it's a popular song with children."

"Are the boys singing it?"

"Only Philip. Is that my . . ."

Before she could finish Marc had sprinted past her and she heard him racing up the stairs. A door banged, and for the first time since she entered the house the sound of raised voices floated down the stairs. Marc's was indistinct, his words impossible to make out, but Philip's was crystal clear.

"I can if I want to," he shouted. "This is my room, can do what I like here."

There was a mumble from Marc.

"I can do it on my own now, I don't need them. You can't stop me."

Judith heard the sound of a slap, followed by screams of temper from Philip.

"I hate her," he yelled. "Why did you have to bring her here? I don't need her, she's in the way. I wish she was dead too."

Judith's back was rigid, and she stood by the small drink table wishing she understood what the argument was about. Whatever it was she knew that she was the woman Philip wanted dead, and remembering his savage temper she was thankful that he was only seven. If he had been older she would have been truly afraid of his hatred. As it was, she pitied him and hoped that in time he would come to like and trust her.

A door slammed again, and this time lighter steps hurried down the stairs. She turned; Philip stood in the doorway, his eyes blazing with fury.

"What's the matter, Philip?"

He stared at her, his dark eyes smoldering. She wanted to tell him that she could help him, be a friend to him, but her head was buzzing and her thoughts were jumbled. The room went out of focus and only Philip's eyes remained sharp and clear.

Her confusion cleared, she knew what she had to say.

"It's all right, Phillip, I'm going. It was a mistake to marry your father. I'll go up and pack."

She walked purposefully out of the room and up the stairs. It was pleasant to be so certain of herself again. As though in a dream she passed the three other boys standing in a group on the landing; automatically she smiled at them but she didn't pause. Round-eyed they watched her go, turning to look down at their brother who stood glaring in the hall.

Slowly Paul shook his head. "Dad! Dad, Judith's packing her case," he called, "I think Philip's upset her."

Marc emerged from the bathroom, toweling his damp hair. He looked along the landing and through the open bedroom door where Judith was piling clothes into an open case like an automaton.

His mouth twisted in anger. The boys flattened themselves against the banister rail as he moved towards the double room. "What the hell are you doing?"

She turned a calm face to his. "I'm leaving. I made a mistake coming here."

He put out a hand, grabbed her by the shoulder and turned her roughly to face him. "You're my wife. You do as I say."

"I should never have married you," she muttered, "I have to get away."

He took one final look at her fixed expression then ran from the room and down the stairs, searching for Philip. Philip had vanished. He flung open one door after another, but there was no sign of the boy.

Alone in the hallway Marc opened his mouth and uttered

a primitive cry of fury. The boys upstairs glanced uneasily at one another.

"Now he's really mad," said Patrick in awestruck tones. "Philip had better look out."

The cry was repeated, and in her cot Kara clapped her hands over her ears and huddled beneath her quilt as silent tears fell from her eyes.

Out in the garden Philip, sitting in front of Sam's new home and watching the dog with sullen eyes, heard the second cry. He lifted his head, as though testing the quality of the sound. Then he rose and moved towards the house, his eyes apprehensive.

As he stepped into the kitchen Marc pounced on him. He lifted the boy in his huge hands and held him suspended at shoulder height. "You bloody little fool," he growled. "Don't you realize that without Judith you won't survive? Can't you tell how far removed from normality you are? You've got to learn. If you're ever going to fulfill my ambitions you have to assimilate all your knowledge. I chose her because of her knowledge of the arts and her unusually strong principles. Take advantage of this. Without absorbing some of her self-control you'll never be capable of adapting to life as it is at present. You have to learn to fit in, to camouflage your superiority. If you go on like this much longer there'll be another tragedy, and next time it might not be kept in the family. How could I protect you then? Do you want to be locked up forever?"

As he spoke he was shaking Philip from side to side. The boy's eyes grew even larger than usual. His face reflected fear, both of his father's rage and of what he was hearing. Marc's fingers dug painfully into his shoulders, and automatically the boy slashed at his father's face with his nails, narrowly missing his eyes.

With a thud Marc let him fall to the hard kitchen tiles. "Don't you dare try your tricks on me ever again," he raged.

Half-stunned by the fall Philip remained where he was, hoping Marc's temper was nearly spent. Marc looked down at his favorite child, and realizing how close the boy was to throwing everything away just when things were goin perfectly, he felt the long subdued primeval fury surge up in him.

Without thinking of the consequences he turned and picked up a heavy iron saucepan from the wooden rack. He lifted it above his head and smashed it down in Philip's direction, uttering a howl of rage as he did so. Philip hurled himself to one side and heard the tiles crack as the saucepan made contact.

"Dad! Don't, Dad, please. I'm sorry. I know it was wrong. Dad, don't, you'll kill me!"

Deaf to the words Marc's hands reached out and closed around Philip's neck. "You ignorant, opinionated bastard! You'll ruin us all if you don't learn to control yourself." As he swore he tightened his grip. Philip struggled vainly, and knew that he was going to be choked to death if he couldn't break his father's grip.

Paul, Patrick and Michael gathered in the doorway. Even Paul was at a loss. He hadn't seen his father lose control for so long that he didn't know what to do. It was the sight of Philip's legs buckling beneath him that finally goaded the boys into action. They ran forward together, hurling themselves on top of their father; grabbing at his arms, pulling on his hair, anything to distract him.

As the five of them wrestled in the cool kitchen Judith continued her packing, a soft smile on her lips as she did so. She felt calm and peaceful, and did not hear any of the noises from below.

The boys were having little effect on Marc, and Philip's eyes were now closed. In utter desperation Paul jumped from his father's back onto the ground, and managed with a final lunge to force himself between his father's legs. Quickly he reached up and grabbed. Feeling flesh between his fingers he then twisted, and continued to twist despite Marc's scream of agony.

The white hot pain forced Marc's hands to loosen their grip. Philip fell to the floor, his chest heaving, his eyelids beginning to flutter. Seeing that he was safe the other boys swiftly retreated; they didn't want Marc's rage turned in their direction. He would understand as soon as his temper had cooled; until then they wanted the safety of their rooms.

Doubled up by pain Marc began to return to reality. He saw the ugly cracks in the flooring, saw too his son lying by the deep freeze, his hands round his swollen throat. With a moan of distress Marc gathered Philip to his chest, cradling the boy's head with his hands, rocking him to and fro.

Gradually Philip's terror receded. He kept close to his father, feeling how his heart pounded in the massive chest.

"I could have killed you," whispered Marc. "How could I have gone on living if I had killed you? You above all of my children must live. You have all of the gifts. I'm sorry, Philip, I lost my temper."

"It doesn't matter," said Philip, his voice hoarse from his injury. "Now I know how important it is that I do as you ask. When I'm a man I must be able to control myself completely, mustn't I?"

Marc nodded. "It's the one thing I never mastered—and neither did your grandfather—and it's what holds us back. That's why Judith had to come and live with us. She's very controlled, very civilized. You must all take advantage of that. I don't know how long she'll be here, and so no time must be lost."

Philip licked his lips and swallowed with some difficulty. The pain was a reminder of this lesson that he would never forget.

"Will she be here long enough to give you sons?"

Marc held the boy at arms' length, "Yes. What do you know about that?"

"Everything. Paul told me after you'd explained it to him."

"Does Patrick know?"

"Not yet. He isn't ready, he'd be embarrassed."

Marc stood up and began to tidy the things that had been knocked to the floor during the struggle.

"Now that you'll be busy learning from Judith, do you think you could leave your mother alone?" He put the question casually, but his eyes were alert.

Philip, on his way upstairs to stop Judith from leaving, paused. "I don't think I can promise you that. I like punishing her. Paul was always her favorite, she hates m bringing her back. She's still tired too!'' He gave an unpleasant laugh.

"That's because you won't let her rest. Well, try not to do it when Judith's around.''

"OK. Shall I go and see to her?''

Marc nodded. "You'd better, or I'll have to start searching all over again.''

The case was packed. Judith had piled the rest of her belongings neatly in one corner of the room and with her cardigan over her arm was checking that she had all she needed. She turned as Philip came into the room and smiled pleasantly at him. "All done. Goodbye, Philip.''

He ignored the extended hand and stared into her tranquil gray eyes. He waited until they had begun to cloud over, and then he left her, confident that all would be well.

She looked at her suitcase in surprise. With a small frown she took in her pile of possessions, the open drawers and closets. What on earth was she doing, she wondered? Her head ached and she felt completely bewildered. Marc came into the room and she ran to him.

"Did we quarrel? I seem to have packed my case, but I can't remember doing it.''

He understood how frightened she must be feeling, and deliberately kept his voice low and soothing. "Of course we didn't! You came up for a rest on the bed, you had a headache. I think you were out in the sun too long. Sun and sea can be lethal, you know.''

As he spoke he was unpacking for her, replacing clothes and toilet articles. Bemused, she watched him. There was something she wanted to remember, something about Philip, but she couldn't grasp it and the harder she concentrated the more it slipped away.

Marc sat on the bed and pulled her onto his lap. "How about some food? You didn't eat many sandwiches at lunch, perhaps you're undernourished!''

"I must be going mad. How can I possibly have packed . . .'' She broke off and gave a gasp as a shaft of pain struck her. Both hands flew to her stomach and she doubled up, crying out as it lanced through her again. Sweat broke out on her forehead and she stumbled to the basin, just reaching it before she began to vomit.

After what seemed an eternity the pain and the sickness passed. Weak and shivering she allowed Marc to pick her up and lay her beneath the quilt.

"It must be the sun," she said. "I must be more careful in future."

He settled her comfortably and drew the curtains. "Yes," he said quietly. "It's a son. I've seen the symptoms before." But Judith's eyes were already closed in sleep. Thoroughly satisfied he left her there, nurturing his fifth son.

Tuesday was again a glorious day. When Judith awoke she felt thoroughly rested. Turning her head she found Marc watching her, his expression affectionate rather than passionate. She stretched lazily.

"Are we going to the zoo today?"

"I don't think so. I go back to work tomorrow, and I thought it might be a good idea to spend the day quietly here so that you feel thoroughly at home before I leave you to the tender mercies of the children!"

"As you like." She sat up. "I'm starving this morning. I suppose it's my turn to cook breakfast."

"You don't have to, not on your honeymoon. However, if you're offering . . ." and he closed his eyes again.

"I'll call you when it's done. Do the boys like cooked breakfast?"

"Yes, so does Kara." He couldn't disguise the amusement in his voice.

Judith flushed. "It must be catching, how else could I forget Kara?"

"The boys swamp her, as you're discovering."

It took Judith nearly an hour to cook sausages, eggs and bacon for seven, and by the time it was ready all her vitality of the early morning had gone. Despite the cool kitchen she was limp and hot.

"Daddy doesn't take that long," said Patrick flatly as he sat down on his stool.

"He's had more practice," retorted Judith, trying to keep her tone pleasant.

Philip started to eat the moment she put his plate down. He ate quickly and with concentration, ignoring the chatter from his brothers. Despite being called Marc hadn't joined them, so Judith left his in the oven and took her place between Michael and Philip.

"When's your birthday, Michael?"

"Next Monday. You did say I could have a hamster, didn't you?"

"I did. Don't tear at your food with your fork like that, cut it up properly."

"He's a messy eater," said Paul, neatly spearing a piece of sausage. "Dad says he'd rather watch animals in the zoo eat than have breakfast with Michael."

Michael's mouth tightened and Judith tried to divert him.

"Are you going to have a birthday party? I don't mind doing tea for some of your friends."

The boys glanced at one another as though unsure how they should react to her offer.

"It's very kind of you," said Paul finally, "but usually we take one or two friends out on a trip with us. Daddy doesn't care for children's parties."

"I don't care for the noise that goes with them," called Marc from the doorway. "Don't make rash promises, Judith. Parties aren't what you imagine, not in this house. They always end in fights and tears."

Michael tugged at her sleeve. "It's Philip's fault," he confided. "He's the troublemaker."

Judith looked at Philip's calm face as he continued eating, ignoring Michael's remark.

"I'm sure it isn't always Philip." She laughed. "You'd better let me know what you want to do as your treat."

Michael mopped around his plate with a piece of bread. "I don't want any friends here this year. I want to have a long talk with my mummy."

The knives and forks were still. Patrick and Philip kept their eyes on their plates. Paul glanced across the room at his father, and Judith remembered the swimming pool and

Elizabeth. Cool air traveled over her shoulders and neck and she shivered.

Marc moved over to his youngest son and laid a hand on the boy's unbrushed cap of hair. "Mummy's dead," he said gently, "it isn't possible to talk to the dead."

Michael looked up at his father in surprise. "But . . ."

"If you've finished, go and brush your hair. We're spending the day here, and if you want to swim you can."

They all slid from their stools, murmured their thanks to Judith and sidled from the room.

Marc took his plate from the oven and sat next to Judith.

"What did he mean, Marc?"

"Since you came the others have taken to talking about Elizabeth more. As he can't remember her he probably feels a meeting would put him on a more equal footing with them! Sometimes he can be very foolish. Where's Kara?"

"She's fast asleep. The seaside must have worn her out. I'm still starving, I'm going to do some toast."

Marc nodded. "That's right, build yourself up."

"I don't need building up, I'm perfectly fit."

He ignored her comment. "I thought we might all try our hand at some tennis before it gets too hot."

"I'm useless at it, but I'll try. Have you got a spare racquet?"

"You can have Mummy's," called Paul as he ran through the kitchen and out into the garden. "She wasn't any good either."

"Thanks a lot!"

Outside there was a shimmer of heat haze, but as Judith changed in her bedroom she was quite cold. It had been hot when she awoke, but now all the warmth had drained away and it was positively cool. She supposed it had something to do with the stone walls of the house.

Kara awoke before Judith could go outside, and it was nearly an hour later when she finally stepped into the garden. The heat hit her like a blast from a furnace and she took an involuntary step backwards. "Heavens, it's hot! I felt cold upstairs."

Marc, bending over one of the bushes glanced quickly at her. "You're never content with the temperature in the house! I'll have to buy you some thermal underwear for indoor use.''

Judith shaded her eyes, looking for the boys. ''Perhaps my blood's thin,'' she remarked casually. ''Where is everyone?''

''Down the bottom, on the apparatus.''

He held out a hand and she slipped hers into it. Kara trotted along behind, chattering to herself.

At the bottom of the garden Michael and Patrick were clambering over the climbing frame. Their feet were bare and they were both wrapping their long toes around the narrow bars. They were like agile monkeys, thought Judith with a smile. She heard an excited yapping sound and turned around. There, in the middle of the big lawn, she saw Sam, but a transformed Sam. She stared in astonishment, unable to believe her eyes.

The elderly dog was gamboling like a puppy, leaping high into the air and circling around Paul and Philip. Paul was laughing, waving his arms around, but Philip's face was thoughtful and he kept away from any contact with the animal.

Sam continued his frolicking. Judith remembered him when she first had him, he had played like this then, but now he was far too old and she felt a stirring of worry. Slowly she walked towards him. As she got closer she could see that whilst he was leaping and yapping like a one-year-old he was frothing at the mouth and his eyes were full of worry. He turned his head to look at his mistress and she could have sworn that he was beseeching her to stop his antics. ''Calm down Sam,'' she said soothingly. ''Sit boy! Sit!''

For a second Sam halted, but then he was off again, leaping manically up at Paul and yapping with apparent enthusiasm. Frowning, Judith stepped towards him, putting a hand out for his collar, but he twisted away from her in mid-air and ran off in the opposite direction, the boys close behind him.

''He's enjoying himself,'' said Marc, coming up behind her and putting his hands on either side of her waist. Her flesh tingled at his touch.

"His tail isn't wagging," she said, puzzled. "He's too old to behave like that."

"He's enjoying the boys, don't fuss." She could see Sam tearing around the edge of the swimming pool; his shrill barking was piercing, as were the shouts of laughter from the boys.

"I'm going to stop him." She started to move, but Marc's hands restrained her.

"Give me a kiss, Judith. You look particularly lovely this morning."

Flattered, instantly responsive, she allowed him to pull her against his body. The kiss had all the fire she would have expected in the privacy of their bedroom and instinctively she pressed herself against him more firmly, feeling his body's response. He laughed deep in his throat and his hands began to wander over her. She was lost in a whirl of sensation, oblivious to what was going on around her.

The howl of pain when it came was too terrible to be believed. Marc's hands instantly left Judith's body. His eyes searched the garden and came to rest on the group by the pool. He gave a regretful sigh and stepped away from his wife. Patrick and Michael ran to them, with Kara only a few feet behind. They all stared towards the pool.

Unaware of her flushed face and swollen mouth Judith looked at Marc in horror. "What was that? It wasn't Sam, was it?"

"I don't know."

She ran towards the pool, her heart thumping behind her ribs. She could not believe that Sam would cry out like that, he had sounded like an animal in his final agony.

Once she reached the edge of the water she knew that she was right. It had been Sam's final cry that had broken through the passion and brought her to her senses. He was lying on his side, mouth open, vomit trickling from his open mouth. The two boys stood together, alert and watchful. There was no sorrow in their eyes, and no pity, simply instinctive self-protection.

In silence Judith crouched next to the dog and touched his warm coat. "Sam! Sam, what happened?" she was crying now, her voice rising as she put her arms around the gentle animal.

"He's dead," she shouted as Marc approached. "He's dead, and it's their fault."

"What did you do to him?" said Marc sternly.

Paul looked into the distance, and it was Philip who met his father's eyes. "Nothing. He was playing with us. Running around, having some fun. Then he just arched his back, gave a howl and fell down. We never touched him."

Marc walked up to them, and kept his voice low. "Stupid! That was stupid! What were you trying to prove?"

"We wanted to see him play," said Philip, equally quietly. "He never did anything, and we wanted to watch him enjoying himself."

In the background Judith's sobs were increasing. "I hope you made the most of it," commented Marc, "because he won't be enjoying himself any more."

Paul looked at his stepmother, huddled on the concrete path. "She's jolly upset, it's only a dog."

"Don't try and understand, Paul. Women feel these things more than men at the best of times. At the moment Judith is particularly vulnerable. He was her link with the past. Now there's nothing of that left. You'd better get yourselves away from here, go on."

They ran off without a backwards glance. Marc knelt down by Judith. "Don't cry like that, darling. It must have been his heart."

"He shouldn't have raced around like he did. What were Paul and Philip doing to him?"

"Nothing at all. He was simply trying to play and it was too much for him. These things happen. Come on now, you sit down in the hammock and I'll see to everything."

Still sobbing she allowed herself to be led to the swing seat. "He wasn't enjoying himself," she cried. "He looked terrified. They were making him leap around, he didn't want to, I could tell."

"You're overwrought," he soothed, handing her a large handkerchief, "otherwise you'd realize how ridiculous you sound. He wasn't used to children and he got overexcited, that's all. I'll get you another dog if you like, but please try and calm down.''

Judith remembered Sam's wretched air of fear and defeat since she had married, and pictured his final, frantic jumping around the garden. She shuddered and moved away from Marc's embrace. ''No more dogs,'' she said firmly. ''I wouldn't want any more dogs here.''

''I think that's sensible. Now, close your eyes for a few minutes while I tidy up.''

She heard the sound of the spade and then some digging further down the garden, but she refused to dwell on it. Sam was gone, nothing could hurt him now. He was free, and in a secret corner of her mind she was relieved. There was no place for a dog in this peculiar household.

Sam's death spoiled the whole day. Despite the heat and Marc's efforts at getting them all to play tennis and swim, the children and Judith were subdued. Kara was inconsolable. She trailed around the garden searching for her new found pet. ''Doggie gone,'' she said at intervals. ''Nice doggie gone.''

''He's gone to heaven,'' explained Marc patiently. ''He's up in the sky now, watching us all.''

She peered up at the sky and shook her head. ''Doggie gone. All gone.''

Judith was not only upset, she was worried. There were too many inexplicable things happening and she needed someone to talk to, someone uninvolved, detached. She decided that as soon as Marc went back to work she would ring Sue and ask her over. Surely Sue would be able to use her commonsense to ease Judith's anxiety.

In addition to her mental fears she also had a nagging pain in her right side that occasionally stabbed fiercely before subsiding to a dull ache. She wished once again that she and Marc knew each other better so that she could confide in him, but she feared that he would dismiss her worries as foolishness, and kept silent.

After tea the pain eased and Judith went into the drawing room and sank into the easy chair where she had sat on her first visit. The others were outside playing badminton on the lawn. She closed her eyes, trying not to picture Sam as he had been that morning.

"Judith?"

Sleepily she turned. "Hello, Paul."

"I wondered if you'd like to look at my photograph album." Under his arm he clutched a red, padded book.

"Are they pictures of you?"

He nodded.

"I'd love to look. Bring it over here."

Placing the book on her lap he sat down at her feet. "I'm sorry about Sam," he said hesitantly. "We shouldn't have played with him."

"It doesn't matter. You weren't to blame." It was true. Judith blamed Philip. She opened the album.

The first photo showed a radiant Elizabeth cradling a small baby in her arms. Her eyes laughed at the camera, her round, glowing face reflected complete maternal satisfaction. "Paul—2 days," said the caption. There were several more in his first month, and in all of them Elizabeth was vibrant with health.

When Paul reached six weeks the pictures began to change. Slowly, almost picture by picture, Elizabeth ceased to look out at the world so laughingly. Her face grew thinner, her eyes were troubled. Paul on the other hand flourished. By three months he was a large, chubby child with placid features and his enormous dark eyes dominated the snaps more and more. Marc wasn't in any of the pictures.

Judith worked her way through the album. With the birth of each child Elizabeth was visibly diminished. A picture of Paul, tall and handsome behind a birthday cake, caught her attention. It wasn't because Paul was so handsome that she stopped, and stared, it was because of the other children. There were three other children in the photo. One was Patrick, smiling shyly; another Philip, his eyes already purposeful for such a young child; but cradled on Elizabeth's lap was a tiny baby, his face screwed up. Judith bent to check the caption.

"Paul's 3rd birthday. Also Patrick (2), Philip (1) and Piers (1 week).

Paul glanced at her, suddenly aware that she wasn't turning the pages. "What one's that, Judith?"

"Your third birthday. You all look so handsome and bright, don't you?"

He wasn't diverted. "I forgot that one. Piers is in that, isn't he?"

"Yes. What happened to Piers?"

Paul tugged on his right ear lobe and frowned. "Has Daddy ever mentioned him?"

"No."

"Well, it's really a secret. There was a terrible accident. He had a fall and hurt his head badly. He died a couple of hours later. I can't remember it very well, and the others don't remember it at all. I know Mummy was very upset, I can remember her screaming all night."

Judith was horrified. "That's dreadful! How old was he?"

"A few weeks. You'd better not tell Daddy you know. He doesn't like people talking about it. Piers is a secret."

"I understand."

She looked again at the photo. By this time Elizabeth was positively slender, despite having just given birth, and her eyes were sunk in dark hollows. There was no vitality left in her, yet she gazed protectively at her children with an almost desperate intensity. She didn't look strong enough to bear another child, but Judith realized with surprise that Michael had been born the following year. She turned the page.

There was only one more photo. Elizabeth was in bed, lying against a mound of pillows, and she had the newborn Michael resting against one shoulder. The other boys were grouped around her. Paul had his right hand protectively on his mother's shoulder and Patrick was looking tenderly at his new brother. Elizabeth looked exhausted, her eyes were half-closed and her hands were like an old woman's where they clutched at Michael. Only Philip was staring at the camera.

He was not touching his mother, he didn't look part of the

family group. His eyes, so thickly lashed, stared out of the page. Even at the age of two you could see the man he would one day become. Hard, forceful, domineering; it was all there in his face. There was no childlike softness about him.

Judith shut the book sharply. "They're very good. Thank-you for showing me."

"That's all right." He saw Judith wince. "Have you got a pain?"

"A bit of a stitch·in my side."

Paul's eyes widened and he smiled. "Have you? Hey, that's really good news."

"Not for me."

"Mummy always had a stitch there when she was going to have a baby."

"Don't be silly, Paul, it hasn't got anything to do with having a baby. Besides, your mummy never did anything except have babies so she probably blamed all her aches and pains on that."

He stepped back from her. The gentle courtesy had gone from his face now. Without it he was no different from Philip. He had the same harshly purposeful air, and she realized it was only his smiles that kept it concealed.

"Don't talk about Mummy like that. Your pain does mean you're going to have a baby, and it will keep on hurting, you wait and see. You shouldn't sound so scornful either, you're only here to have lots of babies and see to Michael and Philip. Daddy loved Mummy, he doesn't love you. Give me back my album."

Numbly Judith held it out, flinching from the fury on Paul's face. "I didn't mean to hurt your feelings, Paul."

"I loved Mummy and I was sorry about what happened to her. I'm not sorry about you. I thought I would be, but I'm not." With a half-choked sob he ran away from her, the book safely beneath his arm.

Judith put a hand to her side and walked heavily into the kitchen. Marc was giving Kara her supper and glanced casually up, then seeing Judith's stricken face he moved quickly to her, putting his arms around her body.

"What's wrong?"

She could feel the tears coming. "I've got a pain, and Paul's upset because he thinks I insulted Elizabeth and he says I'm pregnant."

She was really crying now. "But it can't be that. Pregnant women don't have pain like this, not early on. I don't know what he was talking about. He said you don't love me. He said I'm only here to have babies."

"Don't be silly," soothed Marc. "Come and sit down."

"I won't! Why didn't you tell me about Piers? It wasn't very nice hearing it from Paul. I don't know what's going on in this house but I don't like it. I want Sam here again, I want my dog back!"

Sobbing like a child, she clung to Marc. He called for Patrick to look after Kara and led his wife into the study. There he sat her down and crouched on the floor in front of her, his hands cupped around her face. He tilted her head up so that she was looking at him.

"You're upset, Judith, and you're blowing everything up out of all proportion. There's nothing wrong in this house, nothing at all. We all need you here, and we're going to make you happy with us. We're your family now, your ready-made family."

As he spoke her eyes began to close. She was no longer aware of what he was saying.

"You don't need Sam," he continued. "You don't need anyone else, certainly not Sue. You're safe here, safe and content. You're lucky to be here, Judith, very lucky indeed."

She was completely limp in his grasp. He picked her up easily and carried her to the bedroom where he lay her on the top of the cover. He stared down at her with a fleeting look of pity before leaving her and going to Paul's room.

Paul was sitting on his bed, his album between his knees. Marc snatched it from him.

"You stupid little fool! If you can't look after it then I'm going to destroy it."

"*No!*" Paul leaped up. "I'll be careful, I will. I'm sorry, Dad."

"We need her," said Marc clearly. "How many times do I have to tell you that. She's absolutely necessary for all your sakes. Do you promise me that you'll behave from now on?"

"I don't like her," complained Paul. "She's pathetic. How can she help us?"

"She isn't pathetic, she's sensitive. I chose her because that is where you and your brothers are weakest. Draw it out from her, analyze it and understand it. There will be times when displays of sensitivity are needed if you are to pass unnoticed in the outside world. You don't have to like her, only tolerate her. It will be easier that way when she dies."

"Easier?"

"You won't be so upset, will you? Only yesterday you were worrying about what was going to happen to her."

Paul nodded. "How long will she be here?"

Marc straightened and walked over to the bedroom window. The house was beginning to warm up, evening was approaching.

"Three years or so."

"She's pregnant, isn't she?"

"Yes."

Paul's face twisted in disgust. "I don't know how you can bear to touch her."

"That's no problem. You'll find when you grow up that it's keeping your hands off your wife that's difficult."

"Even if you don't love her?"

"Love doesn't come into it at all. It's instinct, Paul. You'll find out soon enough."

"How soon?" His voice was eager.

Marc glanced at the tall, well-built nine-year-old. "A couple of years. That's when the problems start. Don't wish your time away, you've still got a lot to learn."

Paul nodded. "I know. I'm doing my very best."

Marc reached out and touched the boy on the forehead. "I love you, Paul."

On the bed Judith moved restlessly, muttering in her sleep. "I'm lucky," she murmured as she turned over. "Very lucky," and she smiled.

* * *

The sound of the alarm bell ringing finally forced Judith to open her eyes. At first she was puzzled, and then she remembered that it was Wednesday, Marc's first day back at work. Immediately the pleasantly sleepy feeling was banished; today she had the boys to herself, and she wasn't looking forward to it.

Marc slipped out of bed and went into the shower room without speaking. Probably, reasoned Judith, he wasn't even aware that she was awake. Something nagged at the back of her mind, something important. There had been an incident last night that had increased her natural trepidation about being in charge of the boys. Her inability to recall it infuriated her and she sat up, trying to retrace the evening in detail. Her mind was a blank. Only Sam's death stood out from a day that in all other respects was a haze of sunshine and lazy hours in the garden.

Marc walked back into their room and glanced over at her. "Hello! I hope the alarm didn't wake you. I tried to switch it off quickly, but I was pretty deeply asleep myself."

"It's all right; I can't lie around half the morning letting the boys run riot!"

"True enough. Do you mind if I see to my own breakfast and leave the boys' food to you?"

"Of course not. I'll cook yours if you like."

He smiled. "I only have toast and coffee when I'm at work. You take your time getting up."

"I wish you wouldn't encourage me to behave like an invalid, I might get a taste for being waited on." Judith laughed and swung her legs around until her feet touched the floor.

"Are you going to see about Michael's hamster, or shall I go . . ." With a stifled cry Judith clutched her hands to her right side as once again the pain lanced through her.

She bent double as it increased, and then held her breath in an attempt to get it to go away. That was how she had treated a stitch when she was small, and perhaps this was only a bad stitch, she told herself hopefully. After a few seconds she took a cautious breath. The pain had gone. She wiped her clammy hands on the sheet and stood up.

In the mirror her reflection looked ghostly white. Shivering slightly from reaction she sat down at the dressing table until her legs stopped trembling. She stared into the glass and saw Marc standing immobile on the opposite side of the room. He didn't realize that she could see him, and the expression on his face was unmistakably one of triumph.

In disbelief Judith swung around to face him. "What are you looking so pleased about?" she demanded.

His face was once again impassive, there was no trace of triumph on his countenance now. "Pleased? I don't think I was looking pleased. Puzzled would be more accurate. I was wondering why you were performing exercises so early in the morning."

"I wasn't doing exercises, I had a pain in my side!"

He smiled indulgently at her, rather as though she were one of the children making a fuss about a scratch.

"Probably a pulled muscle. As I said, take your time getting up!"

For a moment Judith had the desire to throw something at him, but there was nothing to hand, and besides, she told herself as she dressed, it was only her dignity that would have suffered.

When she went out onto the landing Michael and Patrick were waiting for her.

"What are you going to do today?" asked Michael, jumping up and down on the top step.

"I don't know. Would you like to go into Stamford and look around the shops? You might see something you'd like for your birthday."

"Shops are boring. Besides, I know what I want. I want a hamster."

"Nothing else? Only a hamster?"

He began to jump down onto the second step and back up again, his feet together. He made it look easy, apparently unaware of the danger of falling down the entire flight.

"Why? Do I get lots of presents? I never have before."

He cast her a quick look from beneath his lashes and she smiled at his deliberate attempt to charm her.

"I don't believe you, Michael! I'm sure you've always had several presents."

He chuckled and clasped his hands above his head, still

continuing the rhythmic jumping. Patrick didn't seem impressed.

"Stop showing off Michael. You'll fall."

"I won't! It's easy, anyone could do it. Anyone at all."

Judith was afraid to step past him in case she caused him to lose his balance. "Mind the way, Michael. I want to go down."

He ignored her, and now instead of jumping straight from one step to the other he began to jump in a diagonal line from opposite corners. As he jumped he sang. The tune was "Nuts in May," but the words she suddenly realized were different.

"I'm not going to let you get away,
        get away, get away,
    I'm not going to let you get away,
        not for the entire morning."

Judith laughed. "Very clever. Now will you please stop."

Still he ignored her, but he began to jump faster and faster, his legs pumping vigorously, his feet landing on the narrow stairs with an accuracy that astounded her. She was so engrossed in this display of gymnastic skill that she didn't hear the other two boys approaching.

"Watch out," she cautioned again, "if you're not careful you'll fall."

"I'm not going to let you get away,
        get away, get away, . . ."

His voice had a sing-song quality to it that reminded her of someone else. She started to think, and then watched in horror as an arm pushed past her and caught Michael savagely in the chest as he was in mid-air. He gave a shrill scream and his hands clutched desperately for the banister but they missed by a fraction of an inch and Judith watched as he started to tumble through the air.

He didn't fall properly, not as she had seen Sue's boy fall, arms and legs thrashing at the air. He curled himself into a tight ball, and instead of bumping from one stair t the other he managed by some incredible stroke of luck to remain airborne until he reached the bottom, at which point he uncurled himself and landed squarely on hands and feet. It was how she would have expected a cat to land, or possibly a monkey, but not a child.

While she marveled at what she had seen Michael raced back up the stairs, screaming in fury. "You pushed me! I could have hurt myself. You're a horrible pig, Philip Farino! A selfish, horrible pig!"

Behind Judith a scuffle took place, quickly turning into a fight.

Michael was still screaming in rage, but Philip was on top of him, pounding at the younger boy's head with his fists. She tried to take hold of Philip's shoulders, but he twisted away.

"Stop it!" yelled Paul, and then he raced down the stairs shouting for his father.

Michael's cries were more feeble now, and Judith could see blood coming from his nose.

"Patrick, help me pull them apart."

Patrick stared at her and stepped back against the wall, unwilling or unable to be of assistance. She was tugging vainly at Philip's arms when Marc shouted from the foot of the stairs.

"Philip! Stop fighting at once!"

His voice boomed around them all. Judith had never heard him use his voice like that before, and she found that she wanted to cover her ears. It echoed around the large house long after he had finished speaking, dying slowly away as the sound waves were absorbed by the heavy stone walls. Philip stopped one arm in mid-swing and released Michael. Slowly he walked to the top of the stairs and looked down at his father.

Marc didn't speak again, but all at once Philip looked away and then walked back towards his bedroom, his shoulders slumped. Once he was gone Judith and the boys, previously immobile, were abruptly released from their frozen postures. Michael started to cry and Judith bent to comfort him. Paul and Patrick, after one glance to make sure that Michael was all right, went down to join their father.

Judith took Michael into the bathroom and made him sit down while she put a cold flannel over the bridge of his nose. The flow of blood quickly slowed to a mere trickle but she left the flannel in place while she put some disinfectant on the various small scratches that covered his face.

"This will sting, but it will make sure they don't turn nasty," she told him. He blinked but didn't protest.

"There! Now you look as though you could do with a good breakfast. How about scrambled eggs on toast?"

He lifted his soft brown eyes to her. "It was the song," he explained. "I shouldn't have sung Philip's song."

Judith nodded. She had no idea what he meant; obviously some private squabble between the boys.

"I'm afraid Philip acts first and thinks later," she said briskly. "He could have broken your neck pushing you down the stairs like that."

Michael smiled sweetly and slipped a hand into hers. "He knew that," he assured her. "That's why he did it. May I have a sausage with my scrambled egg?"

Judith stared at him. "You can't mean that, Michael?"

"I do. I like sausages."

She shook her head. "Not the sausage, Philip. He wouldn't want to hurt you that badly, would he?"

Michael looked up at her and squeezed her hand tightly. "You're nice, I like you, but it's a pity you're not really our mummy."

"Why?"

"Because then you'd understand things better."

"What things?"

His eyes slid past her to the doorway.

"All sorts of things, like me wanting sausages with my eggs. I can have a sausage, can't I, Daddy?"

Judith turned quickly, and found Marc in the doorway.

"What are you two up to?"

"I was stopping Michael's nosebleed and cleaning his face up for him."

"Well, if you've finished the other three are clamoring for some food and I really must get off to work."

She knew that she mustn't mention her conversation with Michael. For some reason Marc was anxious to get her away from the boy before he talked too much. She didn't know what Michael could have talked about, or why she felt suddenly convinced that there was something deeply wrong with the children, something that Marc wanted to keep hidden; what she did know was that if she was to have any chance of finding out then she must pass off the morning's scene as a normal childish squabble with no dark undertones.

"He's fine now," she said calmly. "I've told him that next time he gets in a fight he'd better choose a more sensible place than the top of the stairs. Right, Michael?"

He nodded his small, dark head gravely. "Right!"

"Come on then, breakfast."

"You carry on," said Marc smoothly. "I want a quick word with young Michael."

Judith walked away and down the stairs. She heard Marc's deep murmur and Michael's shrill denial.

"I didn't! I didn't tell her anything!"

Then the bathroom door was closed and there was nothing further for her to hear.

She had cooked breakfast and almost eaten her own before Michael joined them. His eyes were red-rimmed but she tactfully ignored the fact and put his food in front of him. Philip finished his last mouthful and got down from the table. He stopped by his youngest brother's chair.

"Sorry," he mumbled.

"S'all right," Michael mumbled back and they exchanged a fleeting smile.

The boys were out in the garden and Judith was putting the dishes in the machine when Marc came in to say goodbye. He put his arms around her from behind and squeezed her tightly.

"Have a nice day, darling. I won't be late back. Have you any plans?"

"I thought of taking them into Stamford, but probably they aren't too keen on shops. Otherwise I wondered if I could take them over to your sister's this afternoon. Would she mind if I gave her a ring do you think?"

"I'm sure she'd be delighted. Her number's in the book

by the phone. Under "Z" for Zilla. Sorry about this morning, I'm afraid they do get rather physical at times. Take care of yourself, won't you."

She kissed him on the mouth and felt his grip tighten for a second before he stepped away.

"Hussy! Incidentally, I thought I heard Kara while I was shaving."

"I'll go up and get her. Have a good day."

As she walked up the stairs she heard his car moving down the drive. Outside Kara's door she hesitated for a moment, looking carefully around her.

It was the first time she had been alone in the house, with only the children for company, and she had the ridiculous feeling that it regarded her as an outsider. Giving herself a shake she went in to Kara, who immediately stretched out her hands and beamed.

"Wet! Kara wet!"

"Not again you monster!"

Laughing she picked the child up and hugged her. As she stripped the saturated nappy off she wondered why it was that Kara, who had the same father as the boys, was such a normal, uncomplicated child with none of her half-brothers' precocious ways and primitive furies.

"Your mummy must have been very placid," she said as she fastened the safety pins.

Kara laughed and rolled off the mat. She walked over to the window and pointed up at the glass. "Carry!"

"You know how to give orders don't you!" Judith lifted Kara up and they both looked out onto the garden. Kara pointed towards the lush lawn. "Mummy!"

Judith stared at the empty lawn, then tried to see down to the bottom and the gate that Mrs. Watson had used, but there was no one in sight. "I'm afraid not, poppet. There's no one there."

Kara nodded emphatically and pointed again, banging her hand on the glass. "Mummy there! Mummy gone garden."

"Did she like gardening, is that what you're saying?"

Kara looked at Judith and put her thumb in her mouth.

"I don't suppose you even remember her," Judith said

softly, "though how she could leave a lovely little girl like you I just do not know."

"Mummy gone! Nice doggie gone!"

"Not to the same place." Judith laughed, and she moved Kara more comfortably onto her hip. "Come along. Breakfast, and then I'm going to ring your Auntie Zilla."

When Judith finally found time to make the telephone call her nerve nearly failed her. After all her new sister-in-law had made no friendly overtures towards the new member of the family; perhaps she didn't approve of her brother's new wife. Despite this troubling thought, Judith still rang; Marc had sounded so certain that Zilla wouldn't mind, and his sister quickly proved him right.

"How nice to hear from you, Judith." Her voice was soft over the telephone.

"I hope you don't mind us inviting ourselves over."

"I'm delighted. I would have called you, but I knew that Marc was on holiday and I rather thought you'd all like some time alone together."

"We had a nice few days," confirmed Judith, "but I feel somewhat at a loss without him."

"That's quite natural," Zilla assured her. "The only thing is, I haven't very much garden here. Would it perhaps be better if I came over to you?"

"Yes, of course, if you don't mind. I half-hoped the boys would be less boisterous in other surroundings!"

"I doubt it. They don't trouble me, I'm quite used to them. If I arrive about two, would that suit you?"

"Lovely. We'll see you then."

Despite her bright tone Judith was disappointed. It wasn't really because of the boys being boisterous. She had looked forward to getting out of the house for a few hours. Already the familiar chill hung in all the rooms except the drawing room, yet she could tell that outside it was another scorching hot day. She wandered out of the back door and around to the swimming pool. Paul and Philip were swimming while the other two sat on the edge splashing the water with their feet.

"Are you allowed to swim without an adult to watch you?" she queried.

"Well, Daddy prefers a grown-up to be out here, but we thought that we're probably better at swimming than you are so you don't count." Paul spoke very politely, but Philip sniggered and turned his back on her.

"If that's the case then perhaps he'd prefer you not to swim at all until this afternoon."

Patrick turned his head. "Why? Who's coming this afternoon?"

"Your Aunt Zilla."

She saw how Paul and Patrick wrinkled their noses. "Phoo, only her!"

"That's rude, Patrick."

"No, it's not. She's just another woman."

"Women are not second-class citizens." Judith made her voice as commanding as she could manage; she was getting a little tired of their attitude towards the opposite sex.

Slowly all four boys turned their faces to her, and their astonishment would have been comical if she hadn't known who they got their attitude from. The fact that it was her husband made it somewhat less than amusing.

"How can you say that?" asked Paul.

"What makes you so sure that they are?" she challenged him.

Philip climbed out of the water and stood on the concrete slabs, water streaming from his sleek body. "It's obvious that they are. They aren't so well coordinated; they can pass on genetic illnesses to male children without being affected themselves; they are more susceptible to ill health; they . . ."

"Hang on a minute! You've just contradicted yourself."

"No, I haven't. The two statements are not related."

She had to laugh, he was looking so serious about it. "They are related. Besides, some girls are better coordinated than boys. Not all boys can swim like fishes and tear around tennis courts, you know."

"In this family it's true. Daddy says that our aunt was hopeless at games, and so was his mother."

"What about *your* mother?"

He hesitated, and she looked down as Kara came to stand by her.

"That's different," he said at last.

It was hot by the pool, and Judith was suddenly tired of Philip's stubborn insistence on female inferiority and his brothers' unblinking interest in the conversation.

"I think we'll have to call it a draw, Philip. I don't see how either of us can prove what we think; I just wish that you'd stop making such a sweeping statement with such monotonous regularity."

Philip flushed and took half a step towards her before thinking better of it and jumping back into the water. The other boys continued to watch her.

Patrick padded over. "Philip is right. Watch this." In one swift movement he bent down, picked Kara up, turned and threw her into the pool. Kara and Judith screamed in unison, and then as Judith watched Kara sank out of sight beneath the deep blue surface only to emerge briefly, splashing and crying before descending yet again.

"Get her out!" shouted Judith to the watching boys. "Quickly, she can't swim."

"We all could," said Patrick loudly while Paul swam over to his half-sister and began to carry her to the side. "We were all thrown in when we were three months old, and we all swam instinctively. It's only girls who scream and thrash about like that. You ask Daddy."

"I shall certainly be telling your father about this," said Judith furiously as she took the soaking, crying Kara from Paul. "Thanks to you she'll probably never want to go near the water again."

"She couldn't have drowned," said Philip. "Not with all of us here."

"She's rather too young to have appreciated that point. Now you can all come out and get dressed. There'll be no more swimming until I've spoken to your father."

They were all in the water now, a line of four handsome children watching her with interest.

"How are you going to get us out?" asked Patrick politely.

Judith felt herself shaking with fury. "*Get out of that pool!*"

"No!" Their voices blended together. It sounded like one voice.

She cast frantically around for some threat that could be effective. "If you don't come out I shan't teach you anything at all, ever." Even as she said it she was aware of how feeble it sounded. There was nothing they could learn from her, and she knew that and knew that they must know it.

Apparently they didn't. After one brief exchange of glances they all swam to the poolside and climbed out. As they passed her they muttered apologies with varying amounts of grace. Amazingly Philip's apology was the most sincere.

"We didn't mean to upset you," he assured her, "and we won't do it again. It's very nice of you to come here and help us all; we really appreciate it."

Judith waited for him to smirk or snigger, but his face was solemn and he even brought a towel from the house for her to wrap the sobbing Kara in. She stayed out in the sun while the boys went indoors to change. As she soothed the little girl and peeled off her soaking sundress, she wondered in what way Philip felt that she was going to help them. At the moment it seemed to be as much as she could do to keep up with them.

"There you are, Kara. Is that better?"

"Bad boys. Bad boys hurt Kara."

"I'll tell Daddy tonight and he'll be very cross with them."

A look of fear crossed the girl's face. "Mummy tell," she whispered, leaning towards Judith. "Mummy tell. Mummy all gone now."

A tiny black cloud passed in front of the sun and Judith shivered.

"Mrs. Farino! Mrs. Farino!"

Startled Judith turned towards the house. It was Mrs. Watson. She had quite forgotten that the woman would be coming to help her today. Relieved at the sight of another adult she stood up and walked away, leaving Kara staring after her with a worried frown. Finally she put her thumb in her mouth and wandered away across the lawn towards the vegetable garden.

With the arrival of Mrs. Watson the atmosphere in the house changed. The boys were now polite, and their games were quiet and orderly. Judith, watching out of the kitchen window as they set up their cricket stumps, remembered her first impressions of them and wondered how she could have been so wrong. Paul glanced towards the kitchen, and seeing Judith standing there he waved a friendly hand and flashed a brilliant smile at her before turning his attention back to the game. She moved out of sight of the children and gave a small sigh. If the boys had deceived her so easily with their good looks and air of courtesy then wasn't it possible that she had been similarly deceived by their father? The thought troubled her.

"That's a big sigh!"

She had forgotten Mrs. Watson, busy peeling potatoes at the sink. "They tire me out!" It was a casual remark, the first excuse she could think of, but the older woman caught her breath sharply.

"Don't spend too much time with them," she cautioned. "I saw what happened to their poor mother. She sacrificed her life to those children."

"Nonsense! Their mother caught a virus. It was a tragedy, but you can hardly blame it on the boys."

"I know what I know," she retorted, "and a virus is only an explanation for something that doesn't respond to antibiotics. You can't argue with someone if they tell you it's a virus, can you?"

Judith was intrigued. Until now she had always felt that Mrs. Watson disapproved of her, finding her a poor substitute for Elizabeth. Suddenly the woman was being friendly and talking as though she knew things that Judith didn't. But, much as she wanted to hear more, she knew instinctively that Mrs. Watson shouldn't be encouraged. It was easier for her to subdue her curiosity now that Zilla was coming. Surely Zilla must know everything that Mrs. Watson did, if not more.

"I'm sure the doctors did all they could," she said firmly. "I think we had better have lunch by twelve thirty. My sister-in-law is coming here at two o'clock and I'd like everything tidied away by then."

"Very good, madam." The rebuff had been plain, and Mrs. Watson retreated into herself, all desire to confide apparently gone.

Half-way through lunch the telephone rang. Mrs. Watson was upstairs doing the bedrooms and so Judith left the children at the table and went to answer it. The caller, a woman, sounded surprised and tentative.

"Is that Mrs. Watson?"

"No, this is Mrs. Farino."

"Oh!"

There was a silence.

"Would you like me to fetch Mrs. Watson for you?"

"I didn't realize. . . . That is, I didn't know there was a Mrs. Farino any more."

"Who is that?" asked Judith sharply.

"You wouldn't know me, my friend used to. . . ." The voice trailed off again.

Judith gripped the receiver more tightly. She was beginning to feel afraid, yet there was no reason. The voice on the other end of the line was certainly not intimidating.

"Do you have a message? If not I really must get back to the children."

There was another pause. Mrs. Watson closed one of the bedroom doors sharply and began to descend the stairs. Judith glanced up and her worried expression had Mrs. Watson hurrying down the last steps towards her. Just as Judith was about to hand the phone over the unknown voice started to speak again.

"I've called about my friend Felicity. Felicity Green. Does the name mean anything to you?"

"I'm very sorry, I'm afraid not."

"She was housekeeper to Mr. . . that is your husband, for a time."

"There's no housekeeper here now."

"I know. I just wondered if you'd heard anything from her yet. I can't help worrying and I really think that I ought to go to the police."

"The police?"

At Judith's startled exclamation, Mrs. Watson snatched the telephone rudely from her grasp.

"You know perfectly well that you weren't meant to call here again, young lady. There's been no word from Miss Green since she walked out on the children. If you want to go to the police then that's your business, but stop bothering us with your melodramatic fancies. I shall tell Mr. Farino you called, good afternoon to you." The receiver was slammed down and the two women stared at each other in silence.

"Who did she mean?" asked Judith at last.

"She's trying to contact Kara's mother and seems to think we know where she is. All I can say is that if we did, young Kara would be there too. Mr. Farino wouldn't keep her on if he didn't have to."

"But she's his daughter."

"Is she? I've got my own ideas about that."

"You seem to have a lot of ideas about things today. First Elizabeth, now this Mrs. Green."

"Miss Green."

"Miss Green then; it doesn't really matter, does it? She obviously found herself unable to cope with her situation and she must have known that my husband accepted Kara as his own, otherwise she wouldn't have left her behind."

Judith's voice was harsh. The distress in the caller's voice had raised a worry in her own mind as to the whereabouts of Kara's mother. Mrs. Watson sensed this and her own voice was calm, reassuring. "You're right of course, madam. Felicity Green was a born troublemaker, and that makes me over-critical of her, especially when the trouble continues long after she's gone. But if her friend should call again just pass her on to me, madam, don't let her upset you as well."

The kitchen door swung open.

"We've finished our mince. May we have ice cream for dessert?"

"Of course you may, Patrick. I'm just coming." Judith followed her stepson back through the door, and with an annoyed click of her tongue Mrs. Watson returned to her work.

By two o'clock Judith had set out the sun loungers near the bottom of the garden. It was a pleasant spot, right in the sun but with shade from the laden plum tree easily available. Also it was possible to keep an eye on the children whether they were in the pool or playing on the apparatus. A rug was spread out beside the loungers and Kara was busy with a plastic tea set and three small dolls almost as soon as she was put on the ground.

The sound of Zilla's car tires on the drive had the boys sprinting for the back gate, and to Judith's surprise it was Philip who got there first despite being the last to set off. He ran with no apparent effort and only Paul could match him for grace of movement. Idly she wondered if any of the boys would take up athletics seriously; at the moment they certainly looked to have great natural ability.

She rose to greet Zilla who had her arms full of various packages. Once these were distributed amongst the children they ran off, leaving the adults alone, except for Kara who was still absorbed in her tea party.

"It is nice of you to come, Zilla."

"It's nice of you to have me. I'm surprised you're up to visitors on your first day alone with this lot." She waved a slender pale arm in the direction of the boys.

Judith noted the ash-blonde hair cut close to the small, fine-boned head. The blue eyes were alert but tranquil and the tiny hands were continually on the move, the gestures quick and bird-like. Her skin was creamy-white and flawless, with only a trace of laughter lines at the corners of the eyes.

"Why don't you say it? Most people do!"

"Say what?" asked Judith, painfully aware that she had been staring.

"That I don't look like Marc's sister."

"Well, you don't!"

"I know. I look like my mother, for which I'm eternally grateful. Somehow I don't think that if I were a strapping six footer I would have quite the same appeal for men as Marc has for women, do you?"

Judith laughed. "Probably not!"

They both settled down on the loungers, Zilla moving hers back into the shade a little.

"I burn rather easily, that's the only drawback to being fair. How is married life suiting you, Judith?"

"Fine, thank you. Not that I've had long to get disillusioned!"

Across the garden the boys were jumping into the pool.

"Like water-babies, aren't they? Marc's always been a good swimmer too."

"They're very like him, aren't they?"

"Oh yes. I've got photographs taken when he was about their age and you wouldn't know the difference."

Judith looked down at Kara, now busy pulling large daisies from the lawn. "Yet Kara isn't in the least like him."

Zilla turned her head to inspect her niece more closely. "No, but then she wouldn't be."

"Why not?"

"Hasn't Marc told you about our family's little peculiarity?"

"No."

"I can't think why not; perhaps he didn't think you'd be interested."

"Well, I am. What is it?"

Zilla seemed to hesitate. "Maybe Marc didn't want you to know. Perhaps it makes him uncomfortable. I must confess I've always felt we were a bit, well, freaky if you like." She laughed uneasily. The boys continued to splash in the water, the sound carrying to the two adults.

"Do tell me, Zilla. You've really intrigued me now."

"It's nothing that way out. Nothing for you to worry about."

"Please, Zilla!"

"All right then. All the boys in our family turn out like Marc's. You can tell that they're colored and they're always good looking and very physical. They excel at games, run like hares, swim like fishes! Whereas the girls turn out fair, like me or like Kara. What's more the girls don't seem to be particularly good at anything. I never even won an egg and spoon race when I was a child. That's all."

"All? That's incredible. Do you mean to tell me that it doesn't matter who the men in your family marry? That even if your mother had been tall with brown hair you would still have looked as you do?"

"That's right. Why, take Kara for example. Felicity was nearly the same height as Marc and had long auburn hair and hazel eyes, yet Kara could be me at that age. Weird, isn't it?"

It was more than weird. Judith shivered. "Why didn't Marc tell me?"

"I don't know. Perhaps he thought it would take all the excitement out of things when you get pregnant. I mean, this way you know exactly what your child will look like regardless of sex, don't you? Probably I should have kept quiet, but I didn't think that far ahead. You don't mind, do you?"

Yes, I do, screamed a voice in Judith's head.

"Not at all," she forced herself to say quietly. "Is there anything else I ought to know?"

Zilla looked steadily at her. "Like what?"

She wanted to ask her lots of things. Why the boys were so strange. Why Marc wanted more sons. Why the house was cold in the day and hot at night, but as she met her sister-in-law's steady gaze she knew that she wouldn't get any answers. If there were other family secrets then Zilla would keep them; if there weren't then she would make herself sound ridiculous.

"Like why you never married?" she said at last.

"I should have thought that was obvious, knowing what I've just told you. Not many men would relish the idea of marrying a blue-eyed blonde and finishing up with a brood of colored sons."

"You mean that although you're not like Marc your children would be?"

"Correct."

"But that's incredible! What does your family doctor say about all this? I mean there must be some reason for it. How far back does it go?"

Zilla sat up abruptly, nearly tipping over the sun lounger. "We never discuss it with medical people. We don't want to finish up in laboratories being dissected under microscopes. After all, perhaps it's just coincidence."

"It can't be!"

"It is never discussed outside the family. I'm sure you'll respect this, just as Elizabeth did."

Elizabeth. Immediately Zilla mentioned the name Judith recalled the anguished figure in the pool and the sunken face that had looked out at her from the final pages of Paul's album.

"How did Elizabeth die, Zilla?"

"She caught a virus. I think she would have lived if it wasn't for the fact that she was already weakened by childbirth. We were all stunned; she was such a wonderful mother to the boys."

"Marc told me that she'd been ill a lot over the years."

"Mmmm, I suppose so. She got tired easily, but that was perfectly normal."

"Why?"

"Because she was so busy with the boys, why else?" and Zilla laughed.

"Did Marc love her very much?"

"Yes, he did," said Zilla quietly. "He loved her to distraction. We were afraid of what would happen to him when he lost her, but he coped magnificently."

"I saw her photo. She looked good fun."

"Yes; yes she was. She knew how to amuse Marc. He was always inclined to be over-solemn when she wasn't around."

Above them the bees buzzed in the plum tree. Judith felt her spirits sink. How could she ever replace someone who had been loved so much by husband and children alike.

"I don't know why we're talking about Elizabeth," said Zilla brightly. "We should be talking about you. How did you come to meet Marc? He never did tell us."

Judith explained about the bureau, and about her own circumstances.

"So you got married quite quickly?"

"Yes, I suppose we did. When I was on my own in the bungalow I used to worry about that, but somehow when I was with Marc he just carried me along as though it was the most normal thing in the world to marry a virtual stranger!"

Zilla nodded. "They're very forceful, the Farino males. They have a way of taking over, completely dominating a relationship. It can be quite difficult to retain your own personality."

Judith nodded. What Zilla said made sense. Ever since she met Marc she had become a pale shadow of her former

self. She was always too tired or too lazy to try to impose
her own ideas these days, and the brisk, efficient young
woman who had cared for her dying mother for so long
seemed to have vanished without a trace.

"I believe you're right," she said slowly, "and thank you
for pointing it out."

Kara stood up and walked across the lawn towards the
vegetable garden. Judith watched her picking her way dain-
tily past a giant clump of rhubarb, the leaves way above the
child's head.

"What was Kara's mother like? As a person, I mean. It
isn't something I can really discuss with Marc."

Zilla too watched Kara's progress. "I take your point.
Well, she was a nice woman. Very lively, quite fond of a
drink or two, I'm afraid, but only in the evenings when she
went out. She was very good with the boys, although they
never cared for her. She had a sort of animal magnetism
too, and I think it was that which attracted Marc. Elizabeth
had been pregnant for so much of their marriage, and when
she wasn't pregnant she was getting over childbirth, so I
suppose Felicity made a stimulating change. I guessed that
he was sleeping with her, but I didn't blame either of them.
The pregnancy was rather surprising but we all imagined
that they would get married and become one family. However, it didn't happen like that."

"Was Felicity upset when Marc wouldn't marry her?"

"Perhaps she didn't want to marry him. She never confided in any of us, and your guess is as good as mine. I
know that when Kara was born Marc was disappointed; and
from then on their relationship deteriorated."

"So you weren't surprised when she left?"

"Not really. I was surprised she left Kara behind as she'd
always taken the baby everywhere with her. In fact she was
quite fanatical about never leaving her alone with any of the
boys even for five minutes. I suppose she had her reasons.
Nevertheless, she abandoned Kara in the end."

"Has she ever got in touch since? To find out how Kara
is?"

"Not that I know of. I imagine that a small child would

be quite a handicap for someone like Felicity. Besides, she's settled down well, hasn't she?''

"Yes,"

"Does she ever mention her mother?"

Judith turned to Zilla, about to tell her what Kara had said, but she surprised such an intense, searching expression on the other woman's face that she changed her mind at the last moment.

"No, never. I don't think she realizes that she ever had one."

"That's all right then."

Judith looked at her watch. "Four o'clock—would you like a cup of tea?"

"That would be lovely."

"I'll go in and..." With a cry of pain she doubled up, the now familiar pain lancing through her side again. She dropped to her knees, and felt Zilla's cool arms around her shoulders.

"Try to relax, Judith. Take steady breaths; don't fight it, go with it." She followed the instructions, the pain ebbed and then disappeared.

"I'm so sorry. I've had that pain on and off for the last couple of days. I think I'll have to see a doctor about it. Do you know who the family doctor is?"

Zilla smiled and kept an arm round Judith's waist as they went indoors. "Yes, I know their doctor but I shouldn't worry about it. You're probably pregnant."

"Why do you say that?"

"Elizabeth always had a similar pain when she was pregnant."

Judith tried to keep her temper in check. "So Paul told me, but I am not Elizabeth and there is no way that I can be pregnant enough to get a crippling pain. A pain that is not, to my knowledge, a universal sign of pregnancy in any case."

"Of course it isn't; but it was for Elizabeth."

"I'm not Elizabeth."

"But you're carrying the same man's child."

"This is quite stupid. You have no reason to assume that I am pregnant, and even if I am why should it..."

The pain returned. This time it spread down her right leg and was so agonizing that she screamed and clutched hold of the cool stainless steel sink. Her knees began to buckle and she tried to call Zilla's name. Sweat rolled from her forehead and down her face, partially obscuring her vision, but she could see that Zilla was moving away from her, back towards the door into the garden and she thought that she was calling for help.

Now it was difficult to draw breath because every movement of her ribs increased the agony. The kitchen began to darken and she clung on to the sink in desperation. Her breath was coming in short gasps and she felt incredibly hot. Dimly she was aware that Zilla had returned and she tried to ask her to ring for a doctor, but only a croak emerged from her lips.

Then she saw that she had an audience. The children were standing beside their aunt, their dark eyes seeming to glow with a strange luminosity that accentuated the golden flecks around their pupils. They showed no distress at her agony, in fact she saw with a feverish horror that they were beginning to smile. The pain eased slightly, but immediately her stomach lurched and it felt as though all her internal organs were turning around and around, spinning faster and faster until she was certain that she was about to die by some ghastly, internal strangulation. As she lost consciousness she managed to cry out once, a desperate beseeching appeal for the help that was not forthcoming.

The tiles felt cool beneath her face and she was instantly aware that the pain had gone. Above her Zilla was speaking urgently.

"We didn't know what to do. Will she be all right or should we call a doctor?"

"She'll be all right now that it's settled into place. From here on it's plain sailing."

"Another son. You're doing very well, Marc."

"Did you tell her anything?"

"Only what you suggested."

"How did she take it?"

"She was curious, nothing more."

"She ought to be around by now."

Judith gave a slight moan and allowed herself to move one arm. They mustn't know that their conversation had been overheard; they must continue to think that she believed Zilla her friend and ally. But she wasn't; she was her enemy. She and her brother and the children, they were all enemies. Judith didn't know in what way or why, but she knew that she must remember it for every second of every day from this moment on.

Marc bent down to his wife. "Judith? Judith, darling, are you feeling better?" She allowed her eyes to open slowly and looked into his handsome face.

"What happened? Why are you here? You're meant to be at work."

"You had some sort of a fit. Zilla rang me up and I got here as soon as I could. Have you suffered from this kind of thing before?"

"I had a pain, a terrible pain."

"How is it now?"

"It's better."

"Come on then, let's see if you can stand up."

Slowly and with great gentleness he helped her upright, and then he insisted on carrying her upstairs and putting her into bed.

"It must have been something you ate, darling. Food poisoning can be agonizing."

"I only ate the same as the children."

"You look much better now. I'll bring you up a cup of tea if you like."

"No, thank you. I want a doctor."

Marc looked slightly surprised. "Really? I'll call one then. Have you still got the pain?"

"No, but I can describe it easily enough."

"Fine."

She felt better knowing that another outsider would be coming to the house. There was something terribly wrong with her and the sooner she got professional help the better. She didn't doubt now that she was pregnant, Marc and Zilla had been certain enough; what she did doubt was her ability to withstand further attacks like this one, possibly for nine long months.

Within half an hour a doctor arrived and Marc came into the room with him. He was a middle-aged man, with intelligent eyes and a kindly but brisk manner. Judith could tell that Marc wasn't going to leave, even so she intended to tell the doctor exactly what had happened, and what she had been told by her stepson and her sister-in-law. He might think her unbalanced, but he would be bound to examine her thoroughly and when he did she was quite certain that he would find something unusual. Enough to get her put into hospital, if only for observation.

"Now then, Mrs. Farino, describe exactly how this attack of yours happened, would you?" he asked as he quietly checked her pulse.

"Well, I was rather foolish this morning and I ate quite a lot of the gooseberries that I was picking for a tart tomorrow. I think that those combined with the rhubarb I had for dessert probably brought on a nasty attack of colic."

The words came out in an even flow with just a hint of apology and a suggestion of self-disgust. Judith tried to shake her head, to convey to this man that she didn't mean a word of it, but Marc was holding her tightly and movement was impossible.

"I'm very sorry," she babbled on. "I told Marc not to call you but he insisted."

"So he explained over the phone. Still it's better to be safe than sorry. I'll leave a bottle of indigestion mixture and I'm sure you won't repeat your mistake."

"I certainly won't, I feel such an idiot."

The doctor smiled in obvious agreement and Marc opened the door to let him out. Alone again Judith could only sit in the bed shivering with fear. She didn't know where the words had come from or why she had been unable to say what she wanted. It was as though she were going completely mad and she pushed her fist into her mouth to prevent herself from screaming aloud.

She sat staring at the door until Marc reappeared. His face wore its habitual expression of bland amiability; she hardly dared to think any more about what it might be concealing. Defiantly she continued to stare at him until he looked away.

"I don't know how you did it," she said coldly, "but you know perfectly well that what I told that doctor was rubbish. What's more it bears no relation to what I had intended to tell him."

"Which was?"

"Why, that . . ." She stopped, her mind suddenly a confused jumble of thoughts that refused to be processed.

Marc smiled at her. "Yes?"

"That I love you and want you to make love to me."

For the first time since she had met him she saw him throw back his head and roar with laughter until tears streamed down his face. She remembered the boys when she told them she'd been kissing their father, and recalled how they had laughed in just the same way.

"Well, I'll try to oblige you then," he spluttered when he started to recover.

Judith scrambled to the end of the bed and glared at him. At that moment she both hated and feared him. "I love you, I love you," she crooned. It became too much for Marc, and with another roar of amusement he left the room. Once he had gone, her brain cleared and her mind was crystal clear.

Then the door opened again and she spun around defensively, but it was only Kara. Kara clutching a giant stick of rhubarb, its huge leaf trailing the ground behind her. Her face was tear-stained and she held out the rhubarb to Judith.

"Mummy all gone," she whimpered. "No Mummy, only oobarb now."

Judith bent down and picked her stepdaughter up, her mind instantly rejecting the implications of any further horror.

"Tea's ready!" called Zilla from the foot of the stairs. Judith's gray eyes stared into the equally frightened small blue ones.

"We'd better go down, Kara," she whispered. "I'll be your mummy from now on, so don't get upset. You're quite safe with me."

The child nestled against her shoulder, and Judith lifted her head defiantly as she went down the stairs.

The boys were already at table, and as one they swiveled their heads towards her.

"Are you feeling better?" they chorused.

"Yes, thank you, I'm quite well now."

"That's good."

In unison they turned their attention back to their plates. The evening sun glinted on their shining heads and she looked around at their equally handsome father and their petite, attractive aunt. As she took her place at the opposite end of the table to Marc she had never felt so alone in her entire life.

Despite Zilla's attempts at light conversation the atmosphere throughout tea remained strained. The boys kept casting covert glances at Judith, and then turned away as soon as they saw that she had noticed. Marc was strangely silent; all traces of his earlier amusement had vanished and apart from the occasional instruction to one of the children he didn't speak. Judith confined herself to civil answers when Zilla's remarks required them and reasssuring smiles at Kara, who seemed cowed by the unusually quiet meal-time.

"I really must go now," said Zilla at last, pushing her empty plate to one side as though to emphasize the point. Judith did not attempt to dissuade her. As his sister left the room to collect up her cardigan and handbag Marc remained seated, staring down at his plate.

"Aunty's going," said Michael loudly. "Can we race her car down the drive?"

"What?"

"Can we race her car down the drive?"

"Whose car?" Marc sounded irritable.

"The Queen's!"

Philip laughed and Marc looked angrily at him. "Don't encourage your brother in his stupidity, Philip. I've no idea what you're talking about, Michael, but since you're obviously feeling humorous I think you should go to your room and practice your handwriting, which is certainly one big joke at present.''

Judith was surprised, this was not Marc's usual way of dealing with his children. Michael was surprised too. He set his mouth in a mutinous line and remained seated. Marc turned his head and stared at the boy. ''Go to your room,'' he repeated firmly.

''Won't!''

''Either you go yourself or else I make you go. Which would you prefer?''

Michael began to go red in the face and clenched his fists tightly.

''If you hurt me I'll tell.''

''Tell what?''

''About Philip.''

Automatically Judith glanced at Philip. He had his dark eyes fixed on Michael's face, and an expression of intense concentration on his features. She looked back at Michael, who had now stood up and was beginning to shout.

''Right, I'll tell then. I'll tell Judith.''

He turned towards his stepmother.

''Philip is . . .'' he hesitated, his mouth working furiously. ''Philip is . . .''

''Go on,'' said Marc lazily.

''Philip is . . . very kind and helpful. He's the kindest person in the world and I'm lucky to have him as a brother.''

Paul and Patrick were chuckling while Philip continued his steady appraisal of Michael, whose voice was rising all the time. Then, abruptly, Philip looked away.

''I hate you,'' yelled Michael. ''You stinking, arrogant cocksucker!''

''*Go to your room*,'' thundered Marc, and Michael went; running blindly past his aunt who was standing in the doorway.

''My goodness, his vocabulary is extensive for a five-year-old,'' she said casually. ''Well, I'm off now. I do hope you feel better soon, Judith dear.''

''Thank you.'' Judith was too bemused by the scene that the boys had just played out for her to take much notice of

Zilla's false sympathy. She knew only too well how Michael must be feeling at this moment, and although she pitied him she felt a sense of relief that she wasn't the only person in the house who voiced thoughts that were neither believed in nor indeed intended to utter.

She looked down the table at Marc. He was the first to turn away.

"I'll show you out, Zilla. Thanks for coming over. I don't know what Judith would have done without you."

Their voices continued in the hall, but too low for Judith to make out the words. Paul and Patrick slid from their seats and started to leave the table.

"You should ask permission," said Judith.

"Why?" asked Patrick politely.

"Because that's the way well-mannered children behave."

"Oh, right. May we leave the table, please?"

"You may."

They went. Judith was alone with Kara and Philip. "Don't you want to say goodbye to your aunt, Philip?"

"No. She doesn't like me and I don't like her."

"I'm sure that's nonsense. She seems very fond of you all."

"What do you know about it?" he asked rudely. "You're new here."

She cut Kara a slice of sponge cake. "Why doesn't she like you? I assume there is a reason."

His eyes wouldn't meet hers. "I don't know why. It's just one of those things."

"I see."

"Is Michael getting a hamster for his birthday?"

"I expect so."

"Good."

Kara put the last few crumbs in her mouth. "All gone! Me go play now."

Philip laughed. "She sounds like Tarzan in those awful films. 'Me go hunt buffalo,' that sort of thing!"

"All children talk like that at first."

"We didn't."

"Probably not, but most other children do. Don't you want to go out and play for a little before bedtime?"

He nodded and started to walk around the table. When he drew level with Judith's chair he stopped abruptly.

"What's that, Kara?" he asked, pointing at the floor.

"Oobarb. Mummy all gone now."

Philip stared at his half-sister for a moment and then took a step backwards. "It's a pity you didn't go too," he muttered, his eyes still on the thick stalk of rhubarb.

Kara shook her head. "Daddy keep Kara." Then she lifted her eyes to Philip and gave him a brilliant smile. For the first time Judith could see a resemblance between the small girl and her half-brothers.

Philip licked his lips nervously, his normal composure completely deserting him. Kara moved towards him, her arms stretched out and her eyes shining. He stayed motionless and let her wrap herself around his legs, crooning softly. He looked down on the tip of her golden head and then, slowly and awkwardly, he lifted one hand and patted her gently on the head. For a few seconds she pressed herself more tightly to his legs, and then she let go and made her way into the hall.

Philip looked up and saw Judith watching him. He tried to shrug nonchalantly, but it didn't carry any conviction. "I guess she likes me," he said, half defiantly.

"I guess she does."

"I guess Dad knows best."

"Probably."

Then he turned and bolted from the room. Judith shivered. She wondered why the scene, which should have comforted her—showing as it did that at last Philip was willing to accept the previously rejected little girl—should instead have left her full of a sick foreboding which she didn't even understand.

Judith went to bed before Marc that night. He had coped with putting the children to bed and all the routine evening chores while Judith sat in a comfortable chair in the drawing room and longed for someone normal to talk to about her mounting fears. She resolved to ring Sue the very next day and invite her and the boys over for an afternoon. If anyone could dispel the ridiculous ideas that were festering in her brain it would be Sue.

Once she had made that decision she felt easier in her mind and went up to the bedroom. She glanced in at the boys' rooms first; as usual all the rooms were hot and the windows tightly closed. Only Kara's room had any air coming in, but tonight that didn't seem to be enough and it seemed almost as hot in there as in the other bedrooms.

After showering she read a magazine for half an hour and then lay down to sleep, leaving Marc's lamp on for when he came up. Although tired she wasn't able to sleep, and began to toss and turn restlessly. The bedroom was stifling and she thought longingly of cold winter nights.

Marc came in to the room quietly and was quickly in bed beside her. She had her back turned to him, determined not to have any form of contact either verbal or physical. Not after the way he had humiliated her in front of the doctor. When he put a hand on her waist she stiffened and moved to the edge of the bed. He gave a small sigh and rolled away from her. For a time they both lay there in silence.

"Judith?"

She ignored him.

"I know you're awake. I want to talk to you."

"Well, I don't want to talk to you."

"I want to apologize about this afternoon."

His words surprised her. She had expected him to ignore the entire episode, deny it had ever happened. Intrigued, she decided to let him continue.

"Go ahead then," she murmured, but she kept her back turned on him.

"That's all, really. I'm sorry that you felt so ill, and I'm even more sorry about what happened when the doctor called."

She rolled onto her back, staring up at the ceiling.

"You made me tell him all that nonsense about gooseberries, didn't you?"

"Yes."

"How? Are you some sort of hypnotist? Is that how you do it?" She was intrigued.

"In a way. I've always been able to do it, ever since I was a small child. The boys can too."

She remembered Michael's humiliation at Philip's hands.

"Does anyone else know about this 'gift,' or do you keep it secret?"

"We keep it secret, of course. Wouldn't you?"

"I don't know. I can't envisage such a situation, I'm afraid."

"Of course you can't. You're delightfully normal."

"Why are you telling me this? I'm not a blood relation. In fact the more I see of your family the less I want to be any sort of relation at all. Aren't you worried that I'll leave and tell people about you?"

He was quiet for a time and when he spoke his voice was sympathetic. "Poor Judith, don't you realize that you can't leave?"

"Why not?" Her voice was sharp with sudden fear. She imagined being confined to the house for the rest of her life, never able to mix with the outside world again.

"Because you are tied to me now. You're carrying our child, another son, and this time he'll be yours as much as mine. You'll be as protective of him as I am of the four I already have. That's how it was with Elizabeth. She would have died for the children."

He sounded so confident that it was difficult to doubt him, but Judith's commonsense made her reject his words.

"There is no reason why our child should be anything like your other boys," she said reasonably. "Half of its genes will be mine, not Elizabeth's. That's bound to make a difference."

"No, it won't. It doesn't work like that."

"Don't be so stupid, of course it does. All human beings reproduce in the same way, you know. There's nothing special about your family, except for the fact that you seem to bear a remarkable resemblance to each other from generation to generation if Zilla is to be believed."

"You've missed the point," he said softly.

"Which is?"

"Nothing. It's senseless trying to explain further until

you've had the child. I only started the conversation because
I genuinely regretted what occurred earlier."

Judith knew that he was giving her what he believed to be
the true facts, and certainly there was no doubt that all his
family had strong personalities and tended to dominate other
people, but that was all. If Marc was right and she was
indeed carrying a child, then she didn't want to even
consider any more complicated explanation.

All the peculiarities that she herself had noticed, she
resolutely pushed to one side. The tremendous physical
coordination; the terrible outbursts of temper; the apparent
isolation from their contemporaries; the strange temperature
changes in the house: she buried everything deep in her
subconscious. Already, without knowing it, she was trying
to provide a calm, peaceful and untroubled atmosphere for
the embryo that had begun to gestate in her womb.

"There is one thing," she said.

"Yes?"

"Why did you marry me? I mean, why not any of the
other women from the bureau? In fact, why use the bureau
at all? You're very attractive, I'm quite sure you didn't have
any trouble finding women to go to bed with you."

"I found *you* attractive. I liked your appearance and your
personality. Also you had no family ties. That was important. I knew how demanding my family commitments were
going to be and I didn't want a new wife with other
responsibilities. You were perfect in every way, Judith."

"I see. Is that the truth?"

"Yes."

And it was, as far as it went. Fortunately Judith didn't
follow his line of reasoning any further. "It isn't very
flattering," she continued. "It's so practical. I didn't have
any sensible reasons for wanting you, I just fell madly in
love. Even now I don't know why. It wasn't like me at all."

"You sound as though that's all in the past."

"Do I? I suppose it is in a way. Reality has a way of
changing things quite a lot, hasn't it?"

"I'm sorry. I don't want you to feel that you made a
mistake."

"I don't, at least not often. Sometimes I feel rather lonely, that's all."

He could hear that she was lying and he was troubled. He put his arms around her and pulled her to his chest, kissing her forehead gently.

"I'd like to make love to you."

"Would you?"

"Of course."

"I wish I was better at that side of things, Marc. I'm sure Elizabeth was good at sex."

"Why do you say that?"

"Because I get the feeling you and she were very close, and somehow I connect the two things."

"You're being silly," he said quietly as he let his hands roam over her body. As she relaxed and began to respond to his touch she closed her eyes, letting the sensations fill her mind; it was fortunate that she did, otherwise she would have seen the bleak look of despair on her husband's face at the mention of his first wife's name.

Elizabeth. He could remember her so well. Her dark, vital presence. Her eager initiation into all the ways of love-making that he could show her. She had even learned to love the dark side of him; the violent coupling so necessary for the siring of sons had become something she had craved. A craving that he had been unable to refuse to satisfy, even though he knew only too well where it was all leading. He watched as their children sucked her life from her in order to grow and learn; draining her of knowledge and strength as a leech drains blood. Killing her because that was what happened to outsiders, although as yet no one knew why. He wanted to keep her with him but his instincts overruled his commonsense and so he had lost her sooner than was perhaps necessary. But eventually he would have lost her anyway, he knew that, and the bliss that they had experienced more than made up for the loss of one or two years more together. Elizabeth, his one true love.

Judith was so overwhelmed by the peaks of ecstasy that continued to build up in her that she cried out, desperate for final fulfillment. His hands seized her swollen breasts and closed on them like iron bands. At the same time he thrust violently into her, pushing her back to the headboard as he did so, but she was no longer noticing. She opened her eyes and saw his face; saw the brown eyes soft and tender, with an expression of such overwhelming love that all her doubts and insecurities were banished and she gave herself entirely to his demands.

In Paul's hot, stuffy bedroom the three older boys were crouched on the bed. They were all staring at the fourth figure in the room, the thin pale figure who stood before them, her eyes filled with suffering quite beyond their comprehension.

"Let her go, Philip. She looks so sad, I don't like to see her so sad."

"You're soft, Paul. I'm enjoying myself."

The figure shimmered, grew fainter.

"Stop it, Paul," hissed Philip. "I can't do it on my own yet."

Paul was getting angry. "I want to let her go."

The woman stared gratefully at her first-born. Her image trembled and began to fade. Philip concentrated harder than he had ever concentrated before, and slowly she became more clearly defined again. Paul and Patrick gazed in awe at their brother, for now he was doing it entirely alone. They wore impressed, and also afiaid.

Elizabeth watched Philip in horror. She knew how much he hated her, and knew that some of his hate was justified. Even so she had never envisaged torment such as he could now inflict on her. She turned her head; she could feel the emotions coming from the master bedroom. Could feel them and also hear the accompanying sounds. As Judith cried out in pleasure the wraith-like figure in front of the boys opened her mouth in a cry of distress that was all the more terrible for remaining unheard.

The thin hands were lifted to the almost transparent head and the stick-like fingers tried unavailingly to cover the ears. The boys continued to watch as their mother shook her head from side to side, her mouth still open in her anguish. She knew that until Philip lost interest and allowed his concentration to waver she would be forced to remain in the bedroom, listening to her beloved husband and his new wife.

Back in their father's bedroom Judith closed her eyes in sleep. Drenched in sweat and completely exhausted she lost consciousness immediately. Marc, his memories of Elizabeth now shut away again until another time, lay down beside her. The room was silent except for their even breathing.

Paul, Patrick and Philip saw their mother's hands slowly drop to her sides. The anguish in her eyes dimmed. She watched her sons attentively, waiting for release. Paul and Patrick bent their heads, ashamed of what they had witnessed, only Philip continued to stare at her. Eventually, realizing that the worst was over for her he emptied his head of every memory of his mother until his mind was a complete blank and Elizabeth immediately vanished.

Philip got down from Paul's bed and stretched. "I'm exhausted. That was jolly hard work. If you two aren't going to help me any more then I shan't let you see her."

"I don't think we want to see her," said Paul. "It's not nice; she's always crying."

"I like seeing her cry."

"Well you would!"

Philip's eyes began to close and he stumbled to the door. After he had gone the other two looked fearfully at each other. "He's very powerful isn't he?" said Patrick at last.

"Yes. Daddy says he's going to be the leader."

"He's the leader now."

"I think Daddy meant the leader of everyone who's like us. Or perhaps even the country; the Prime Minister or someone important."

"We'd better not annoy him any more then," said Patrick fearfully.

"No, but he still has a lot to learn."

"Not from us."

"Of course not. From Judith. I think he ought to hurry up and learn, I'll tell Dad tomorrow."

"Yes. Dad will know how to handle him."

"Of course he will."

But both boys sounded doubtful, and in need of reassurance. It took them longer to go to sleep than usual, whereas Philip slept immediately and was untroubled by any dreams.

The next morning Judith noticed how unusually subdued the older children were, and Philip looked tired and unwell. He brushed off her anxious query with a casual "fine," but he played alone all day and she was certain that he was about to come down with something within the next few days.

Despite this she telephoned Sue and invited her and her two boys over for an afternoon. They arranged the visit for the following Tuesday, the day after Michael's birthday.

"How are you coping?" asked Sue. "I've been thinking about you."

"Quite well. I've got lots of things to ask you when you get here."

"Great. Look forward to seeing you again. Take care, love."

Judith smiled and put the receiver down. As she turned away, she almost fell over Patrick who was crouched on the floor.

"Good heavens, Patrick. I could have broken my neck! What on earth are you doing there?"

"Just thinking."

"Well, do it somewhere else before you cause a nasty accident."

He stood up slowly. "Who were you talking to?"

"A friend of mine. She's coming to visit us next week and bringing her two boys with her. That will make a nice change for you, won't it?"

"Depends on what her boys are like. They're not those noisy ones who came to the wedding, are they?"

"Yes, but I'm sure you'll all play very well together. Now please move out of the hall."

For the rest of the day she scarcely saw the children except at meal-times. Even Kara was included in their games and when Marc arrived home at six Judith was able to say with complete truth that they hadn't been any trouble at all.

"I expect they're getting used to me," she said cheerfully.

"Maybe. How have you felt?"

"Great. I rang Sue this morning, and she's coming over next week."

"That's nice," he said flatly, and she decided not to mention the visit again. She was determined not to lose touch with her friend, but that didn't mean Marc had to be included in her plans. Obviously evenings out with Sue and Dave were not going to become part of their social life, but her days were her own, whatever Marc's feelings on the matter.

The next few days were all peaceful and uneventful, and then it was the morning of Michael's sixth birthday. It started well. All the children swarmed into their father's bedroom as soon as he called them, and then sat watching as Michael jumped up and down clamoring for his presents.

"Presents? Do you think you deserve them?" joked Marc.

"It's my birthday!"

"Why didn't you remind us?"

Judith laughed; Michael had mentioned the fact at least ten times every day for the past week. As the presents were brought out and Michael's shrieks of excitement grew more piercing she felt very reassured. This was a normal, happy family scene and all her fears, all the strange incidents since her marriage suddenly receded. This was the reality.

The hamster was brought in after everything else had been opened. It was crouched in the corner of its cage, half-hidden by the straw.

"They sleep in the day," explained Judith. "Just wait until tonight. He'll be whizzing around on his wheel and driving you mad."

The boys gathered around to look at the tiny, golden creature. Michael put a tentative finger between the bars and made quiet clicking noises. Instead of hiding more securely the hamster was galvanized into sudden frantic movement and began to run around and around the perimeter of its home, squeaking loudly.

"Leave it alone," said Marc. "You're frightening it."

"I'm not, I'm not doing anything," protested Michael and Judith saw that he had removed his finger and was merely watching. The hamster continued to run, blundering into one of the wooden sides and then panting heavily with shock.

"Look, I think I'd better move it somewhere quiet again," said Judith, worried by the animals' obvious terror. "Perhaps it's the sight of so many of you that's upsetting it."

She picked the hutch up and carried it into Michael's room, placing it carefully on top of one of the corner units. Then she peeped inside again. The hamster was back in its corner, whickers twitching furiously, but at least it had ceased its running.

Michael was late for breakfast because he had been looking at his new pet, which he decided to call Albert.

"Was he asleep?" asked Judith as she gave him his cereal.

"Not really, as soon as I went up to him he started racing around again. It's nice isn't it? I mean, it's better if he's awake in the day and sleeps at night the same as me."

"I suppose so." She was doubtful Albert would last long if he continued to be so nervous but she hadn't the heart to say as much.

During the day she checked the animal from time to time, and whenever she went in alone he was sleeping peacefully. The two times that Michael went with her Albert immediately sprang to life, much to Michael's delight and Judith's worry. She continued to hope that the animal would get used to his new home.

In the evening the whole family went to see *Return of the Jedi* at the Oakham cinema, with the exception of Kara who was looked after by Mrs. Watson. Michael sat between his father and Judith and was enthralled by the whole film, but the other boys lost interest after the first half hour and twice Marc had to tell them to keep quiet.

On the way home they were told off.

"If you can't behave in a cinema then you won't be taken again, it's as simple as that," said Marc angrily.

"Sorry," they chanted.

"I liked it, I was good," clamored Michael.

"Yes, you were." Judith had enjoyed it as well. "Why didn't you like it, Paul?"

"I thought it got silly. Besides, it was sad the way they killed all those creatures off. They were really great."

"They were grotesque." Judith laughed. "I've never seen such horrible freaks!"

The boys became silent. She turned her head to look at them, sitting side by side on the back seat. They turned their identical dark eyes towards her.

"They weren't freaks," said Paul politely. "That's the way they were supposed to look where they lived. It was a different galaxy, you know."

"I know that! But they were repulsive, ugly mutations."

"What's a mutation?" asked Michael.

"A divergence from the racial norm," said Marc shortly. Judith started to enlarge his definition. "That means..."

"We know what that means." Philip's voice was cold and precise.

"Good. Do you know what it means, Michael?"

"Of course he does."

"I wasn't asking you, Philip."

"I thought we were..." began Michael tentatively.

"Were what?" asked Judith.

"You know, that word. But we're not grotesque, are we?" His anxiety made his voice quiver. Judith laughed. "Whatever gave you that idea? You're just ordinary, mischievous boys. A mutation is..."

"Drop it, for Christ's sake!"

Marc's shout took her by surprise and when she glanced at him he was gripping the steering wheel tightly in annoyance.

"There's no need to shout. I don't know what's so wrong in talking about monsters from a space film."

"You stupid woman!"

The words were muttered but unmistakable. To her distress she felt tears at the back of her eyes and had to blink furiously. They drove the rest of the way in silence.

Judith put the children to bed and then went to find Marc. There was no sign of him downstairs and she thought that he must have gone to bed himself. Afraid that he wasn't well she went to look in on him but the bedroom was empty. An hour later there was still no sign of him and so she went to bed herself; she felt exceptionally tired even though it was only ten o'clock.

After showering she walked naked to the windows and opened the largest one, glancing out into the garden. It was still fairly light and she could see a figure at the bottom by the vegetables. Realizing that it must be Marc she leaned out further. He had his back to the house and was staring down at the ground, his hands thrust into his trouser pockets and his shoulders slumped as though he were feeling as tired as his wife.

She was about to call out to him when he sank to his knees on the edge of the grass and spread his arms out in front of him. Judith drew back. This was something that she knew instinctively she wasn't meant to see. It looked to her as though his hands were moving in the earth, digging or scraping with slow measured movements. Intrigued she waited for him to pull something out of the ground, but he didn't. After a time he stopped digging and rested his hands on his knees. Then, through the still heat of the night air she heard a strange sound; strange, but unmistakable. Marc was sobbing.

Judith put a hand to her mouth and pressed it hard against her lips. He was the last person that she would have imagined crying, and it was all the more terrible for taking place where it did and in such secrecy. Her heart thumped heavily against her ribs and she moved cautiously back from the open window. When he turned she didn't want him to see her. Whatever the cause of his distress she knew that it had no connection with her.

"Where have you been?" she mumbled when he eventually came to bed.

"I ran Mrs. Watson home and then went around to Zilla's for a few minutes. Go back to sleep."

She wondered what he would say if she told him that she knew he had been kneeling in the garden crying. Quite probably he would deny it or refuse to give any explanation. In any case she wouldn't dare mention it. The longer she spent in this large stone house the more she grew to fear her new family.

Gradually, in the back of her mind, she was beginning to

consider the possibility that one day she might need to leave. It was a remote possibility, one that she scarcely liked to admit even to herself, but it was there.

When she awoke the next morning she was still feeling troubled, and it was with a great sense of relief that she realized Sue was coming over. There would be no harm in telling Sue about what she had seen; it would be wonderful not to keep everything bottled up inside her. She would tell her about the pain as well, and Zilla's strange behavior. Perhaps Sue could even think of ways in which they might try and contact Kara's mother, if only to let her know that Kara was well and happy.

Greatly cheered by the prospect of company, Judith managed to cope cheerfully with Marc's moody silence at breakfast and a particularly difficult meal-time with the children as the boys continually needled one another with whispered comments and quick pinches and pokes. Finally she chased them all out to play, and then when Mrs. Watson arrived, the two of them set about turning out the boys' rooms, where toys and clothes made it impossible even to reach the beds.

They started in Paul's room. "Heavens, it's stuffy!" exclaimed Judith, drawing back the curtains and opening the windows. "I'm looking forward to winter nights."

"The heating's on at night in the winter."

Judith stared at the older woman methodically folding up pairs of shorts and placing them in a drawer.

"All night? Marc keeps it on day and night in a house this size?"

"Not in the day. Just at night."

Mrs. Watson moved to the bed, stripping it back and smoothing the bottom sheet.

"That's ridiculous! It must be freezing in the day."

"It is, but that's how they all like it."

"Well, I'm certainly not going to walk around muffled up every day. Perhaps it's only because there hasn't been a woman here all the time."

"There was Felicity."

"Of course. Did she complain?"

"I didn't know her very well. Shall we do Patrick's room next?"

"Yes. Did you know Elizabeth?"

"I used to help here from time to time when she was alive."

"Was it the same then?"

"The boys were younger, their rooms were naturally tidier."

"I didn't mean that! Was it cold in the winter when Elizabeth was alive?"

"I'm afraid I don't remember. Did you know Paul was reading this?"

Judith reached out and took the book from Mrs. Watson's hands. "The *Kama Sutra*! I don't think he's quite ready for that at nine! I wonder where he got it from. Someone at school perhaps."

"I've no idea. Perhaps we should separate. I'll do Patrick's room while you do Philip's."

It was plain that Mrs. Watson didn't want to talk any more, and so Judith agreed, and after taking the book into her own room and slipping it into one of her drawers, she turned her attention to Philip's room. This was by far the neatest one of all and when she had finished it ahead of Mrs. Watson she went into Michael's, which looked as though a bomb had hit it. There were toys and books and clothes over every surface, and he had even put a box of board games on top of Albert's cage.

Judith paused in front of the cage. The hamster had seemed quieter when she looked at him before breakfast but his food bowl had been empty and she had reminded Philip to fill it up. Now she decided to check that he'd remembered. To her relief the bowl was full of seeds, and the water bottle was freshly topped up. Albert was asleep in the straw.

"Getting used to them, Albert?" she whispered as she took the box of games from the cage. Her hand knocked the back and the cage started to tip off the unit. She grabbed it and pushed it back. "Sorry! Bet that gave you a fright."

To her surprise Albert hadn't woken, but he had moved

He had slid along the sawdust that covered the floor and was now lying by the bars, still fast asleep. At least, she hoped that he was only asleep.

She watched the animal closely for several minutes, but there was no movement. It looked to her as though Albert was dead. She lifted the hatch and put her hand in. The golden body was cold as she pulled it out of the cage and cradled it in her hands. He had obviously been too nervous from the start, but Michael would be heartbroken.

"Mrs. Watson!" called Judith, wondering what she should do.

"Yes?"

"Come in here a minute. Poor Albert's died on us."

Mrs. Watson took the animal in one hand, grasping it around the middle of its body. The head flopped limply and at a most peculiar angle.

"Do you think it was fright?" asked Judith hopefully.

"A pretty bad one to break its neck."

They stared at each other.

"It must have fallen off its wheel," said Judith at last.

Mrs. Watson shrugged. "You'd better ask the boys. I've just got time to do the bathroom before I go."

Judith nodded and reluctantly took Albert back. After a moment's thought she carried him downstairs and out into the garden.

Paul, Patrick and Michael were playing cricket on the lawn. There was no sign of Philip or Kara. The three boys ran up to her.

"May we have an ice cream? It's boiling out here."

"What's that, Judith?"

She looked at Patrick's inquiring face.

"I'm afraid it's Albert. He's died."

"Died?" Michael's eyes opened wide. "My hamster's died already? That's not fair. Why did he die? He didn't starve to death, did he?"

"No, there was plenty of food in his cage. Where's Philip?"

"Here I am."

Philip strolled around the side of the house; Kara was close behind him, her face flushed by the heat.

"Philip, was Albert all right when you fed him after breakfast?"

"He was fine. Scampering around all over the place."

"Well, he isn't now, he's dead!" and Michael began to sob.

"I know he is."

Michael stopped crying, and he and his brothers looked quickly at Philip.

"How do you know?" asked Judith.

"I can see him lying in your hands."

"Aren't you surprised?"

"Not really."

"Why not?"

Philip shrugged and looked defiantly at her.

"Why not, Philip?" she repeated.

"Because I thought I might have killed him."

"When?"

"This morning, when I fed him. He was so ungrateful. There I was, feeding him and giving him a drink to make sure he was comfortable and do you know what he did? He bit me! Stupid animal. I was the one who was looking after him, and he didn't appreciate me one bit."

"What did you do?" whispered Judith.

"I wrung his neck. Well, I was angry. It jolly well hurt where he bit me. It bled a lot!"

Judith's stomach lurched and she felt nauseous. She looked into Philip's indifferent face and wanted to scream at him, but it was obvious that no words of hers would reach him. He had followed his instinct and saw no reason for shame.

"You don't change, do you?" said Paul. "Wait until Dad hears about this."

Philip flushed. "I wouldn't have done it if he hadn't bitten me. I like animals, you know that."

"Yes, animals and small children."

"Shut your mouth!"

"Make me."

"I bloody well will too."

As they began to fight Patrick looked anxiously at his stepmother.

"What did Paul mean?" she asked. "What small children?"

"I don't know. Shall I take Albert for you? Michael and I will bury him in the garden and have a pretend funeral."

Judith didn't want to stay outside a moment longer. She thrust the dead hamster into Patrick's hands and backed away from the children. Away from the fighting of Paul and Philip and away from Michael's silent tears. The one consolation was that Sue was coming. She could tell Sue all about it after lunch.

As soon as she had gone the fight stopped. While Patrick and Michael buried the hamster at the edge of the vegetable garden, the other two stared watchfully at the house. Finally Philip slipped silently in through the back door and hid himself beside the large fridge, his eyes intent upon Judith's back as she peeled potatoes.

Judith checked that she'd done enough and reached for the saucepan lid. Her hand stopped in mid-air and slowly she walked towards the hall. She picked up the telephone and dialed. When the receiver was picked up at the other end she spoke quickly and firmly.

"Sue? I'm sorry, the boys seem to be coming down with something and I think we'd better postpone this afternoon. I'll ring you again when they're better."

"I am sorry," said Sue. "Have they got any spots?"

"No, nothing like that. I must go now. Bye."

She replaced the receiver firmly and returned to the kitchen where Philip stood waiting.

"Who were you talking to?"

"My friend Sue. I told her not to come today."

"Why?"

"I suddenly decided that I didn't want all the bother of entertaining her."

"Oh. What's for lunch?"

"Wait and see."

As she stood by the stove he raced out into the garden again. "It's all right, it worked. They won't be coming."

He and Paul linked hands and glanced down at Kara.

"Come on," said Philip. "You come and have a go too. It's great, you'll enjoy it."

"Won't she tell?"

"No, she enjoys it."

"OK, then."

They disappeared around the side of the house, shepherding their half-sister in front of them.

"What time's your friend arriving?" queried Mrs. Watson as she washed up the lunch dishes.

"She isn't coming after all. I telephoned her and cancelled. I think the business with the hamster must have upset me more than I realized; I just don't feel up to seeing anyone."

"You don't want to lose touch with all your friends," cautioned Mrs. Watson as she emptied the water down the sink and started to dry the stainless steel drainer. "That's what they want."

"Who?"

"The children, of course. They want all your attention for themselves, they're a possessive lot. Their poor mother couldn't call her soul her own."

Judith shook her head. "I'm quite sure that isn't true. I get the feeling the boys resent me; they'd prefer to see less of me, not more."

"Try to get out sometimes," continued the other woman, ignoring Judith's comment entirely. "Ask your husband to take you out to dinner one evening. I don't mind babysitting now and again if their aunt can't manage it. It's not natural you coming here straight from the church and not setting foot outside from that moment on. There, I've finished for today, so I'll get along home if that's all right with you?"

"Of course."

Left to herself, Judith gave some thought to what had been said. It was true that she hadn't been out of the house and garden without the children yet, but that was because there was so much to do here. It was taking time to get used to running the home and coping with the family, she hadn't felt the need to go elsewhere. All the same Mrs. Watson had a point. She resolved to speak to Marc in the evening, and she would remind him about the honeymoon at the same time. The boys would soon be back at school and he had promised that once they were, the two of them would go away on their own.

It was six o'clock before Marc did arrive home. He was in an extremely cheerful mood, even spending half an hour with Kara before taking her up to her room himself.

Judith had fully expected Michael to rush to his father and tell him about the hamster, but he didn't. None of the boys mentioned Albert, and when they were all upstairs and she was alone with Marc Judith found it difficult to raise the subject. In the end Marc provided the opening she needed.

"How was Sue this afternoon?"

"She didn't come."

"Not ill, I hope?" His tone implied the opposite but Judith ignored that, taking the words at face value.

"No, she's fine. I didn't feel up to visitors. I had a bad morning."

"In what way?"

"When I went to clean out Michael's room I found Albert dead."

"Do you fancy a drink? Sherry; wine; whiskey?"

"No, thank you. Did you hear what I said?"

"Yes. You said Albert was dead. Well, I'm sorry, but it isn't a major catastrophe. We'll get Michael another one."

"Philip wrung his neck."

Marc's back was turned to her and he was reaching into the drinks cabinet for glasses, but as her words sank in he seemed for a brief moment to physically shrink. His shoulders slumped and his chin dropped down onto his chest. Then, with an obvious effort he stood up straight again and continued pouring himself a drink, but he didn't turn to face Judith.

She waited for him to speak. At last he returned to his chair, a tumbler of whiskey held tightly in his right hand.

"I take it you didn't want anything. Cheers!"

"Marc, did you hear what I said?"

He stared at her, his eyes probing her face as though searching for a clue as to what his response should be.

"For God's sake, Marc! Aren't you shocked?"

He glanced down at the floor. "Yes, very. I'm not all that surprised though. If you remember I didn't want Michael to have a hamster in the first place. None of the boys are very good with animals. If you recall you were the one who thought it would be nice for Michael to have a pet."

"If I'd known that this sort of thing might happen I'd never have suggested it! It isn't normal, you know. This doesn't happen in an average household. Do you know what Philip said? He said he wrung its neck because it bit him when he was the one looking after it. He's seven years old, Marc. Old enough to appreciate that an animal can't reason things out. There's something wrong with Philip, he ought to see a psychiatrist."

"That's utter rubbish!" His voice was harsh. "All children are cruel, they don't mean to be, it's in their natures."

"It might be in your children's natures, but it isn't in most. A two-year-old might do it by accident but not like Philip. Not a calculated killing."

"It was a hamster, Judith; a hamster, not anything that mattered."

Judith stood up, infuriated by his attitude. "And that makes it acceptable? What about next time? What happens if Kara annoys him, or one of his classmates? Will that matter? What's it going to take to get you to face up to your responsibilities?"

"There's no need to shout. I know my responsibilities. I appreciate that Philip hasn't matured quite as I would wish, but he's had a very unfortunate childhood so far. Elizabeth never took to him and he was always on the fringe of things; never loved as much as he needed to be loved. I hoped you'd make up to him for that."

"Has it never occurred to you that Elizabeth might have had good reason to reject him? Perhaps she could see how destructive he was. Was that it? Did she try and tell you only to have you ignore her, just as you're ignoring me?"

She was breathing quickly, her hands clenched at her sides. Marc's eyes slid over her from her head to her toes and there was an expression of surprise on his face.

"I thought you were placid and easygoing; I didn't realize you had such a temper."

"You sound as though you've been cheated. What's

wrong? Do you want to send me back to the bureau under the Trades Description Act?''

"I can't, can I? You're my wife, carrying my child. It's a little late to ask for an exchange!''

Although he laughed Judith knew that he was more put out by her display of anger than he was by his son's behavior. She refused to let him divert her from the problem.

"Never mind my faults, Marc. What about Philip?''

He stopped laughing. "Yes, Philip. Well, you're quite right, of course. Elizabeth did have a good reason to dislike Philip. You see, he killed Piers.''

Stunned, she looked longingly at the glass of whiskey on the small coffee table, and remembered Paul telling her that there had been a terrible accident.

"How?'' she whispered.

"He didn't wring his neck, if that's what's worrying you. He was only a baby himself, barely one year old. He didn't understand what he'd done but Elizabeth never forgave him.''

"What did he do?''

"Elizabeth wasn't feeling very well. Piers had kept her awake most of the night, and as a result she was very short-tempered. Philip had hurt his head and went to her for some sympathy; she didn't give him any, told him it was his own fault or some such thing. She was resting in bed and she saw him walk out of the bedroom. The next thing she knew there was a terrible crash, and when she managed to get herself out onto the landing she saw Piers' wicker cradle lying at the foot of the stairs. He had been pitched out of it onto his head, and he died a few hours later in hospital.''

"How did she know Philip had done it?''

"He was still standing at the top of the stairs and kept making throwing motions with his arms.''

"Did he say anything?''

"At twelve months? No, according to Elizabeth he stood waving goodbye at the baby than turned to her and smiled. She went into hysterics of course, she was ill for weeks.''

"What did the doctor say?''

"It was the police who asked the most questions, but that was really only to make sure that Elizabeth hadn't done it herself and then used Philip to cover it up. Once they'd satisfied themselves on that point there was nothing for them to do. A one-year-old isn't held responsible for his actions by even the most zealous policeman. It was recorded as an 'accidental death.' "

"But that's ghastly. Poor Elizabeth. She must have been terrified to take her eyes off Philip when Michael was born."

"She was, although I knew there was nothing to worry about. Philip was older, he had learned better by then. She didn't believe me, any more than you do, but I knew I was right. He's always been very good with Michael."

"But not animals? You don't trust him with animals, do you?"

"I don't trust any of them with animals."

She hesitated a moment. "Why not? What's wrong with your children?"

It was out at last. The question that had haunted her ever since she became properly acquainted with the family.

Marc smiled smoothly. "There is nothing wrong with my children. They're all bright, lively and athletic. They are splendid specimens, and I'm proud of them."

"Specimens? You mean specimens of boyhood, I take it?"

"Of course."

"I don't think that's quite how I'd describe them."

"Indeed? How would you describe them?"

"A rare species."

"Species usually applies to animals!"

"I am aware of that."

Marc's heavy brows drew together in a frown. "Don't get carried away by your vivid imagination. We all appreciate your artistic streak, but carried to extremes it could be tiresome."

"Don't patronize me," flared Judith. "You must know that they're different."

"I'll be interested to see what your attitude towards them is once you've given birth to your own rare specimen."

"We don't even know that I'm pregnant yet."

"You're pregnant. If you don't believe me go to the doctor and find out."

"We're meant to be talking about Philip and the hamster," she reminded him in annoyance.

Marc sat down with a sigh. "You're certainly tenacious. Very well then, I'll speak to him about it."

"Is that all?"

"Yes, it bloody well *is* all. If you hadn't been so sure you knew best none of this would have happened. I knew the boys weren't ready for a pet, but you had to insist they were. In a few months' time it would have been all right, but you couldn't wait, could you?"

"How do you know it could have been all right in a few months?"

"Because that's what you're here for, to civilize them."

"How? Give a series of talks? Exactly how am I meant to do it?"

"All you need to do is be around them, they'll pick it up from you instinctively."

"You're talking nonsense and you must know it. I suppose that this means we won't get away for our honeymoon?"

"Honeymoon?" He looked genuinely bewildered.

"We didn't have a honeymoon, Marc. You said that we'd go away once the children went back to school."

"I'm sorry, I remember now. Well, of course we can if you feel up to traveling. Why not wait until you've seen the doctor, take his advice on it."

Judith knew that he had forgotten and she was surprised how much it hurt. She wanted time alone with him, away from the children and their problems.

"I'll go next week," she said quickly, "then we'll have time to arrange everything in advance."

Marc stood up and came over to her. She was still flushed from their argument and her eyes were bright. Slowly he put out a hand and smoothed her hair. She stayed quite still, refusing to respond. She wasn't a puppy, he couldn't put everything right with an affectionate pat.

"You're really angry aren't you? Angry and hurt too. I'm sorry, it's all my fault and I really regret it."

"Regret what?"

"Involving you in all this. I needed someone so desperately and you were obviously kind and caring, but perhaps I shouldn't have married you. It was selfish of me, and I'm sorry, more sorry than you'll ever know."

Despite his size and his normal air of self-sufficiency he was suddenly insecure. He pulled her towards him, seeking comfort from her physical closeness and she felt him tremble as she eased away from his chest to look up into his face. She lifted a hand and stroked his neck gently. To her horror his eyes filled with tears and he caught her hand in his own and held it away from him.

"Don't make me love you," he said softly. "I couldn't cope with that a second time."

"What do you mean?"

"It's the sense of loss. When Elizabeth died I discovered what being alone really meant, I couldn't face that again." He was crying now, but he didn't seem to be aware of it. Judith wanted to wipe the tears away but he had her hands too tightly gripped in his.

"I'm not going to die," she said clearly. "I shan't leave you like Elizabeth did. We'll grow old together."

He looked at her open face, her fine gray eyes, and struggled to regain his composure. She was so defenseless that it pained him to look at her.

"I wish I could believe that," he said at last.

"I'll make you believe it."

"I hope you can."

"As long as we learn to truly love each other then everything will work out," she assured him. "You wait and see."

They made love on the rug in front of the fireplace and this time she was as much the aggressor as he, her previous restraint banished by this evidence of his need for her. Even the specter of Philip was banished for a time, and she was content.

She fell asleep on his shoulder and he covered her with his jacket so that she shouldn't catch cold. He looked at her features as she slept, and they were gentle and vulnerable. As he thought of all that lay ahead of her he gave a muffled groan and his face twisted in anguish. He wished that there were another way, but knew that there was not.

The pattern was predetermined and remorseless; however much he might want to change events his instinct would drive him on, just as it had his father and would his sons. Nature was implacable when it came to the survival of a new species, a fact that Marc appreciated only too well.

A week later Judith sat opposite Dr. Fullick and heard him confirming the pregnancy that Marc had already taken for granted.

"April 11 according to my calculations," he said with a smile. He was a pleasant, middle-aged man with steel-gray hair and kindly brown eyes. This was the first time that Judith had met him.

"What happens now?" she asked tentatively.

"Have a word with the receptionist on the way out. She'll tell you when you need to make your first visit to my ante-natal clinic. No problems so far? No early-morning sickness?"

She remembered the pain in her side, but that no longer troubled her, was in fact something that she wished to forget, and so she shook her head.

"Fine. Naturally you'll contact me if anything untoward should crop up. You tell me you have five stepchildren, so your husband must be quite an expert on these matters by now." He laughed genially.

"I suppose so. Don't you know the children?"

"I can't say that I do. They probably see one of my partners. Good morning, Mrs. Farino."

"Good morning, and thank you."

Outside on the pavement she wondered what she had to thank him for. He hadn't told her anything new, and her next visit wasn't for three months.

Over dinner that evening she waited until the children all left the room and then told Marc about her visit. His eyes gleamed and he reached out to press one of her hands tightly.

"Darling, that's wonderful news. We'll have a drink to celebrate."

"It's hardly a surprise, you've been telling me I'm pregnant ever since that horrible wedding night."

"What? Oh that! Well, now you know that I was right. Anyway, it's always nice to have it officially confirmed."

She watched him pour brandy into two glasses and add a squirt of soda to hers before placing it on the table in front of her. He raised his glass and smiled.

"To our son!"

She raised hers. "Or daughter."

He shook his head in mock reproach. "Oh ye of little faith!"

They sat with their own thoughts for a few moments, then Judith put her glass down and looked carefully at her husband.

"Didn't Dr. Fullick look after Elizabeth during her pregnancies?"

"No. As a matter of fact I hadn't intended you to consult him. He's good enough for routine illnesses but all the boys were born here, which Dr. Fullick doesn't allow. I know a very good private chap who encourages home confinements. Never mind, you can easily change. I'll give him a ring."

She felt a swift stab of fear. "No! I don't want a home birth. Too many things can go wrong. I'll stay with Dr. Fullick."

"As you like, darling. April's a long way off, you might change your mind by then."

"I might," she conceded, but inwardly she knew that nothing would induce her to give birth in this house.

At the end of the week she made an appointment to see the nearest dentist. "Dr. Fullick's receptionist said I ought to have my teeth checked every four months while I'm pregnant," she explained to Marc.

"I don't think Elizabeth bothered."

"I am not Elizabeth."

"I realize that! We've never had the need for a dentist before. I hope this one you've chosen is good."

She was astounded. "Haven't the boys ever been to a dentist?"

"No. Their teeth are perfect."

"How can you tell? I'm taking them with me for a check-up when I go."

Marc stirred uneasily in his chair. "I don't think that's necessary."

"Well, I do. Michael's second teeth are just coming through and the gap between his top front ones looks far too wide."

"All the boys have a gap between their front teeth."

Judith paused and tried to picture them. "So they do! That's what makes them look so alike, that and their coloring. Well then, it's all the more important that they see someone."

"I'd rather you didn't take them, Judith."

"Surely it's better that they go now when there's nothing wrong, rather than wait until they're in pain and have them afraid of the dentist for ever more?"

"They won't need fillings, well, it's unlikely. Zilla and I have perfect teeth."

"Were Elizabeth's perfect too?"

"She had a couple of fillings, but that's beside the point."

"I think they should come."

Judith could tell that Marc was weighing up whether or not it was worth opposing her, and finally he conceded the argument, but he didn't look pleased. That night in bed he made no attempt to put his arms around her or even kiss her goodnight. His opposition puzzled her, but she wasn't unduly worried. Once the visit passed off without any trouble he would accept routine visits to the dentist as part of her care of the children's welfare; or so she thought.

The following Tuesday she arrived at the spacious surgery and shepherded four somewhat subdued boys towards the reception desk.

"Name?" asked the girl.

"Farino."

"First visit?" She sounded extremely bored.

"Yes, it is."

"Fill in these forms please."

It took her some time to manage the five forms and by

then a white-coated girl was waiting at one of the wooden
doors and calling, "The Farino Family," in loud carrying
tones.

"That's us," said Paul, tugging at Judith's arm. "Come
on, the dentist's waiting."

When they walked in the door of his surgery the dentist
looked a little taken aback. For the first time ever the boys
were unsure of themselves and grouped closely around Judith,
their eyes wide and unblinking as they gazed around the
room.

"I'm Mr. Osborn," the dentist volunteered. "Which one
of you is the oldest?"

Paul stepped forward. "I am."

"Fine. Up on the chair then, and we'll take a look at you.
Have you ever been to a dentist before?" he asked as he
tilted the chair back and handed a pair of dark glasses to
Paul.

"No. My father says we didn't need to come today either,
but Judith insisted. She's our stepmother."

"A very wise one too. Now, open your mouth for me
would you, Paul?"

The dentist prodded and examined Paul's mouth before
tilting the chair upright again. "That's marvelous. We'll
need an X-ray before you go, just to see why those front
teeth haven't closed up yet. Which one of you is next?"

This time Patrick stepped forward and Judith saw how
Mr. Osborn's forehead wrinkled slightly as he examined his
teeth. She was fully expecting to hear that he needed some
treatment, but the examination was speedily completed and
Patrick was released.

"Same again," murmured the dentist to his nurse who
was sitting taking notes.

"Have I got to have an X-ray?" Patrick demanded.

"Yes, and for the same reason. Your mouths are identical
which is quite unusual, I can tell you."

Patrick glanced at Paul and moved to his brother's side.
He didn't care for the dentist's patronizing tone and he
didn't particularly want an X-ray either. He and Paul began
to mutter to each other.

Philip got quickly onto the chair and reached up for the glasses.

"Now then, Philip. Let's see what's going on in your mouth, shall we? How old are you?"

"Seven."

"You've got a lot of second teeth for seven, haven't you? Do you ever get toothache?"

"No."

After a brief examination Mr. Osborn glanced at Judith. "This gap in the front teeth is very pronounced. It's a pity they weren't brought to me before."

"She's only just arrived," said Paul coldly.

"I see. Right, young man, down you get. Another X-ray for that one, nurse, please. Now for the baby of the family. Hop on the chair, young man. Which one are you?"

"He's the only one left," drawled Paul.

"His name's Michael," put in Judith, shooting a quelling glance at the other boys who were once again muttering together in the corner.

"And how old are you, Michael?"

"I'm just five. I had a hamster for my birthday, but it died."

"Only just five. Big enough to have new front teeth, I see."

He bent closer to the small, pearly-white teeth. "Amazing! Their mouths are identical. It will be interesting to see what the X-rays show. Nurse, would you take them along to the X-ray room while I have a look at Mrs. Farino?"

Michael slid from the chair and ran to join his brothers.

"We're not going to be X-rayed," said Paul loudly as the nurse approached. "Daddy doesn't want us to be X-rayed, not ever."

"No. He says X-rays are dangerous," chimed in Paul. "They can damage your blood."

"Not this sort," said Judith. "Now go along and stop being silly."

She had just leaned back in the chair when the boys started to scream. Startled she jumped to her feet, half-stumbling as she did so. Paul and Patrick were hanging on to the work surface nearest them and screaming on one shrill note as the nurse tried to coax them out of the room. Philip began to dash from side to side, knocking instruments to the floor as he did so. Michael ran to Judith and buried his head against her, screaming loudly from the safety of her skirt. It was complete bedlam. The dentist and his nurse stared in amazement as the four previously well-behaved children turned into demented animals before their eyes.

Judith tried desperately to keep calm. She closed her eyes and took two deep breaths before raising her voice enough to reach them through their own cries.

"Stop it at once! Behave yourselves. You're acting like little savages."

She hadn't really expected to make any impression on them, but to her astonishment Paul and Patrick were immediately silent and Philip ceased his frantic movements. Only Michael continued to howl, and she smoothed his hair automatically as the other three looked to her for guidance.

They were genuinely puzzled, she could tell that; puzzled and very scared. She cursed Marc for not letting them go to a dentist before. Now they had built up visions of some terrible treatment that she had to dispel if order was to be restored permanently.

"I'll come with you," she said quickly. "I'll have my check-up another day. Perhaps when I come for the X-ray results?" she queried.

Mr. Osborn, his eyes fixed on the boys lest they start to run riot again, nodded. "A good idea. You could come alone if you liked. There's no need for me to see the children again just yet."

"Thank you. Come on boys, the nurse will show us the way."

She was thankful that for some reason they continued to obey her. They were reluctant but they trooped along behind her, down the corridor and into the X-ray room.

The nurse explained what would happen and showed the small machine to Paul. "There'll be a buzzing noise when the picture's taken, that's all," she assured him, her smile strained.

"We're not *afraid*. Our blood is special, and we know our father wouldn't want X-rays to be taken."

"Special blood! My goodness me, we must be very careful then mustn't we?" and the nurse smiled condescendingly.

"I am not afraid," insisted Paul, insulted by the suggestion.

"Of course you're not; not a big boy like you."

Philip sighed heavily and Patrick began to giggle.

"That's enough," interjected Judith. "I don't want any more nonsense from you four. One such display is quite sufficient."

The door opened and Mr. Osborn came briskly into the room. He looked both surprised and relieved at how easily they submitted after their original scene, and he was smiling amicably as he ushered them out. Judith thought about apologizing, but decided to wait until her next visit when she could explain without the children listening.

Once out of the swing doors all four of them went mad, rushing down towards the path screaming and shouting as though they'd been cooped up in their rooms for a month. They narrowly missed cannoning into an elderly gentleman and then ran four abreast down the pavement and around the corner into the High Street.

Judith watched them carefully. It could be the relief; they had been afraid at the dentist despite their denials, but somehow she didn't think it was just relief making them so wild. It was their reaction to being brought into line in the surgery. They waited for her at the Post Office steps, jumping sideways up and down them.

"May we have a drink in a restaurant, please?" asked Paul.

"I don't think so. No wonder your father never took you to a dentist. None of you know how to behave in public places."

Philip jumped casually from the bottom to the top, his arms stretched out wide so that momentarily he gave the appearance of flying. "Yes we do. At least, sometimes we do. This was new though. You can't expect us to know what to do in new places."

"I'd like a milk shake." Michael said.

"I do expect you to know how to behave in new places. Politely. That's easy enough to remember isn't it?"

"A strawberry milk shake."

"He frightened us," Patrick put in. "We're not supposed to be X-rayed."

"And is that meant to excuse your disgraceful outburst?"

"With ice-cream on top and a straw in it."

"We did behave, once you'd shown us how." Philip sounded almost proud.

"What do you mean, shown you? How did I show you?"

"All whipped up in one of those machines."

"Will you shut up about your bloody milk shake," shouted Judith.

The four boys stopped their jumping and stared at her in amazement.

"You mustn't swear like that," reproved Paul. "You're meant to be civilized. How can we learn self-control from you if you haven't got it yourself?"

He sounded most put out, as though she had committed an unforgivable social gaffe.

"Don't be such a stuffy little prude," she snapped as her head began to throb. "No one's perfect."

"Not yet," said Philip as he started to walk along the pavement towards the bus stop. "But if someone could learn to be perfect think how well he'd get on in life," and he shot a crafty glance at her from the corners of his eyes.

"It might be a woman," said Judith, her good humor returning.

"A perfect person would probably be allowed a milk shake." Michael's voice had a wobble in it and she relented.

"Come along then, let's go and have a drink before we catch the bus."

Marc had barely stepped in the front door that evening before the boys were upon him, all talking at once in high excited voices.

"We had to have an X-ray, Dad."

"We told her you wouldn't allow it."

"He was a horrible man."

"Do we have to go back again?"

He looked over their heads to where Judith stood quietly waiting. "What are they on about?"

"Their visit to the dentist this morning. The dentist wanted X-rays of their mouths, and they all went berserk. Why on earth are they so frightened of an X-ray?"

He pushed the children aside. "Get away the lot of you. I'd like five minutes' peace before you start bringing me your complaints. Why not go upstairs and play. I'll come up when I've had a drink."

They went quickly and silently, refusing to glance in Judith's direction. As soon as they were out of sight she let out a sigh of relief.

"I told you they should have been to a dentist before, Marc. If they'd been used to going regularly none of this would have happened."

"If they hadn't gone today it wouldn't have happened either. Was there anything wrong? Did they need fillings?"

"No, but the dentist's worried about the gap between their front teeth. That's why he took X-rays. I'm to go back next week for my check-up and the results. He couldn't look at me today, I was too busy trying to control the boys."

"In what way control them?"

"If you come in the kitchen I can tell you while I finish getting dinner."

Marc perched himself on the kitchen stool and listened without comment as she related the scene in the dentist's surgery. When she stopped talking and looked to him for an explanation or apology he simply shrugged his shoulders and stared at her.

"Is that all you've got to say? A noncommittal shrug! They behaved disgracefully, and I think you should punish them, or at least give them a telling-off."

"They were only doing as they were told," he said flatly. "I don't agree with X-rays."

"That's ridiculous. Suppose they broke an arm?"

"In that case they would have to be X-rayed, but unnecessary ones like these should be avoided. What on earth's the point? Plenty of people have a slight gap between their front teeth, I don't know what all the fuss is about. You'd never noticed it until I pointed it out."

"I'd noticed it on Michael. He's got a very large gap."

"So had the others at first, but they close up. I've got no sympathy for you, it was your idea to take them and perhaps in future you won't be in such a hurry to change their routine."

"Marc, you married me so that the boys would have someone to care for them. That doesn't just mean washing their clothes and tidying their rooms. It means visits to doctors, dentists, opticians, schools; all the routine things that every mother has to do in order to help her children grow up as fit and capable as possible."

He stood up. "I'm going up to talk to the boys. I had hoped that your concept of caring for them would mean a somewhat broader program than the one you've outlined, but obviously I over-estimated your intelligence."

Judith was so shocked that she was incapable of replying, and she stared after him, wondering why he had felt the need to be so unkind.

The subject of the dentist was not brought up again, not even by Michael—usually incapable of keeping anything to himself—and the next week Judith set off for her own check-up without mentioning it to anyone except Mrs Watson, who was looking after the children for her.

Mr. Osborn smiled warmly at her as she sat down on the leather chair. "A lovely morning, Mrs. Farino. How are the boys today?"

"They're fine. I'm sorry about last week, they completely panicked and were very ashamed afterwards." She didn't think that the lie mattered, in her opinion they should have felt ashamed, certainly the dentist would expect such comment.

"Not to worry. They must be quite a handful for you, and now you're expecting one of your own. When is it due?"

"April. Did the X-rays show anything?"

"As a matter of fact they did. It's the most incredible thing I've come across in twelve years of dentistry. All of your stepsons have a mesioden which is causing the gap between their front teeth. This does happen sometimes, but to find it in four brothers is a fantastic coincidence. I imagine it must be quite unique."

"What is a mesioden?" Judith was beginning to have an unpleasant feeling about the conversation. She didn't like the dentist's air of excitement.

"It's an extra malformed tooth, in their case of conical shape, that often doesn't erupt. In other words it doesn't come into the mouth but stays up in the gum causing the gap but remaining undetected until X-rays are taken. It is most interesting to find it in four brothers like this. I hope to write a short case history and send it to one of the dental journals. Human development is quite amazing, don't you think?"

"I'm quite sure my husband wouldn't like you to write about the boys," said Judith quickly.

"No need to worry, I shan't mention them by name. Now open wide and lets take a look at you."

She put on the dark glasses and as his voice murmured away above her she tried to make sense of what she'd been told.

"Upper left eight."

The boys were not normal. The more she learned about them the plainer this became.

"Upper left seven, missing . . ."

Marc knew that they weren't, which was why he was so against the visit to the dentist.

"Upper left six, MOD filling needing replacement."

They were abnormal physically and mentally. They didn't know how to fit in to society, and that was why she was there. To show them.

"Five and four all right; three distal pallatel filling."

Which meant that Marc couldn't teach them himself. Why not?

"Two, porcelain jacket crown. One, sound."

Because he was exactly the same. He couldn't teach them because he didn't know himself. The hairs on the backs of her arms prickled.

"Upper right eight, missing."

She remembered her wedding night, the almost animal ferocity of his assault.

"Upper right seven, all right."

That was how the children behaved a lot of the time, like animals.

"Six, distal occlusal filling, restoration sound."

Animals knew there was something wrong with them; Sam and Albert had known, and they had both died.

"Five and four sound."

It wasn't just a malformed tooth, they were malformed children.

"Three, two and one, sound. Lower right eight, missing."

And she was carrying another of Marc's children. Another son for him.

"Seven, MOD filling needing replacement."

Sweat broke out on the back of her neck and trickled down her spine. She trembled.

"Nearly done, Mrs. Farino."

She wasn't aware of him any more, she was only aware of her fear. The boys' faces were so clear to her: the smooth features, the dark eyes with flecks of gold when they were angry or afraid. Four identical children, or were they really children? If not, what were they?

"There, finished at last. Three fillings, I'm afraid, so perhaps you'd make an appointment on your way out."

She handed him back the glasses and tried to stand up but the room swam dangerously. The nurse pressed a glass of water into her hand then opened a window.

"I'm sorry, I felt very hot."

Mr. Osborn smiled. "It does get warm when the sun's out. Incidentally, do you happen to know if either of the boys' parents have the same gap?"

"Their father hasn't. Their mother's dead, but I'll try and find out for you."

"I would be grateful. The more information I can get the better the paper I can present."

Judith didn't care about his paper or his excitement, she only cared about the child she carried. If it was abnormal then she didn't want it. However handsome and intelligent it appeared to be, she would loathe it if it wasn't normal, would want to reject it as Elizabeth had rejected Philip.

The receptionist called a taxi for her and when she got home she went straight to the bedroom ignoring Mrs.

Watson, Kara and the boys who were all anxious to talk to her. Then she lay down on the bed and tried to calm herself.

The door opened and Paul came in. "Aren't you feeling well? Did the dentist hurt you?"

"No, he didn't hurt me; I just feel a bit faint. It will pass off."

"I expect it's the baby. What did he say about our X-rays?"

She turned her face away from him. "You've all got an extra tooth in your gum that's keeping your front teeth apart."

"Is he going to take it out?"

"He didn't say so."

"Do lots of people have it?" He sounded anxious.

"No, not a lot, but a few."

"He didn't think it odd? He didn't ask anything about us?"

She pushed herself into a sitting position and saw his worried expression.

"Nothing at all. Well, only if either of your parents have the same gap."

He let out a small sigh and sat on the edge of the mattress. "That's good."

"Why are you worried?"

"It's bad enough being colored, we don't want anything else wrong with us."

"Being colored isn't having something wrong with you."

"It jolly well is. I get called a wog at school."

"Oh, Paul I am sorry. Try and ignore it. If you don't let it worry you the other children will soon give up."

"Who said it was the children? If you come down now we can all have a swim. You don't have to come in, but you're meant to keep an eye on us. Would you mind?"

"I'll be down soon."

Paul had given her something different to think about and her earlier panic faded away. She hated to think of adults being so bigoted, but knew this was naïve. It was something all the children would learn to live with and she must help them. Wondering the best way to go about it she started to get changed. She decided to take her drawing materials with her.

Out in the garden Paul, Patrick, and Philip were in a group near the pool.

"I think the dentist must have said something, she looked very odd, but I've got her mind onto something different now. The old persecution tale, that's usually good enough to distract anyone."

"But she'll think about it again another time. You can't keep her mind on something else."

"Dad will be able to deal with it properly when he gets home. I think he's getting quite keen on her. Have you noticed?"

"Perhaps she's good in bed," suggested Philip and sniggered.

"That's all you think about these days." Patrick sounded bored.

"It's all you'll think about once it happens to you. You're a very late developer, aren't you? Is Dad worried?"

In a fury Patrick leaped on his younger brother and started to fight. Judith came out from the back door with Kara at her heels.

"If you want to go swimming, better get changed. Lunch is in half an hour."

"Just you wait!" threatened Patrick as Philip ducked out of his reach.

"You can't touch me, I'm stronger than you!" jeered Philip as he ran to the pool.

The other two glanced at each other. "I wish he'd slow down a bit," muttered Paul. "At this rate he'll be grown up in a few years."

"Only if he takes advantage of having her here," and Patrick nodded towards his stepmother.

"I sometimes think Philip isn't going to bother with getting civilized."

"In that case he won't survive. Remember what Dad told us about Uncle Saul?"

"We're not meant to talk about him. Race you into the water."

They dived in cleanly causing scarcely a ripple.

* * *

"Well then, what did he say?" inquired Marc as they walked around the garden after dinner.

"Who?"

"The dentist, Osborn, is it?"

"Yes, Mr. Osborn." She glanced towards the climbing frame where the boys were risking life and limb in their usual casual manner.

"Actually it was rather odd."

"In what way?"

"He said it was the most incredible thing he'd come across in twelve years of dentistry."

"What was?"

"The X-ray result. All of the boys' X-rays were the same. Each one showed an extra malformed tooth up in their gum causing the gap between the front teeth. He couldn't get over finding four cases in one family."

Marc looked critically at the honeysuckle climbing the wooden fence down the side of the vegetable garden. "This isn't growing as fast as it should. I wonder why?"

"Marc, he wants to write a paper on the boys."

He swung around to face her, a look of fury in his eyes. "Tell him from me that he isn't to do any such thing. What a bloody nerve, trying to make a name for himself out of my children. It's a great pity you ever started all this."

"Marc," she put a hand on his arm trying to soothe him, "he won't use their names, he just wants other dentists to hear about them."

"What the hell for? What good will it do them?"

"I don't know, none I suppose. It's more a matter of interest."

"I fail to see how it can be of interest to anyone. What sort of a man is he?"

"Just an ordinary one. He's very nice."

"Nice! How extremely perceptive of you to know that he's nice. On what do you base this observation?"

"There's no need to get annoyed. You asked me what he was like and I've told you how he appeared to me. Go and see him yourself if you're so anxious to find out more. He'd be only too pleased to see you. He wanted to know if you or Elizabeth had the same malformation."

"Certainly not."

Judith saw how Philip was running along the top rung of the frame, hotly pursued by Paul. Michael was busy throwing himself off one of the side bars and turning a somersault in the air before he landed, while Patrick hung upside down at the end of the bar, his knees curled casually around it. He had an open book on the grass and was reading it from his, to Judith's eyes, hideously uncomfortable position. She studied them all briefly before turning to Marc again.

"He gave me the impression that this extra tooth is some kind of genetic freak, and not a thing that you'd expect to find repeated in a family unless . . ."

"Unless what?"

"Unless the children were genetic freaks."

Marc stood perfectly still. "Did Osborn say that?"

"No. I'm saying it."

Without another word he turned his back on her and walked briskly away to the front of the house.

Judith's eyes fell on the giant rhubarb leaves and automatically she started to look for Kara. She found her standing at the side of the swimming pool.

"Come on, darling. Time for bed."

"I want to swim."

"Daddy will teach you soon, when you're older."

"Now!"

"It's late and I'm tired, don't start playing me up."

"I want to swim *now*."

Judith bent down and sharply slapped Kara's left leg. "I don't want any more argument, come along in."

She stooped, picked the little girl up and turned towards the house. The boys stood in front of her, their expressions hostile. Startled she clutched Kara tightly.

"Where did you all spring from? I'm just taking Kara in to bed."

"Goodnight Kara," they chorused and Kara beamed at them. Judith forced herself to walk through them and then moved as quickly as she could, anxious to get away although she didn't know what she feared.

By the time Kara was in bed Judith was exhausted. She sat down on the top stair, unable to face trying to coax the boys through the evening routine. Below her Marc came out of his study and glanced up.

"Are you all right?"

"Only tired."

He started to walk up the stairs towards her. "What did you do with yourself this afternoon?"

"Nothing much. I read through some of my old A.A. Milne paperbacks to see if the boys would like them and I did a bit of sketching, just quick drawings of the house and garden. Nothing tiring."

"You look rather white. Why don't you have a rest on the bed while I see to the boys and then we can watch some TV or play some records for a couple of hours."

It sounded perfect and without any argument Judith left Marc to get on with everything himself. It must be her pregnancy, she reasoned as she closed her eyes, she had no other excuse for feeling so utterly drained.

Her thoughts drifted pleasantly while she lay there, the sounds of the boys splashing in the bath and arguing with each other providing a by now familiar background. Michael was always the first into his pajamas and she heard him pattering around outside the bathroom door where the others were still busy. He was chanting to himself and sounded very cheerful. She tried to make out the words.

"Mumble mumble mumble all his buttons undone."

Startled she sat up, ignoring the way the room swam in front of her eyes. She strained to hear more.

"Good bear learnt his twice times three,
    but bad bear never used his handkerchee."

He laughed loudly and sniffed.

"Shut up, Michael," called Patrick. "She'll hear you."

Judith's fingers dug into the palms of her hands but she didn't even notice the pain; she hardly dared to breathe lest she miss his next remark.

"Good bear learnt his twice times four,

but bad bear's knickerties were terrible tore!''

Then there was the sound of a scuffle, a door slammed and
Michael was silent. She wanted to go to him, wanted to find
out how he'd known the rhyme, and determinedly she
pushed herself off the bed. Her legs wobbled, but she made
it to the door and reached out for the knob. Before her hand
could reach it the door swung open, nearly knocking her
down. She screamed and Marc's arms grabbed hold of her.

"What's wrong? Are you feeling ill?"

She shook her head, trying to struggle free. "I must go
and see Michael."

"Why? Can't it wait until tomorrow, you're dead on your
feet."

"But he was reciting from 'Twice Times'."

"From what?"

" 'Twice Times'. It's A.A. Milne, from *Now we are Six*.
One of the books I was reading this afternoon."

He lifted her up without any effort and placed her back on
the bed.

"Obviously he already knows it; I'm afraid you were
wasting your time."

"But he didn't. I asked them all if they knew any of the
A.A. Milne books and they'd never heard of them."

"Children often don't know authors, just the stories.
What are you in such a state about?"

Judith pulled herself away from him and moved to the
other side of the bed. Marc was worried, she could see it in
his eyes, and in the way his hands moved restlessly over the
duvet cover.

"I want to ask him how he learned it so quickly. He's
only just five."

"He didn't learn it today, did he? You said you read to
yourself, not aloud."

"I think he did learn it today, but not from me. At least,
not by me reading it to him."

Marc reached for her but she evaded him and refused to
look him directly in the eyes. When she did that her
thoughts were often changed, she had learned that much
already.

"I'm afraid I don't understand you," he said at last. "You're very over-wrought, perhaps I should get the doctor to prescribe a sedative."

"You do understand me, you understand me only too well. I believe Michael knows that verse because I read it to myself today. He learned it from me without my knowledge. He literally picked my brains, just as Philip did when he watched me sketch. He wasn't watching my hands, he was staring at my head when I drew that day at Peakirk. Obviously Michael was somewhere near me this afternoon. That's how they learn isn't it? That's how I'm supposed to civilize them; by example. I'm a very civilized person, I was strictly brought up and my natural reaction to a situation is a very restrained, nonaggressive one. That's really why you chose me isn't it? To turn your offspring, for want of a better word, into reasonable imitations of young human beings. But they're not, are they? I don't know what they are, but they're not normal children."

Marc stared at her, his eyes wide and incredulous. She stared aggressively back at him, refusing to react to his apparent astonishment.

"My dear Judith, if you could only hear yourself! I hope you haven't been talking this sort of gibberish to other people, they might get quite concerned about your mental health if you have. My children do go to school, they mix with their peers, they catch colds and chickenpox and they sometimes learn bits of verse from books on their shelves; in other words they're normal children and no one has ever suggested otherwise."

"Until now. Now I'm suggesting it."

"Darling, look at me please. There is nothing wrong with the children. I know it's hard for you after . . ."

She heard his voice droning on and felt herself slipping away from reality. His eyes, the flecks of gold shining distinctly, held hers. "*No!*" Her scream was forced from her throat and took him by surprise. She had managed to break the contact and she jumped from the bed and ran towards the door. He leaped after her, catching hold of an arm and holding it tightly.

"Judith, for your own sake don't go out there like this.

Stay here with me. Listen to me, then everything will be all right. Just lie still and let me explain things to you. I promise you you're wrong. Don't go out there. I beg you, don't . . ."

"Shut up," she shouted. "I'll show you I'm right."

She ran from their room and straight into Philip's. He was standing by his window and turned towards her, his face was no longer young, despite its childlike smoothness. There was knowledge and awareness in his eyes; there was also hate. She stopped abruptly in the middle of the room. He raised his eyebrows slightly, then started to recite.

> "King John was not a good man,
>   he had his little ways,
> And sometimes no one spoke to him,
>   for days, and days, and days."

"How do you know it?" she whispered.

"We all know it. We know all the books now."

She turned to find the other boys in the doorway. Behind them stood Marc, his eyes filled with compassion.

"But how?"

"We learn from you. We are the sum of everything you know."

Judith shook her head. "Why me?"

"Not just you," explained Patrick politely. "We learn from everyone. Facts and figures, but emotions as well. Love, hate, anger, fear, we learn it all. That's how we grow."

"We absorb you." Philip's voice was hard, filled with suppressed anger.

"We're like sponges, and we'll suck everything out of you until you've nothing left to give us."

"That's enough!" Marc's voice cut across Philip's, temporarily silencing him. Philip shrugged.

"What then?" asked Judith frantically. Philip turned his back on her. She looked around at his brothers but none of them would meet her eyes.

"*Tell me*!" She was almost demented with fear.

Philip turned slowly back to face her. "Why, then you die, of course."

"*No!*" she screamed. "I won't stay here that long. You can't make me. I'm not staying in this house a minute longer." Crying and babbling to herself she lunged through the children and past her husband. In the bedroom she paused only long enough to slip on shoes and take a cardigan from a drawer before running back to the top of the stairs. Marc and the boys were grouped by the top step but they made no move to stop her.

Trembling from head to foot she started to descend the long flight of stairs. Half-way down she heard a sound and spun around in terror. It was only Kara, rubbing the sleep from her eyes as she joined the group on the landing. Despite the look of loneliness in the little girl's eyes, Judith knew that she had to go on, had to get free. The stairs seemed endless, but at last she was safely in the hall.

She gave one final look back. The rest of the family had remained motionless; they were watching her journey with a detached curiosity that she couldn't understand but was desperately thankful for. Her shaking fingers curled around the front door latch and it swung slowly open. The fresh air rushed into the over-heated hall and she took her first step outside.

As her foot touched the outer step her stomach lurched violently. Then, without warning, she suddenly felt as though hundreds of fingers were pulling at her. Not externally but internally. Her back arched as though her bones were forcing the flesh out behind her. Her ribs seemed to cave in with a terrible pressure and she began to cough and choke for breath. Her feet continued to move forward but at a terrible cost. Her eyes pressed inwards until she thought that they were going to touch the back of her skull and in a frenzy of terror she sensed her tongue curling back in her mouth and tickling the back of her throat.

She began to retch, bile rising in her throat and stinging her mouth with its acid. Then as she fought against the nausea and the pain in her head, there began excruciating sensations in her abdomen, as though someone were plucking relentlessly at her intestines, using them to pull her back to the house. Still retching and doubled up with agony she tried with all her power to force herself forward for a few more steps so that she could reach the safety of her Mini which was parked on the drive. She fumbled with the door catch; her coordination had gone completely and her fingers felt like giant sausages, but just as she despaired of ever managing it the door opened and she toppled into the driving seat.

She didn't have enough strength to pull the door closed, instead she let it swing to and rest against the side. If she could only get away, out onto the public road, then she was sure that she would feel better, but she had to put a distance between herself and the children. Her instinct told her that the children were to blame for all her agony.

The intense pain was causing her to sweat, and beads of perspiration ran down from her forehead partially obscuring her vision. She was terrified that Marc would come after her and pull her from the car, but when she glanced nervously in the direction of the house there was no sign of anyone.

It took three attempts to start the engine, but as it came to life she drew a sigh of relief. Now she only had to negotiate the drive and she would be free. Even this small accomplishment was almost beyond her. All her muscles were pulling her back, dragging her body in the direction of the house again, and as the car inched forward she screamed aloud at the terrible tearing pain that threatened to consume her.

Her heart was pounding frantically with the strain, and although she was now nearly blinded by sweat and tears she didn't have enough strength to lift her hands and wipe her eyes clear. She told herself that it didn't matter. She knew the drive so well; one long, gentle curve. All that she had to do was keep her nerve and she would be safe.

An extraordinarily vicious streak of pain jabbed through her stomach and she started to double up in an automatic attempt to ease her agony. Keep going, she urged herself, you're almost there. As she eased the car around the final part of the bend she was driving purely by instinct. She could not stand such pain very much longer and she knew it, so she put her foot down on the accelerator in order to cover the last few yards as fast as possible.

The knowledge that she was almost safe elated her, and she managed to lift her head up to check for oncoming traffic as she drove through the gates. Her brief moment of triumph vanished. She threw both hands up in the air, trying to protect her face, as the Mini crashed into the heavy wrought-iron gates. Gates that, to the best of her knowledge, had never before been shut. As the windscreen shattered and glass showered around her head she continued to scream.

When the car came to rest Marc walked swiftly out of the front door and then ran lightly along the gravel path. He pulled open Judith's half-open door and his fingers went immediately to her wrist as he checked her pulse. What he felt there seemed to satisfy him, because the look of strain vanished from his face and he took his time extracting his wife from the badly crumpled front of the car.

Lifting her easily in his arms he turned and walked slowly back to the house. She was unconscious as he stepped inside the front door with her but she was beginning to stir.

The watchers at the top of the stairs glanced at one another.

"He's pretty strong," commented Philip at last.

"So was she," said Paul admiringly. "Felicity didn't manage to get that far."

Judith's eyes began to flutter and Marc silenced them. "Get into bed all of you. I'll look after her." Silently they dispersed.

Judith opened her eyes tentatively, terrified that the assault on her body would begin again, but it didn't. There was no pain, not even discomfort, and her muscles slowly relaxed. Marc put an arm beneath her shoulders.

"Can you walk into the living room if I help you?"

She nodded and as they made their slow progress across the hall she automatically looked up the stairs. Only Kara remained standing there. When she saw Judith looking at her she smiled and clapped her hands together in obvious joy.

"Judy home safe now!"

'Yes, she's safely home. Go back to sleep, Kara, or I shall get cross." The sound of Marc's voice was enough to send her scuttling to her room but she was still smiling to herself as she went.

Shivering with shock Judith was grateful now for the warmth of the room. Marc watched her for a moment and then disappeared into the kitchen. A few minutes later he was back carrying a large mug of tea.

"Come on, drink this. It's sweet tea and will do you the world of good. You've had a nasty fright."

She gave an imitation of a laugh that rang hollow to both of them. "A fright has to be the understatement of the year. I was petrified with terror. It felt as though . . ." As memory flooded back she trembled from head to foot and Marc had to hold the mug to her lips.

"Don't think about it. Come on, drink this."

Her teeth chattered against the rim but she managed a couple of swallows. The scalding liquid burned the back of her throat and she choked and pushed his hands away. "That's enough. I'll have some more in a moment. My throat hurts."

The cardigan that she had snatched up before her attempted escape was on the hall floor and Marc went and collected it then draped it around his wife's shoulders. He allowed his hand to remain resting there but she pushed it off. She didn't want him touching her.

The sounds of boys' voices drifted down into the living room. They were laughing and talking and from time to time a door would bang. Normal family noises, only they weren't a normal family. There was a brief silence and then the sound of Kara's voice.

"I don't want to. I'm too tired."

Judith lifted her head and Marc turned his face towards the door. A voice, probably Paul's, could be heard talking softly, the words unintelligible.

"No. Kara sleepy."

This time there was no soothing voice, only the abrupt, shocking sound of a sharp blow against naked flesh followed by Kara's startled scream. Before Judith could speak Marc had gone racing up the stairs. He kept his own voice low but Paul's was raised in argument.

"It wasn't my fault. Philip sent me."

A long murmur from Marc resulted in Paul's voice rising even more.

"How can I? You do it. You're stronger than him, aren't you?"

Another door slammed and then Marc's and Philip's voices mingled in a furious inaudible argument. Judith clutched her arms around herself and tried to forget what had happened earlier. It was easier to involve herself in what was happening now. Easier and less frightening.

Something brushed against her thigh. She jumped and opened her eyes. Kara was leaning against her leg, a dark blue bruise already appearing down the left side of her face. She touched it with tiny fingers. "Hurt," she whispered. "Paul hurt Kara."

Judith stared in astonishment. "Why did he do that? It isn't like Paul to be so unkind." But perhaps it was, she thought, perhaps he was no different from Philip, merely better at disguising it.

"Don't want to play with boys." Kara laid her golden head on Judith's knee and rubbed her face against the fabric of her skirt. Automatically Judith's hand moved over the soft curls, soothing and reassuring the child.

"It's far too late for any of you to be playing. Your Daddy is telling the boys off now so you'd better get back to bed."

Unnoticed by them, Marc had returned, and his voice took them by surprise. "Quite right, come along, Kara, I'll carry you up."

"Paul hit her on the face," said Judith. "I hope you told him off."

"I've dealt with the matter, yes. Come along, Kara."

Exhausted by the horror of the evening, Judith fell asleep before he returned.

When she finally woke it was quite dark. He was sitting in one of the armchairs, his head resting on his hands as he stared into space. One lamp glowed behind him, outlining his silhouette and throwing light into a small circle that ended just beyond his chair. She was able to watch him for a considerable time without his knowledge and she thought how tired and lonely he looked. There was no sign of his usual magnetism. All at once he glanced towards her, and immediately straightened his back and switched on his normal air of surging vitality.

"You're awake, then. I thought you ought to sleep, it's the best cure for a lot of things."

"Not in my case. I'll never be cured if I stay here, will I?"

"I wasn't aware that you were ill."

"Nor was I. The tiredness, the terrible lethargy that I've been experiencing, at first I put it all down to new circumstances and then to my pregnancy, but that isn't true is it? It's the boys who are making me tired. How did Philip put it? 'We'll suck everything out of you until you've nothing left to give us.' Very apposite, I imagine."

"He was over-dramatizing as usual. He likes to impress people."

"Don't," she said softly. "Don't pretend any more. There's no point. I was right about the children, wasn't I? That is how they learn, and you brought me here to do exactly what I am doing."

"Which is?"

"Provide them with a fresh source of knowledge. A different type of knowledge from that provided by Elizabeth. I'm to give them an awareness of the arts and smooth away their rough edges. Apparently, when I've civilized them as much as I can, they will then kill me and you'll choose another lonely woman with different attitudes and interests. Your task is quite easy. You provide them with an 'all-around' education. It would be funny if it wasn't so horrific."

She began to laugh hysterically but managed to control herself. "Why couldn't I get away? Was that you? Is it another of your unusual abilities?"

"No. I could have stopped you physically, you must have realized that, but I knew there was no need. The child stopped you."

"The child?"

"Our son. He knows that he needs to be near his siblings to survive. From the moment of conception these children have a tremendous will to live. He knows that away from us he wouldn't have a chance, he probably wouldn't even manage to endure the birth. The birth of these children needs specialist attention."

"Yet you wanted me to give birth here, without proper facilities."

"I don't mean specialist medical attention. Someone who understands has to help. Someone with knowledge of what to expect."

Fear tightened her throat and chest; breathing was difficult, speech almost impossible.

"What happens?" she managed to ask. "What else do I have to face before this child of yours can be born?"

He gave her what she assumed was meant to be a reassuring smile.

"Don't panic. As far as you're concerned it will be perfectly normal. No different from any other birth. It's the child who needs special care."

Her head ached violently and she didn't want to hear any more. She knew that she was close to breaking down, hurling herself frantically around the room and screaming at the top of her voice. It was too much for her to absorb and accept, even though she had already half-guessed at a lot of it. Wondering, fearing, was one thing. Knowing and living with the knowledge was quite another.

In any case there were other things that she still didn't understand. The disappearance of Kara's mother. The vision of Elizabeth in the pool with her family. The death of Sam. All of these things needed explanation, but even more important she sensed that there was a purpose behind it all. That Marc had a goal and his children were necessary to achieve it. Why else would he go on and on producing these human mutations when every birth, every incident, increased the risk of discovery.

Marc watched her while her thoughts flickered over her face, her expression changing from fear to puzzlement and back to fear. Finally he stood up and walked over to her chair. She shrank back.

"You've no need to fear me, the last thing that I'd do is hurt you. I spent a long time looking for you and I've no intention of letting you be harmed. There are a lot of things that I will have to explain to you, but not tonight. It can all wait until you're feeling stronger."

He put his hands down to help her to her feet and she pushed them away.

"I'd rather do it on my own, thank you."

"You're still weak, let me carry you."

He reached out for her as she stood up. She loathed his presence; he was alien and repulsive. Instinctively she slapped him around the face.

"I said don't touch me."

He gave a snarl and put his hand to his burning face. "Don't do that again," he warned as he placed an arm around her waist. She hit out blindly at him, catching him behind his left ear. Slowly he expelled his breath with an eerie sibilant sound. His hands closed on her throat, his thumbs pressing hard against the carotid arteries. She struggled feebly and briefly before losing consciousness.

As soon as she slumped Marc released her, letting her fall in a heap at his feet. He tried to take deep breaths to drain his anger away. Her mistake had been in hitting him, it always brought a surge of primitive fury when he was hit and he was still powerless to control such an attack. It continually puzzled Marc that all people of the new, advanced race to which he belonged were subject to these primeval bursts of temper. It was as though their powers of telepathy and mind control and their physical prowess had been obtained at the expense of all normal emotions. Love; tenderness; sympathy; compassion; all of them virtually absent in their makeup, and all to be learned, while aggression and violence were theirs in abundance and control was difficult if not impossible to master. It was their weakness, and he knew that it must be eradicated from his sons if they were to become leaders in the future. Judith would help him fulfill this desire and ultimately achieve his great ambition, even if she would no longer be there to share in his triumph.

That thought sobered him. The last of his rage ebbed away. Gently he picked his wife up and carried her to their bedroom, relieved when she stirred and murmured before curling up beneath the quilt. He could so easily have killed her by accident and lost another son. Piers had been the first tragedy, then the second secret loss. A third death would have been an unforgivable disaster.

Before he fell asleep he spared one final thought for his wife. From now on her life would be one of increasing terror and desperation, and there was nothing he could do to help her.

Judith slept until ten the next morning, and when she finally opened her eyes the sun was shining through the window and the children's voices could be heard from the garden. She struggled to remember what day it was, certain that it was a weekday and wondering why Marc hadn't woken her when he left for the office. She was still puzzling over it when he came into the bedroom carrying a breakfast tray.

"I thought you'd probably have woken by now. This is my apology for last night."

"Last night?"

"We had an argument."

Vaguely she recalled an exchange of words, she remembered trying to push him away from her; but there was something else, something far more important that she was unable to recall. Marc smiled at her.

"Don't look so worried. Try and eat something, you need regular meals now you're pregnant."

Then she did remember. Everything. Marc watched the color drain from her face and saw the dark shadows beneath her eyes. He sat next to her, noticing that she tried to edge away and wondering how long it would be before she realized that she only had him to turn to for protection.

"You'll get used to it," he assured her as he handed her the knife and fork. "In time you won't want to leave, you'll realize how much you're needed here."

The scrambled eggs on toast no longer lookéd appetizing. "If I stay here I die, that's what Philip said. How can you expect me to accept that?"

"He was talking nonsense. He's obsessed with death."

"Perhaps he's seen too much of it."

Marc ignored the sarcastic note in her voice. "That's perceptive of you. I'm afraid he has. First Piers, then his mother; it's bound to prey on his mind. Aren't you going to eat anything at all?"

"You're forgetting Felicity, aren't you? Not to mention Sam, and poor Albert."

"Felicity left us of her own free will. Come on, darling, at least drink the tea."

He looked so concerned, his forehead creased in a frown, that she managed a sip of tea and then nibbled at a slice of toast.

"Why aren't you at work?"

"I phoned in and told them you were ill. I thought you could do with a good rest today."

"I seem to rest a great deal, but it doesn't stop me getting tired."

Abruptly he stood up and went over to the window. Judith studied him intently. Even seen from the back he was impressive; the huge shoulders and the narrow waist and hips; the way his dark hair curled neatly into the nape of his neck; the casually relaxed stance that hinted at great power; it was only too obvious why he had managed to attract women as and when he needed them. It was doubtless a trick of nature, a way of ensuring he was able to continue producing children throughout his life, and had nothing to do with the man himself. That might explain why he had never behaved as other unusually handsome men. There was no trace of vanity in his behavior, no masculine pride in his attraction for women. She had to get away from him.

"Can we go out for a ride?" Her voice interrupted his thoughts, and he was pleased at the diversion.

"Of course. Where would you like to go?"

"I don't mind."

"With the children?"

"Naturally! I might as well get used to having them around me all the time if that's what I'm here for."

"I'll think of somewhere while you're getting dressed."

She found that she felt very weak when she was on her feet but she was determined not to give in to it. The only times that she got out of the house were when Marc was with her, and so she would encourage him to take her out as much as possible. Eventually the child within her would become accustomed to this, and ultimately it might provide her with her only chance of escape. Hugging the thought to herself she ignored the trembling of her limbs and the nagging headache and forced herself through the routine of washing, dressing and makeup.

When she looked in the mirror she was horrified. Her face was paper white and there were enormous blue-black circles beneath her eyes. Her skin looked dry and her hair was dull and lifeless. It was the face of a woman of forty. I must get away, she thought; Philip was speaking the truth, and Marc is not to be believed.

Mrs. Watson was vacuuming in the living room when Judith finally decided that she had made herself presentable enough to go out.

"You look peaky," she remarked, destroying Judith's optimism with the three small words.

"I'm fine. Oh good, there are the drawings that I did yesterday," and she took them from the coffee table where they were neatly stacked. But they weren't her drawings, they were far better than anything she could do.

Her mouth felt dry as she leafed through them. Firm bold strokes had deftly captured the view of the back of the house and the garden in starkly simple terms. Everything that she had attempted was repeated in the drawings she held, repeated and improved. She stopped at the last one, staring in disbelief.

"We did those."

"Why Patrick, you made me jump! I was just admiring them. Which one did you do?"

"The one of the front and the driveway. Philip's are the best, I expect you can tell which are his."

Of all the boys it was Patrick who made the least impression on Judith so far. He seemed a less assertive figure than Paul, and far quieter than his two younger brothers. He was altogether a more gentle child and she wondered if he was any different from the others.

"Can you?" he demanded.

"Tell which are Philip's? Yes, I think so. This first one, and this." Patrick nodded.

"Is this his as well?"

She held up the final drawing, the one that had caused fear to chill her once again. He looked cautiously at it, glancing from the page to Judith's face and back to the page.

"Yes," he admitted reluctantly.

"It's his bedroom, isn't it?" Patrick nodded. "But what's happening? I can see you boys are all there but who is the other figure? The thin one?"

Patrick shuffled his feet. "It's only a drawing," he mumbled.

"That's our mother," said Philip clearly from the hall. "I thought you knew what she looked like."

"It isn't very like her," retorted Judith as calmly as she could.

"It is, it's exactly how she looks now."

"What do you mean?"

Philip smiled at her, a most unpleasant smile. "You'll find out in time. I don't think I'd better tell you though, Dad doesn't want you to get upset again. Not yet, not until our brother's born."

"What's going on?" called Marc as he came briskly in to join them.

"I was admiring the boys' drawings."

"Let me see." He glanced quickly through them, drawing in his breath when he came to the final one. "I suppose this is yours, Philip?" Philip nodded. "Well, if you continue to twist everything that you learn and to abuse all your talents the way you do at the moment, then I doubt very much whether you'll survive. Bear that in mind next time you get a desire to be clever."

Philip slunk away and Marc put the drawings down. "I thought we'd take them over to Belton House. It's on the outskirts of Grantham, quite a little drive, but there's a huge adventure playground there which the boys will enjoy. The house and grounds are attractive too. Have you been there?"

Judith was still looking at the drawings and quickly Marc

turned them facedown. "Right, let's get everyone orga-
nized. You're sure you're up to going out?"

She thought of the haunted face in the picture and knew
what her fate was if she stayed here.

"Of course I'm sure."

Marc tipped her face up to his. "Try not to let Philip
upset you. I'm afraid he has a very unkind streak in him."

"It's in all of you isn't it?"

His eyes filled with pity. "Don't make it more difficult
than it has to be. I can understand why you're so antagonis-
tic but it won't help matters."

"It helps me."

"Well, I suppose you have to come to terms with it in
your own way."

"I can't come to terms with it at all until I know the
truth. There's still so much you haven't told me."

"Tonight," he promised. "This evening I'll try and
explain it all."

He was relieved that she wanted to know. He imagined
that it was a sign of her acceptance.

The outing proved a great success. Out in the fresh air
surrounded by other, normal people, Judith's forebodings
eased a little. Marc was affectionate and attentive, his hand
lingering in hers, his eyes never leaving her. Although she
knew why he was doing it she enjoyed the attention, took
pleasure from the envious glances of other women.

In the huge adventure jungle the boys were in their
element. They climbed everything that there was to be
climbed, swung from ropes and scrambled over netting.
There was one rope bridge to a tree house from which the
only exit was a fourteen-foot metal pole. Paul, Patrick and
Philip all had a go while Michael went on one of the
enormous see-saws made out of a log with small metal
handles at each end. Marc had Kara on his lap at the other
end and bumped Michael high into the air as he screamed
with delight.

When he got off the other boys showed him the pole and
the rope bridge.

"I want a go on it," he clamored.

"Go on then," said Marc. "You can do it on your own can't you?"

"Of course I can. Watch me!"

He ran over to the pole, fastened his hands and feet around it and then shinned swiftly up it, much to the consternation of a young girl who was waiting to descend.

Marc and the boys laughed so much that they cried as Michael then pushed his way through the tree house and walked down the bridge, regardless of all the other children walking up it and calling out at him. He ran back to his family, flushed with success.

"That was easy! Can I have another go?"

"You did it all wrong, stupid!" Philip jeered. "You're meant to come *down* the pole after you go *up* the bridge. What a nincompoop you are!"

Michael looked back at the obstacle and studied the other children. "I don't see the point of that," he said at last. "That's stupid, it's too easy to be any fun."

"Not for most children," put in Marc, still laughing.

"Not for normal children," said Judith softly. Michael turned his small, oval face to hers. "I wouldn't know about them, would I?" he said politely. Judith's pleasure in the outing immediately vanished.

Marc gave a weary sigh and looked at his watch. "Come on then, time to go back."

"Kara hasn't been on anything," said Paul.

"She's too small," Judith objected. "She isn't like you."

Marc glanced at his daughter. "Do you want to go on anything, Kara?"

She hesitated, torn between her own fear and her desire to emulate the others.

"Go on," encouraged Patrick. "We'll help you."

Finally Kara pointed to the tree house Michael had just tried. "Up there!"

The boys clapped. Judith frowned and shook her head. "That's much too dangerous for you."

"I'll take her," offered Marc and held out his hand. Together the large man and the diminutive child climbed the swaying bridge.

Judith and the boys stared up to the top of the pole waiting for Marc and Kara to appear. When it was their turn Judith expected Marc to come down with Kara holding on to his neck but to her horror he was showing Kara how to hold the pole herself. The child moved forward but at the last moment drew back, her fear obvious to the onlookers.

Marc's huge hands rested on Kara's shoulders and propelled her lightly back to the exit. He bent down and whispered in her ear but she shook her head and looked across for Judith. Judith started to step forward only to feel hands holding her back, gripping her arms at the elbows. Paul and Patrick were on either side of her, restraining her from interfering.

"She'll be all right," promised Paul. "He can help her do it, but you mustn't break her concentration." At last Kara put her hands on the pole, watched closely all the time by her father. His eyes never left her back, and finally she jumped into space and her legs waved wildly in the air for a moment before fastening themselves securely around the pole. After that it was easy and she slid slowly and safely to the ground.

As she landed Judith was released and she ran straight to Kara, hugging her as tightly as she could. She felt Kara wriggling in protest and finally released her.

"That was very clever, darling. I was frightened for you."

Large blue eyes looked directly into Judith's gray ones. The child's plump prettiness appeared sharper, more mature and her expression was not as guileless as usual. She put her head on one side and continued to study Judith for a moment before putting out a small hand and patting her face.

"Daddy helped here," she explained, pointing at her head. "Kara all safe."

"Of course you were," agreed Marc coming up and putting his arms around his daughter. "You were splendid, just as I expected."

Kara looked up at him from beneath her lashes, her mouth curved in a smile that was almost an invitation.

"Daddy love Kara?" she queried, and gently slid a hand up her father's leg.

"Come along," Judith said loudly, discomforted by the small scene.

Kara ignored her and rubbed her face against Marc's right knee while she tried to reach higher with her hand. He looked quizzically at her and then over to where the boys were standing.

"What's all this then?" he said softly, picking Kara up and walking towards Paul.

"All what, Dad?" The eyes were too wide, too innocent. Marc gave him a searching look and Paul colored up, moving nervously from one foot to the other.

"I'll talk to you later," concluded his father. "Time to go home now."

Judith stood where she was. If she had understood the scene correctly there were still worse things for her to learn about the children. Things that not only affected them but innocent people like Kara. Kara, who was already changing, withdrawing from Judith and turning towards her half-brothers, attracted by something she recognized but couldn't understand. She would be corrupted whether Judith was there or not, and there was nothing her stepmother could do to stop it.

Judith shivered and glanced about her. Marc and the children were on their way out, there were plenty of people near, people who could help her get to safety. She wouldn't return to the house. Her decision made, she looked about her. Sitting on a large log nearby were a pleasant-looking couple in their mid-thirties. She decided to sit by them. Marc couldn't drag her away screaming without drawing unwanted attention to himself.

As she lifted her foot for the first step she felt it. A light, tugging sensation in her stomach. Not yet a pain, but a subtle reminder of the night before. She persisted; surely it wouldn't dare do the same thing to her again, not in public. As the first step was completed her throat began to close and her breath rasped noisily.

The man lifted his head and sprang to his feet, staring at the young woman in front of him who looked as though she was about to pass out. "Come and sit down, quickly. Try and put your head between your knees."

She could hear him, but she couldn't comply. Her head was being forced back, the sinews of her neck standing out like knotted cords. Frantically she gasped for air, and then magically hands were on the back of her neck easing the pressure and her throat expanded again.

". . . been very ill. She must have overdone it. I'm sorry you were troubled." Marc's voice was full of concern, his South African accent stronger than usual. The man on the log was relieved to have the problem solved for him.

"Hope she'll be all right . . . plenty of rest . . ." His voice tailed off.

She was too tired to try and fight him, too shocked at the speed of the child's reactions. She slumped against her husband and allowed him to help her all the way to the field where the car was parked. He put her in the front seat and fastened her safety belt for her. The children were in the back, subdued and silent.

"That was silly, darling," he said gently as the car slid down the drive and out onto the road. "You ruined a lovely day and all for nothing. Now you're exhausted again and you'll have to spend the afternoon sleeping." He laid a hand on her right knee in a gesture of affection and she didn't even have the strength to knock it away. She closed her eyes and tears slid silently down her face. Tears that if noticed went unremarked. She didn't remember arriving home or being put to bed. She wasn't aware of anything else until Marc woke her at seven to inquire whether she wanted any dinner.

"I said that if you were hungry dinner was ready," Marc repeated.

Judith glared at him. "Keep your bloody dinner! You can make me stay here but you can't force me to eat."

"Don't be foolish. You have to eat; don't forget the baby."

"As though I could! In any case I don't have to do anything. I've decided that I'm not hungry."

"As you choose. Perhaps you'll fancy something at supper-time."

She turned on her side ignoring him and heard the door close quietly as he left. Once she was certain that he'd gone she got out of bed and went to her dressing table. One glance in the mirror confirmed her fears; she looked worse than ever. There were small lines at the corners of her eyes and on her forehead and her pallor had if anything increased despite the morning in the sunshine.

The sight of herself gave her the strength to make the decision. She would not allow the child within her to live. The existing children were already sucking her life from her, she had nothing to lose by starving herself and the new life within her to death. It would be a victory of sorts, the only kind within her power and the thought of it delighted her.

Judith stayed in bed the rest of the evening and feigned sleep whenever Marc came to look at her. She heard the children go to bed and heard too the sound of the telephone as Marc made some calls, to people from the office she assumed, probably telling them that he would be off again the next day. She wondered how long it would take him to realize what she was doing and how he would deal with the situation.

At ten o'clock he came up to bed. "I know you're awake, Judith. Is there anything you want before I come to bed?"

"Nothing."

"You'll regret it."

She didn't bother to answer. A few minutes later she heard him moving about the room as he prepared for bed and she tensed herself for some form of argument but he lay down beside her without a word and was quickly asleep.

The next morning he didn't even offer her breakfast and she lay curled up in the large bed, her stomach rumbling and with a sense of increasing nausea. She dozed on and off and her dreams were full of food; plates of roast beef and vegetables, bowls of fresh fruit salad and cream, picnics of salmon and cucumber sandwiches and cheese flans. Eventually she forced herself to stay awake, unable to face the food that her subconscious mind conjured up for her.

The day passed slowly. No one came near her. She could only tell the hour by the sounds of the household, for Marc had taken the clock away with him and she had forgotten to wind her wristwatch the night before. When night fell and Marc came to bed again she glared at him ferociously.

He laughed at her scowling face. "I don't know why you're so annoyed with me, this is all your own idea!"

She knew that; and she too found her steadily mounting rage inexplicable. Surely she should have been feeling languid and uncaring, not charged with energy and full of ferocious anger. When Marc put an arm around her to kiss her good night she heard her own snarl of fury with disbelief. It couldn't be her making that noise. It had to be a trick that her hearing was playing on her. The children snarled when they were annoyed, perhaps it had been one of them.

And then she realized. It *was* one of them. It was the child; the child was expressing its fury in the only way it could, through her. She shuddered.

"Good night, darling. Pleasant dreams."

She kept her lips tightly pressed together, afraid that another primitive emotion might reveal itself if she gave it any opportunity.

The hours passed and as her hunger grew so did the rage within her. It grew until it filled her body; a terrible, malevolent rage that throbbed in her veins and drummed inside her head until it possessed her entirely. The force of the emotion alarmed her almost as much as the emotion itself. She wondered how such a minute creature could wield such power. Still she held on, it could frighten her but that was all. She had the ability to destroy it and that gave her the ultimate power; the power of life and death. As she consoled herself with that thought there was a brief respite from the rage, a few seconds when she was herself and herself alone. She breathed more easily, relaxed a fraction and immediately it struck.

With a growl of rage she flung the duvet from her and leaped from the bed. She didn't put on slippers or a dressing gown, she couldn't spare even that much time. Her feet had never covered the ground so fast, she ran along the landing, down the stairs and through the hall hitting the kitchen door with the palm of one hand and hearing it crash open.

She looked around her like a wild animal, her eyes wide and staring as they darted from table top to working surfaces. There was no food in sight. A scream of anguish came from her mouth and she flung open a cabinet door. There was an apple pie on the shelf, freshly baked that afternoon by Mrs. Watson. Grabbing it with both hands she stuffed it into her mouth, the pastry crumbling to pieces in her fists and pieces of fruit spilling out onto the tiled floor.

The pie was gone in a moment. Everything else in the cabinet was in tins. She screamed again and ran to the fridge. The fridge was full. Judith fell to her knees in front of it and began to devour a pound of cheese that was on the top shelf. It eased the hunger, but didn't sate her. Picking up a bottle of milk she put the top to her mouth and drained the contents, licking the surplus from her lips when it was empty. Finally her eyes fell upon three large pots of yogurt. Again her hands shot out, she didn't bother with a spoon, she simply tipped back her head and drained the contents into her mouth one after another. Then, when the last pot was empty, she finally felt content. Wiping the back of a hand across her mouth she gave a huge sigh and sat back on her heels.

"My goodness me, I take it you fancied a little snack!"

Judith turned her head to find Marc standing by the table. She smiled softly at him. "Yes, I wanted a glass of milk."

"Couldn't you find any glasses?"

She didn't understand why he was looking at her in such a strange fashion. Surely she was free to get up in the night? She followed the direction of his gaze and saw for the first time the terrible chaos in the kitchen. The mangled remains of the pie, the empty milk bottle lying on its side, the crumbs of cheese on the floor and on her clothes and finally the empty yogurt pots rolling by her feet.

"No!" Her voice was a whisper. "I didn't do that . . . I couldn't have done . . . I . . ."

"My poor Judith, when will you stop trying to fight it?"

It was the tender pity in his look that defeated her. She felt the tears pricking her eyelids and the sobs rising in her throat and as she began to cry she ran towards him, searching for some sort of comfort, someone who would understand. As he soothed her, held her and reassured her, she reached the point that he had been waiting for. She realized that he was the only protection she had. From that day on she would be guided by him and cling only to him. Her need of him became as great as his of her and they were joined in a truly indissoluble union.

From that night on Judith accepted that there was no escape for her. The child would make sure that she remained with Marc and his children, and if she attempted to thwart it then she would be the one to suffer. Therefore, she would try to stay calm, preserve her strength as much as she could, and as soon as the child was born she would leave. Leave Marc, Kara, the boys and the baby and return to her old life. Never again would she attempt marriage; from now on she would be quite content to live alone, and she prayed that she would get the opportunity.

At the end of the week, Marc had to spend a night in London on business. Judith was terrified at the thought of being left alone with the children; to her relief Marc arranged for Zilla to sleep in the big house for that one night.

"It will do you good to have some feminine company," he commented as he kissed her goodbye, and secretly Judith agreed with him. Zilla, however, was less than stimulating as a companion. She occupied herself with the children all day, and in the evening settled down silently opposite her sister-in-law and pulled a half-knitted matinee jacket from her bag.

"Don't do that!" exclaimed Judith, "you make me feel so guilty. Why don't we have a drink now the children are in bed?"

Zilla glanced placidly across the room. "As you like. Won't it make you ill?"

"No. In fact, brandy seems to suit the pair of us!"

"I think I've over-filled it." Zilla laughed as she passed a glass to Judith. The glass was nearly half-full. "Never mind, it means I won't need a second!"

For a time there was silence while the two women enjoyed their drinks.

"The only trouble with brandy"—laughed Judith—"is that it makes me even hotter!"

Zilla's cheeks were flushed, "I feel rather warm too. I must admit I'm not used to drinking. It's a dangerous habit when you live on your own."

Judith waved a hand at the brandy bottle. "Have some more. We've got plenty. You can top mine up while you're about it!"

"I suppose you notice the heat at night," commented Zilla as she sat down with her glass nearly full.

"Yes, I can't understand . . ."

"At least I'm spared that now that I'm away from Marc. It's about the only advantage there is," she added ruefully.

"You must get very lonely," said Judith softly. "Has there never been anyone that you wanted to marry?"

Zilla stared into the distance. "Oh yes. Two or three. They were really nice men, I could have been very happy with them, but of course it was out of the question."

Judith kept silent. Zilla seemed almost unaware of her sister-in-law's presence; it was as though she was talking to herself.

"I couldn't explain," she continued. "I expect that they thought I was a horrible tease who lost interest in them once they got serious, but how could I tell them the truth? Could you, if you were me?"

"No," said Judith, desperately hoping that was the right response.

"It was hard. After Timothy, the third one, I went and had myself sterilized. At least that removed the fear of giving birth to a deformed child, but it didn't really help. Marc had spoiled me for other men."

"I don't understand what you mean," said Judith questioningly. "How has Marc spoiled you? And why should you expect to give birth to a deformed child?"

Zilla's hands closed tightly around the stem of her glass. "Hasn't Marc explained about the women in our family yet?" Judith shook her head. "Well, he ought to have done. After all, you're the one who's going to have to explain to Kara. Poor Kara. Mind you, she'll have some fun as well," and she giggled to herself.

"Why don't you tell me?" urged Judith, anxious to take advantage of the effect of the brandy on her sister-in-law.

"Good idea! That's what I'll do, I'll tell you the story of my life! First of all I think I'll have another drink."

She went unsteadily to the drinks cabinet and poured out more brandy. As she sat down again she stared thoughtfully at Judith. "You're sure you want to know?"

"Yes, please."

"Well, unfortunately the women in our family don't have children like Marc's boys. No potential leaders of men for us! Something else goes wrong and they're physically malformed as well. Repulsively, so I understand. Horrible, isn't it?" and she took a mouthful of her drink.

"When you say 'as well', what do you mean? As well as what?"

Zilla laughed. "Don't try to pretend innocence! You know perfectly well that Marc's boys aren't normal! Your son won't be normal either."

"Don't say that!" Judith jumped to her feet. "I won't listen to you."

Zilla stopped laughing. "But you already know," she said gently. "You've worked it out yourself, otherwise why are you getting so upset? It's better to face these things."

"What things? I'm tired of hints; tell me exactly what's wrong with the boys."

Zilla let out a small sigh and settled back in her chair. "Do you find Marc a good lover?" she queried. Judith's face flushed. "I'm sorry if I'm embarrassing you. It isn't just idle curiosity, I'm an interested party. You see, until he married you he quite often shared my bed, but since then he hasn't been near me and I have to confess that I miss him." She paused for a moment. "God, how I miss him," she added and there was despair in her voice.

Stunned, Judith could only stare at her sister-in-law. It was almost impossible to believe what she was hearing; almost, but not quite. She remembered Kara at Belton, and Marc's lack of concern. She recalled occasional glances between brother and sister that even at the time had seemed over-intimate.

"Now I've really shocked you, and I'm sorry. It must be

the drink, I'd never normally have told you. I think Elizabeth guessed, but we never discussed it. She was grateful, of course. While she was ill it was a relief for her to have someone else cater to Marc's needs. That's part of the trouble; the men in our family have very strong sex drives, but I'm sure I don't have to tell you that!''

''I'm not very experienced in these things. There was only one man before Marc, but certainly there was no comparison. You do realize it's illegal for a brother and sister to have your sort of relationship?''

Zilla started to laugh and then began to cry as well. ''Illegal,'' she said through her tears, ''if only that was all I had to worry about. I've never had a proper life of my own, and I never will. From early childhood I've been used to satisfy Marc's sexual curiosity, just as Kara is now being used by Philip and Paul. It's the only reason we're allowed to continue living, I'm convinced of that. We've no other abilities, there's no logical place for us other than in bed.''

With a sickening lurch of her stomach Judith remembered Kara on the night she crashed the car; Kara saying that she was too tired to play with the boys. All at once the scene took on a very different meaning.

''You shouldn't allow it,'' she said, leaning towards Zilla's chair. ''Why don't you move away? You're still an attractive woman, you don't have to miss out on marriage just because of what's happened in the past. You don't owe Marc anything. Get away while you're still young enough to enjoy life.''

For a moment Zilla seemed to consider the suggestion and then, with electrifying speed, her mood changed. Her mouth curled in a sneer and she stood up. Nervously Judith retreated to her chair.

''Yes, you'd like that wouldn't you? You don't want to think of him making love to me while you're fat and pregnant. The thought of his arms around me, his body on mine, it's unbearable to you, isn't it? Isn't it?'' she repeated loudly.

Judith began to cry, rocking to and fro. She found the visions that Zilla's words were conjuring up utterly repulsive, and yet strangely erotic. The contrast between Marc's dark strength and Zilla's fragile blonde beauty made the scene all the more piquant.

"Shall I tell you what it feels like?" persisted Zilla. "Would you like to hear what he says to me? He's always in a hurry to begin. He's got his own key to my house, and usually he turns up in the middle of the night. I enjoy it, the urgency. I like to feel . . ."

"*Shut up!*" screamed Judith. She picked up her glass. "Get out of here, now. Get out of my sight or I'll throw this at you. I mean it, I really will; then perhaps Marc won't find you so attractive."

Zilla's face twisted in a grimace, the glittering excitement dying out of her eyes. "Perhaps you should," she whispered. "At least that would put an end to it all."

Torn between pity and repulsion Judith simply stared at the other woman, but she kept tight hold of her glass. "Go away," she repeated.

With a small sob Zilla turned and walked slowly towards the door. Judith could hear the sound of her feet dragging up the stairs, but it wasn't until the bedroom door closed with a bang that she put the glass down and allowed herself to cry without restraint.

The next morning Judith wondered how she was going to face her sister-in-law, but amazingly Zilla behaved as though the scene had never happened. She was her usual pleasant, placid self and showed no trace of self-consciousness.

Over breakfast Judith explained that she had to go to the dentist to have her fillings done.

"I wondered if you'd still be here when I got back? It doesn't matter; Mrs. Watson will be looking after the children."

"Why don't I take you to the dentist? It will be company for you and save you having to drive."

Judith felt this was probably an attempt to make up for the night before, and felt obliged to accept the offer. In any case she was grateful as she felt extremely tired. She managed a brief smile.

"Thanks, Zilla. I'd appreciate a lift."

As Zilla pulled the car into the dentist's drive she put her hand lightly on Judith's. "I'm sorry about last night. I'll never drink brandy again!"

"It doesn't matter."

"Of course it does. My only consolation is that you had to know, I just wish I'd broken it more gently. We are still friends?"

Judith knew that she needed friends, and she didn't have many. She managed a smile. "Of course!"

"That's a relief!"

There was only a short wait before Judith was led into Mr. Osborn's surgery. He greeted her like a long-standing friend which somewhat surprised her.

"And how are the children?" he asked after the normal pleasantries.

"They're fine. I hope my fillings aren't big ones."

"No, quite small. I'm getting on well with my paper. I wondered if you'd like to read some of it? After all, it does concern your family!"

Judith had been about to lean back in the chair but now she stopped. "Mr. Osborn, my husband is quite adamant that he doesn't want the boys mentioned in any paper. He is very annoyed with me for bringing them to you in the first place, and all this talk about them only gets me into more trouble. I do wish that you'd let it drop."

"Why does he feel like that?"

"I've no idea, but he does."

"You see, it really is quite extraordinary, Mrs. Farino. I've spoken to one or two colleagues and they're as amazed as I am. It can't be a coincidence, there must be a reason for this abnormality. Is there anything else different about them?" he added casually.

"Like what?" asked Judith sharply.

"Well . . ." he hesitated, then decided to go on. "To be frank, they did seem very excitable children."

Remembering their frenzied behavior at the dentist's Judith felt that he was showing great restraint. For a moment she was tempted to confide in him. He was a professional man, surely he would be able to help her. It was already obvious to him that the boys weren't normal, so he would be the ideal person to help her escape from the house. She tried to think how to word her request for help.

"How about their parents?" he pressed. "Are you quite certain neither of them had the same malformation?"

"Their father says not. Mr. Osborn . . ."

"Yes?"

There was a warning tug of pain in the pit of her stomach and her mouth began to go dry.

"Nothing," she said lamely. The dentist noticed how pale she'd gone.

"Are you sure there isn't anything wrong? You're not in trouble?"

She gave a brittle laugh. "Trouble? What kind of trouble?"

"Silly of me! Let's get on with your teeth, shall we?"

She could have cried with frustration, but she knew better than to ignore the warning signs. Besides, was it fair to involve an outsider? When he had finished and she signed the form she found he was watching her closely.

"If I do learn anything more, about their parents' teeth I mean, then I'll let you know," she said quickly.

"I'd appreciate that. You can ring me any time."

They exchanged glances. Two normal human beings unable to communicate with words and lacking the ability to communicate in any other way. For the first time Judith appreciated what a great advantage Marc and his relations had over everyone else.

"Goodbye," she said reluctantly. He smiled, but the smile vanished when she walked out of the door and he looked troubled. Before he saw his next patient he took a file of papers out of one of his drawers and placed it carefully in his briefcase. He thought they might be safer at his home.

"Was it painless?" asked Zilla as they drove home.

"Yes, he's very good. Zilla, did Marc have a gap between his front teeth when he was young?"

Zilla nearly jumped the lights by mistake. "Dear me, that won't do! As a matter of fact he did. I remember he had to have a brace on them when he was about twelve. Why do you ask?"

"Just a brace?"

"No, I think he had to have a tooth out as well. It was a spare one if I remember rightly. Why?"

"It's only that all the boys have the same problem."

"So there is a physical deformity in the male line after all; how very comforting!" and Zilla gave a short laugh. Judith remained silent, and wondered why Marc had denied all knowledge of any such malformation.

There were a lot of traffic hold-ups going back, and very soon Judith found that the palms of her hands were sweating and she was beginning to tremble. She longed to get back to the house. The other cars, the lorries, even the hurrying pedestrians on the crossings, seemed to offer a threat to her safety.

Zilla sensed her discomfort. "Don't worry," she soothed. "We're nearly home now and you won't need to go out very often any more."

"But I'll have to go to the doctor's clinic, my first appointment's next month."

"Marc says he suggested that you have the child privately, by-passing the National Health system, but you weren't keen. If you agreed, the doctor would always come out to you. Wouldn't you prefer that?"

Judith knew that she shouldn't agree. She sensed an ulterior motive behind Marc's offer, something of which she was ignorant, and it frightened her. Besides, if she gave in to this impulse to stay indoors then when the chance finally came to get away she might not have the courage to take it. Yet, somehow, the suggestion proved too attractive to resist.

"I suppose it would," she conceded reluctantly. "I can't think what's wrong with me. You don't think it's agoraphobia, do you?"

"Not at all. It's perfectly natural, a sort of nesting instinct."

"I've never heard of it before."

"It happens a lot in our family."

The two women glanced at each other and then away. They never again talked about how things were; both of them pretended that this was a normal child within Judith and that she was delighted with her pregnancy.

* * *

In the middle of October the new doctor came to the house. Zilla was there to let him in and act as chaperone and Judith was grateful. He was a strange man who made no attempt at any bedside manner. Very tall and thin, he examined her efficiently in complete silence without once looking her full in the face. She thought that he was in his early forties but it was difficult to be sure. When he had finished he took out his prescription pad and started writing.

"Is there something wrong?" queried Judith.

"You're rather anemic, but that's to be expected. Your blood pressure's very low, we'll have to keep a watch on it. At least you shouldn't have any of the problems associated with high blood pressure. All in all you're doing fine."

"I wish I didn't feel so tired all the time."

"Try not to worry about it, get plenty of rest. It's to be expected."

He was too glib, his words delivered without apparent thought.

"I'm even afraid to go outside the house. I become faint and giddy if I make the effort."

"Perfectly normal."

"To be expected?"

For the first time he smiled, a brief flash of even white teeth. "Exactly!"

He began to leave the room. "Your name?" called Judith. "I didn't catch your name."

"Franciscus. Dr. Piers Franciscus."

Judith looked carefully at him. "Do you live around here, doctor?"

"Not far away."

"But you aren't a local man? You're not from these parts?"

"No, Mrs. Farino, I'm from South Africa originally. Until next month then."

Another flash of teeth and he was gone.

When Zilla returned she found Judith highly agitated.

"He's one of you, isn't he? All that talk about private doctors, you've managed to find one of your own kind to attend me. What is he really? An engineer? An insurance salesman? Don't you care what happens to me?''

"Don't be foolish, your health is of paramount importance to Marc. Dr. Franciscus has an excellent reputation in all fields of gynecology.''

"But he is one of you?''

"He's from South Africa, if that's what you mean. I'll take the prescription to the chemist before I go. Mrs. Watson will bring you your lunch. Perhaps you might try getting up for the afternoon if you feel strong enough.''

"Wait," called Judith. "Don't go. There are things I want to ask you.'' The door closed firmly and she beat at the soft, feathered duvet in frustration.

That evening she was downstairs when Marc arrived home.

"How nice, to see you up and about! Feeling a bit better today?''

"Not particularly. I had a visit from the specialist.''

He hung his coat on the hook and glanced around for the children.

"Did you hear what I said, Marc?''

"Sure. Where are the boys?''

"In their rooms. Marc, you must talk to me. There's so much that I don't understand. I shall go mad if you persist in keeping secrets from me. I have a right to know.'' She sounded near to tears.

"There's no need to get upset. If you're that desperate then I'll talk to you tonight, as soon as we're alone.''

"You'll tell me everything?''

His eyes widened, his face open and without guile. "Naturally.''

She knew then that he wouldn't, not unless he was forced, but at least she would learn something.

"Tonight, then," she confirmed. He watched her thoughtfully as she walked away.

It was eight-thirty before they sat down in the study. Judith's face was strained with tension, Marc's an expressionless mask. He leaned back against the cushions.

"Now then, what exactly did you want to know?"

"I want to know what my child will be like. I want you to tell me all about your family."

He smiled. "It's difficult to know where to start. I told you that my father was a Cape colored, of Portuguese extraction. Well, by the time he was four or five he was far bigger and brighter than his seven-year-old sister and when another baby boy came along soon after that he too was unusually advanced in every way.

"When my father—his name was Carl—was twelve he got a girl pregnant. There was a lot of unpleasantness, the girl's father got killed, and in the end Carl and his brother Christian had to leave. I think their parents and grandparents realized that if they stayed, their precocity could only lead to even worse problems, and so they turned them out in order to survive themselves.

"Eventually, after God knows what experiences, they made their way to this country. When my father married at twenty he had already started his own grocery store, helped by his brother. My mother had three children; Saul, myself and finally Zilla. Each successive pregnancy left her more and more exhausted but Saul and I had a wonderful childhood. We all got on pretty well, we had some marvelous games with Zilla once she was on her feet." He smiled as he remembered it.

"I know about that," said Judith with disgust. "Zilla told me."

"Did she? How extraordinary!"

"It made me feel physically ill. It's the most unnatural thing I've ever heard of."

"To you perhaps, but it was perfectly normal for us. It was a mistake as it turned out because our mother caught us all in Saul's room and threw the biggest scene imaginable. She called us 'perverted animals' and said we shouldn't be allowed to grow up and breed. It was all very silly, but Saul allowed it to annoy him.

"She kept on and on at us, I think really she was using us to let her hatred of my father escape, but she wouldn't keep quiet and in the end Saul attacked her. I was sure he was going to kill her, which seemed quite the best solution, but then it went wrong. My father came home unexpectedly and walked into the middle of all this. He always carried a gun, probably a legacy from his early troubles, and he took it out immediately. He probably only meant to fire a warning shot over our heads, something like that, but it all got out of hand and Saul was shot. He died instantly."

"Your father shot him?"

"It was a mistake, a terrible accident. Once he realized what he'd done he simply turned the gun on himself and fired into his mouth. As you can imagine there was complete chaos after that. The house was full of neighbors, police and ambulance men. It was an overnight sensation. My mother told the police that Saul and my father had never got on—which was a complete lie—and that by the time the rest of us went into the bedroom the two of them were already dead. There was no reason to disbelieve her; they probably wrote my father off as an excitable foreigner.

"Mother sold the chain of shops and bought herself a big house with extensive grounds and there she's stayed ever since. She was quite happy really, she'd got rid of a husband she loathed and feared and a son whose very existence was anathema to her. I suppose she felt that in a large house she could forget all about me, and when I look back I rarely saw her. I had Zilla of course, but I was very lonely until I met Elizabeth."

"And then?"

Marc smiled. "Then it all changed. She was beautiful, so vivacious and cheerful. I was captivated. I spent months pursuing her and I learned a tremendous amount from her as I did so. I didn't realize that by doing this I was actually draining some of her vitality away, no one had explained that to me then. I don't think my mother ever fully understood that her husband and children were different, all part of a new race of human beings, a race which is a natural progression from human beings as you know them. She merely found us difficult and exhausting."

"You say 'part of' a new race. You mean there are others like you?"

Marc looked impatient. "Of course. There are small communities in every inhabited part of the globe. Nature is wise, we stand more chance of surviving that way. As I was saying, with my father and brother dead and my mother ignorant there was no one to explain to me about the damage we inflict on the people from whom we learn.''

''By the time we got married Elizabeth was already tiring easily, but we put it down to the excitement. I was worried when she didn't show any signs of picking up after a couple of weeks, but of course she couldn't. I was learning so much from her that I was tiring her at a tremendous rate. We had a fantastic sex life in those early days. Then—I can remember it so clearly—I suddenly found myself feeling quite differently about her. It was a Saturday night, and all the time I was watching her undress I could feel this suppressed rage simmering inside me. Not only rage, also a desire to take her by force. To throw her on the floor and force myself into her; I didn't want our usual loveplay, I wanted to violate her, show her that I was someone to be feared as well as admired.'' His voice faltered as he recalled the shock and fear in Elizabeth's eyes.

''I went ahead,'' he continued, ''and followed my instincts. In the middle of it all, above her cries and my sounds of triumph I suddenly knew that I was siring a son. That this was what lay behind it. I still loved her as much as I always thought, but my body knew what to do and this was a necessary part of our married life.''

''Poor Elizabeth,'' said Judith quietly, remembering the horror of her own wedding night.

''Yes, I'm afraid she took it very badly. In the end I had to send for my Uncle Christian. He tried to explain to her that it wasn't my fault, that it was an instinct more powerful than anything I had learned from ordinary people. She was only partly convinced. Then Zilla came to stay. She spent days talking to Elizabeth, I don't know everything that was said but slowly she came around.

''I expected her to shrink from me at first, but she didn't. She actually felt sorry for me, her tears were for me, not for herself. I thought how fortunate I was in my choice of wife, and I imagined us together as our children grew up, getting closer with the passing years.

''You see, I didn't know that she would die. I didn't

realize that each successive child drained her more. I imagined that the source was unlimited; that because she had knowledge she could impart it without diminishing herself, but it isn't like that. For some inexplicable reason we weaken normal human beings, it's as though we nourish ourselves on their life force. As we thrive so they sicken, and the process is irreversible.''

"But why didn't you leave her alone? Why did you have so many children?''

Marc looked thoughtfully at her. "You might understand better once you have your own child. She didn't want me to leave her alone. She understood the importance of a large family, and she was devoted to the boys. In the end she was as much one of us as any outsider can ever be. It wasn't even approaching death that distressed her, it was the thought of leaving us all.''

"I saw you crying in the garden once. Is Elizabeth buried there?''

He stared blankly at her and then gave a small yawn. "I don't think there's much point in telling you any more.''

"But you haven't explained anything yet. Why did I see Elizabeth? Why is the house hot at night? Tell me what happened to Felicity.''

He tilted his head. "Is that one of the children calling?''

"You know perfectly well it isn't. All right then, if you won't tell me any of that, at least tell me why you want so many children.''

"My dear Judith, haven't you worked that out for yourself? Our race will provide all the future world leaders. My children will have the key positions in this country; Prime Minister, Lord Chief Justice, Head of the Secret Service and so forth, there will be just one person behind them, holding the country in the palms of his hands.''

"You," said Judith flatly.

"Correct.''

"Is that what you want? Absolute power?''

"I must admit I'll enjoy it but I've worked hard at educating them; finding suitable mothers, teaching them to adapt. I think I'll have earned my reflected glory. We're meant to be the rulers; it's only society's aversion to anything remotely different from normal that's prevented us from thriving as we should, but we're growing fast now. A new species to supersede homo sapiens. You should feel proud to be involved at such a vital stage of our history."

"I'm afraid I'm not," said Judith. "Your lack of humanity, your disregard of anything decent or honorable, entirely negates your so-called gifts in other directions. You're just parasites, living off other people. Your world would be one of anarchy and violence."

"You're quite wrong, but I've no intention of having an argument with you. I've filled you in on background information so that you understand our child better when he's born, but I don't intend to discuss anything else. There's no need for you to know everything."

"You really do think of me as a second-class citizen don't you, Marc?"

"Not at all, my dear," and he flashed her one of his swift smiles.

"You despise women," she continued. "If you didn't you couldn't possibly treat Zilla so badly, or allow your sons to do the same things with Kara. You disgust me, you and the children."

"You'll get over it. Right now you're the most important person in this house, you ought to make the most of it!"

She stared at him. He looked so handsome and sure of himself. His life was going perfectly, and she hated herself for assisting him in any way.

"I don't feel proud of carrying your child," she said coldly.

"Wait until it's born. You'll feel quite differently then."

"I'm afraid I don't intend to allow that to happen."

With a quick movement she smashed her brandy glass against the edge of the coffee table and thrust the jagged piece of glass against her throat. There was a brief stinging sensation and then something warm and heavy began to trickle down her neck.

She heard Marc's exclamation and felt him pressing his hands against the wound, but she was too weak to struggle. She prayed fervently that she had been quick and accurate enough to ensure success. After all that she had heard, death

was the only course of action open to her, and she wel-
comed the encroaching oblivion.

She could hear them talking although she was unable to
open her eyes. Her eyelids felt heavy, leaden weights
beyond her control. She strained to hear what was being
said.

"Can we keep her like this right through until April?"
Marc was asking.

"As long as I'm careful there shouldn't be any problem.
It seems to me to be the only solution. How else can we be
sure she won't damage herself?"

Judith knew the second voice, but couldn't place it.

"I can see to all the nursing side of things," put in Zilla's
voice.

"That would be most helpful." The unknown person
sounded very grateful. "I'll call in after breakfast tomorrow
and give her another injection. You can see how it's done,
and that will enable you to give her the midday one
yourself."

"Thank you, doctor."

Immediately she heard that Judith placed the stranger. It
was the doctor, Piers Franciscus. All at once a hand was
placed on her forehead and she jumped with fright.

"You are awake then?" said Marc. "I rather thought you
were. Try to go to sleep again. Sleep is the thing you need
most at the moment." His voice was gentle and kind but she
was terrified and strained to open her eyes. It was impossible. She opened her mouth to speak, but no words came
out.

"You've had an injection, darling. You won't be able to
talk. Just go to sleep. I'm here, you're quite safe."

But she wasn't. She was trapped by people who cared
nothing for her except as the mother of a child they wanted.
Petrified with fear she found herself in desperate need of the
bathroom and she pushed feebly at the bed covers. She did
manage to sit up, but immediately the room whirled around
her and she fell back again. Unable to speak and communi-

cate her needs she lost consciousness again, even as she realized that she was soiling the bedding beneath her.

It was light when she next awoke and immediately she remembered what had happened to her earlier. To her relief she could open her eyes, and she glanced at the bedding. She was lying on clean linen and had on a clean nightdress. Relieved but humiliated she saw Zilla standing by the window.

"Zilla!" It came out as a faint croak, but her sister-in-law heard and came over to her at once.

"Judith! You're awake at last. I was quite worried about you."

"The bed. I made a mess last night."

"Don't worry, it wasn't your fault. Marc and I saw to everything."

Judith turned her head away.

"Don't get upset, Judith. We don't mind looking after you. You've got to rest, the doctor said so."

She knew very well what was really happening. They were keeping her a prisoner here in the bedroom so that she couldn't try and kill herself again. She put a hand to her throat and felt a large dressing.

"That was silly," reproved Zilla. "Now you'll have a scar for the rest of your life."

She didn't care; she wished bitterly that she had been successful. The door opened and Marc came in. His expression was serious until he saw Judith watching him, and then he smiled at her.

"You're awake! Would you like some breakfast?"

"No, thank you."

"I think you should. After all, it wouldn't be very pleasant to be force-fed by the doctor, would it?"

"All right then. Marc, you can't keep me in bed forever."

"I rather think we can. You haven't left us much choice after last night."

The morning dragged by until at midday the doctor arrived. Zilla left him alone with his patient.

"Now then, Mrs. Farino, I expect you'd like a nice long sleep again," he said as he undid his black case.

"I don't need to sleep, thank you. I need some exercise."

"That's right, plenty of sleep. Let's have your arm."

She pushed her arms behind her back and he stared at her. "Surely you're not going to be difficult? Remember how dependent you are upon us to keep things nice for you. I understand that even last night there was a small accident."

She hated him so much that she wanted to spit in his face, but fear stopped her. Fear of how he and Marc might retaliate. He reached for her arms again.

"Please don't," she said quickly. "I don't want to sleep. I don't like losing consciousness."

"There we are, in it goes!" He plunged the needle into her arm, and then smiled at her. "Good girl! I'll see you tomorrow."

She wanted to call him back, ask him what damage the drug would do to her, but before he was out of the door her tongue was swelling and she was unable to form the words. She began to feel sleepy and lay still, waiting to drift right off. She heard the door creak lightly, and her eyes flew open. Philip was creeping into the room. He stood by the bedside and stared down at her, his dark eyes cold with dislike.

"I know you can't talk," he said clearly, "and I'm glad. You can hear though, so from time to time I'll come and talk to you. I expect you'd like that."

She was hypnotized by his gaze. She didn't want him anywhere near her and struggled to tell him so. He smiled unpleasantly. "I thought you would! I'll come every day, will that please you?"

Against her will her eyes began to close. The thought of not being able to see what Philip was doing nearly unhinged her and she moaned aloud.

"I'll keep you up to date with the news," he said chattily. "That way you won't feel so out of things. And if you die—because you might, you see, the doctor isn't sure about the drugs—then I'll make sure you're buried near my mother and Felicity."

Her eyes opened. It was difficult to make out his features but she could see that he was still standing close to her, his arms folded casually over his chest.

"In the garden," he added. "That's where they are. Buried in the garden. I told Kara about her mother. Her mother's underneath the rhubarb. Where would you like to be put, I wonder?"

"Philip!"

Philip jumped in surprise. He hadn't heard his father come in.

"Yes?"

"What are you doing here?"

"I thought she might be lonely."

"She's meant to be sleeping. You can come and see her later."

Reluctantly Philip left his stepmother's side and Judith's dreams were full of Kara trailing leaves of rhubarb behind her around the house.

The days became a nightmare of drugged sleep and spells of semi-consciousness. It seemed that the doctor had no sooner given her one injection than Zilla was beside her administering another. She became so doped that it was impossible to eat even when she was awake: the sheer effort involved in handling the cutlery was too much for her.

After some time, she had no idea of the exact number of days, the injections were decreased. Now she had quite long spells of wakefulness, but there was always someone in the room with her, and she was kept too weak to leave the bed without assistance.

In the evenings, after tea, Marc would usually sit with her for a couple of hours. Because of the amount of time he had to spend with Judith there were often phone calls that he needed to make from home, and eventually he had an extension put into the bedroom. This gave Judith her first glimmer of hope. It provided her with a form of contact with the outside world.

One day, when she awoke from her morning sleep, she found herself alone. Her head ached, as it generally did these days, but her mind was clearer than of late. She guessed that someone had made a mistake with the drug, that she had woken earlier than usual and in a more alert state of mind. The telephone was on Marc's side of the bed. Judith glanced at it and then began to edge her way across the mattress. She was half-way there when she heard footsteps on the landing. Immediately she slumped down and closed her eyes.

Zilla came into the bedroom and looked at the bed. She was relieved to find Judith still sleeping but noticed that she had slipped off her pillows. She carefully lifted her sister-in-law up and then, because she was so obviously deeply unconscious, went back downstairs to go through the cabinets before making out the shopping list.

Judith's heart was pounding but at least she was alone again. Once more she inched her way towards the telephone. The bed seemed vast, the distance incredible, but finally her fingers fastened around the receiver and she slipped it from the cradle. It dangled on the wire, and for a moment she felt too weak to grasp it again. Then, terrified that someone might lift the downstairs receiver and realize the extension was off the hook, she willed herself to take hold of it.

Her fingers were reluctant to turn the dial; it took her so long that she felt certain she would be discovered, but at last she heard the familiar ringing tone.

"Hello?"

It was Sue's voice; she had remembered the number correctly. Tears of relief ran down her cheeks.

"Sue," she whispered. "It's me, Judith."

"Judith? Speak up, love, I can't hear you properly. What have you been doing lately? Whenever I ring up you're out. I thought perhaps you didn't want to speak to me."

"Sue, I'm in terrible trouble." Her voice was shaking; she was sure that she could hear footsteps on the stairs.

"What sort of trouble?"

"You must come around. Come and see me. Don't let them put you off. Please, Sue! You must help me!"

"Judith, what's wrong? You sound terrible. Are you ill?"

There was a crash as the bedroom door was flung open. Judith screamed and dropped the receiver as Zilla crossed the room with Philip close behind her. Zilla flushed with annoyance and replaced the receiver.

"That was very wrong of you, Judith," she said sternly. Judith stared helplessly at her. The entire episode had exhausted her and she was trembling from head to foot. Philip smiled at her obvious fear and distress.

"I heard the bell ting downstairs, didn't I, Auntie?"

"Yes, fortunately for us, you did. Did you reach anyone, Judith?"

She shook her head.

"Well, that's lucky. I shall have to tell Piers, and he'll probably increase the amount of drugs you have. It's a pity, but it's obvious you're not to be trusted."

Judith tried to moisten her dry lips. "How can you let them do this to me, Zilla? Haven't you any compassion?"

Zilla turned awkwardly away. "You stay here for now," she said to her nephew. Judith's heart sank. She didn't want Philip pouring more poison into her ears, but he was already pulling a stool close to her bed and Zilla quickly left the room. Judith stared after her, wondering how she could allow another woman to suffer without trying to help.

"She's glad you're drugged," said Philip bluntly. "It means Dad goes to her for sex. You didn't know about that, did you?"

"Yes," she said, pleased to disappoint him on at least this one point. She closed her eyes, but without the injection there was no chance of sleep. She hoped that Philip wouldn't know this and would keep silent.

"I know you're awake," he continued remorselessly. "I wonder what you think about all the time. Do you think about Sam at all?" Resolutely she kept her eyes closed; even if he hurt her she wasn't going to give him the satisfaction of knowing it.

"It was great fun," he went on, "watching that fat old dog gamboling about like a six-month-old puppy! We made him think he was one; he was so boring most of the time we thought it would be more fun. It was too, until his stupid old heart gave out."

He watched his stepmother and saw her face twist with grief. Encouraged he elaborated. "Animals hate us anyway. Even if I hadn't wrung that hamster's neck it would have died. We confuse them; they don't know if we're animals or humans!" and he laughed gleefully.

Judith opened her eyes and looked him straight in the face.

"You're animals," she said clearly. "All of you are animals."

She heard his sharp intake of breath, and knew that she had annoyed him.

"You'll be sorry for that," he hissed in her ear. "When you die I shall help Daddy cut you up, like we did Felicity. She was having a baby just like you, and then she spoiled it by killing herself. Daddy was livid, that's why he cut her up. She's improved the rhubarb a lot," he added thoughtfully.

Judith didn't want to hear any more. "If you don't go away, Philip, I shall tell your father that you're making me ill."

"I have to stay, you're not allowed to be left on your own."

"Then keep quiet."

"I hate you," he muttered, but after that there was silence.

Soon Zilla arrived with the inevitable needle and after that there were more hours of sleep. When she awoke it was dark, but she could hear voices in the hall. She stirred and Marc appeared beside her.

"You've got a visitor, Judith. Your friend Sue. She's very insistent upon seeing you. I imagine that you managed to contact her over the telephone?"

Judith nodded.

"I've told her that you're pregnant and have to remain in bed but she won't go away. Under the circumstances I've no choice but to let her up."

She was elated and hauled herself to a sitting position. Almost at once Sue came in, with Zilla behind her and all the children following. The boys made a semi-circle at the foot of the bed but Judith ignored them. She had never been so glad to see anyone and smiled in welcome.

"I came as quickly as I could, love. How are you?" asked Sue.

"I'm fine. I'd really rather you hadn't bothered."

Aghast her eyes flew to the children. Their faces were all fixed in a concentrated stare which they were directing at her. To their left stood Marc, and he too was watching Judith. She could no longer remember what she wanted to say. They were forcing words into her head, words that she desperately wanted to reject, but their strength was immense.

"But you called me earlier, begged me to come around. I've left Dave with the boys. I nearly brought the police with me, you sounded in such a state!"

"As you can see, I'm fine. You must have been the victim of a practical joke. I never called you."

Sue took a step towards her. "Of course you did! I do happen to know your voice."

"Have you been drinking?" asked Judith coldly. Sue went white and looked at Marc who smiled apologetically.

"I did warn you. This pregnancy seems to have unsettled her, she's not herself at all."

Sue frowned. "Shouldn't she have help? It doesn't seem right you having to look after her, and she looks terrible."

"Just push off and mind your own business," snapped Judith. Marc shrugged helplessly and escorted Sue to the bedroom door. She turned for a last look at her friend.

"Will she get over it, once the baby's born?"

"The doctors aren't sure. I'll let you know if there's any improvement. That is, if you'd like me to?"

Sue nodded. "I'm sorry I was so rude to you downstairs, but I imagined all sorts of horrible things."

"Don't worry; you acted in good faith, we all realize that."

As she left the boys broke their semi-circle and danced around the bed while Judith wept hopelessly.

"She's always crying," sneered Philip. "She's as bad as Mummy!"

There was the sound of a blow as Marc hit his son around the ear.

"Get back downstairs, and stop tormenting Judith. She needs peace and quiet. You want another brother, don't you?"

They all nodded.

"Off you go then." He walked over to the bed, ignoring Judith's glare of hatred.

"I'm sorry, darling, but we had no choice."

"I hope your clever doctor friend knows what he's doing. I feel so ill all the time now that I wouldn't be surprised if he killed me himself by accident. That really would be ironical, wouldn't it?"

"He won't," said Marc confidently; but as he looked at her thin, pale face and bloated body he wondered if his confidence was misplaced.

The weeks passed by. Philip spent hours crouched silently by his stepmother absorbing what he could in case she died giving birth. Every visit decreased her strength, and when Marc found out he repeated his instructions about leaving her alone, but Philip was not to be denied. Sometimes he would sit by her in the evenings and then she would find the room becoming so over-heated that she lay bathed in perspiration until he left. It was obvious now that at night the children absorbed most of their knowledge, and as a result gave off some form of heat that only dispersed in the morning. The more that she learned about them the more she hated them.

Some time after Christmas Marc came to see her at lunch time, such an unusual occurrence that she immediately suspected something was wrong. He held a paper in his hand and spread it out on the bed for her.

"Can you read that?" The print danced in front of her eyes and she shook her head. "I'll do it for you. It says, 'Local dentist killed by intruder.' I expect you know who the local dentist is?" Judith stared at him, her eyes full of horror, then slowly she nodded. "I thought you would, your great friend Osborn. He disturbed a burglar they think. Terrible times we live in!" With a smooth smile he refolded the paper and took it away with him, leaving Judith feeling completely alone.

Sue had been driven off and Mr. Osborn removed. There was no one else who could help her. It was probable, she thought, that they expected her to die in childbirth, and in her weakened state she decided that this was the best solution. They would never allow her out of the house again, and she could not possibly spend the rest of her life trapped within four walls surrounded by Philip and his brothers. Even now it was difficult to keep hold of her sanity.

The nightmare continued remorselessly. Her head ached continually and, despite the careful nursing, she developed bedsores. As a result, Marc would help her to walk around the room in the evenings, but she was scarcely aware of what was happening and longed for her bed again. She grew desperately thin, and this, coupled with the exceptionally distended abdomen, gave her a grotesque appearance that sickened Marc. There were moments, as he dragged her whimpering from the bed, when he wondered if they were doing the right thing. Perhaps it was morally wrong to abuse a woman to such an extent in order to produce another of their own species. The only possible justification would be the arrival of a perfect boy child, and as the time for the birth approached he found himself hoping desperately that this new child would be the best so far. If it were he felt that would excuse everything they had done.

He no longer thought of Judith as his wife; it was quite impossible to see any resemblance between the creature in the bed and the shy young woman he had first met. It also seemed unlikely that she would ever recover completely from all the treatment over the past months, and if the ordeal of giving birth was severe then he doubted if she would survive for very long. This was of great concern to him, as the child would need her badly at the start, but quite separate from this worry he found himself distressed on her own account, and he realized with a shock that—over the months—he had become quite fond of her.

Philip, watching his father's face from day to day, also came to this conclusion, and he hated Judith all the more for managing to work her way into Marc's affections. Just a few days before the child was due Philip came home from school and went straight into the master bedroom. His stepmother was lying staring blankly at the wall, her puffy hands resting outside the covers. She gave no indication that she knew he was there until he leaned over her, and then she winced and tried to edge away.

"You look terrible!" he exclaimed with mock solicitude.

"The baby will be born soon, did you know?" She didn't answer him. "Probably not,"he continued quickly, "you're almost feebleminded now, or so the doctor says." Her eyes darted towards him and there was a spark of hatred in them.

"I think you'll die soon, Judith. Try not to worry about it, it will be a relief for you, won't it?" Still she kept silent. "You needn't worry about leaving us," he continued chattily. "I'll bring you back to see us now and again." Judith's head turned slowly towards him, and at last he was pleased to see absolute terror on her features.

"You saw my mother that day in the pool, didn't you? Well, that's what it will be like for you. I've absorbed enough of you to be able to do it, and I'm sure you'd like to come back and visit us, see how we're all getting on. Why, I'll even let you see Daddy's new wife. I mean, he's bound to get another one and I expect you'd like to make sure he was happy with her! What fun it will be!" He chuckled and reached out to touch her.

As his hand approached her she gave one terrible scream and then groaned as a pain flicked through her stomach. Philip turned away and ran downstairs calling for his aunt as he went. He had heard all about the way the children were born, and he didn't want to stay around to see it.

When Zilla entered the bedroom Judith was turning restlessly on the pillows.

"It's time," said the older woman calmly. Judith stared at her, her eyes wide open.

"What is it?" asked Zilla.

"I'm afraid," she said softly.

"There's no need to be afraid. The doctor and Marc will be here all the time; they're quite used to this, nothing will go wrong."

"What happens?"

Zilla smiled encouragingly. "The usual things. First-stage contractions, second-stage contractions and then delivery. Try to relax, that will help you more than anything."

Alone again while the doctor and her husband were being summoned, Judith's mind raced frantically. They weren't telling her the truth, she was sure of that, which meant there was something terrible to hide. Her imagination began to work overtime, conjuring up horrific visions of her body splitting wide open to release this mutation into the world. She moved her head fretfully. If only she had a mother or sister to comfort her, but in that case she wouldn't be here. They had needed a woman alone.

As her fear increased she started to cry, and when Marc arrived he was horrified to discover how upset she was. Sitting down next to the bed he put his hands on either side of her face. Then he stared down at her, forcing tranquillity into her mind. Gradually her terror eased, her eyes flickered and she gave a yawn. Satisfied, he stood up and left her half-dozing.

The doctor arrived soon after that and the two men exchanged a few words before Marc left. Piers Franciscus checked his patient's heart and blood pressure and then settled down to wait.

Two hours later the first real pain struck her. It jabbed through her right side and with a cry she tried to double up. The doctor glanced at her and then went to the top of the stairs.

Philip was standing there.

"Go and fetch your father and aunt, tell them it's nearly time."

"Is she in pain? A lot of pain?"

An expression of distaste crossed the doctor's face. "Just do as I ask."

"OK. I only wondered."

In the bedroom Judith was gasping for breath. She had pain in her side and pains around her stomach; agonizing pains that followed hard one upon the other giving her no opportunity to recover. Ignoring her cries the doctor stripped the duvet from the bed and spread a large white sheet beneath her naked body.

She wanted to ask for a nightgown, something to protect her from complete exposure but the pain gave her no opportunity to speak. She was aware of Marc and Zilla joining the doctor and she tried to signal with her eyes to her husband but Marc was watching her body, not her face.

Zilla brought an armful of pillows to the bed and pushed them behind the panting woman.

"You'll manage better sitting up," she soothed, but all Judith wanted to do was curl into a ball to try and assuage the pain.

Marc quickly pulled her up, moving her without effort and she screamed as she saw the way the skin across her abdomen was rippling from side to side. The tissue beneath seemed to gather itself into excruciating knots of agony for a few moments and then spread out again—which didn't stop the pain but only altered the quality.

For the next hour her anguish continued unabated, until all that she was aware of was her suffering. The instructions she received, the words of comfort, none of them touched her. Her world consisted entirely of agony. Once, as Marc bathed her forehead and moistened her lips she managed to speak.

"Pain relievers," she gasped. "Let me have something."

"We can't, they harm the child. It won't be long now."

Giving another scream she clutched at the sheet beneath her and silently cursed the child.

By eight-thirty she was losing her grip on reality. She moaned and cried still, but more feebly and without making sense. She no longer recognized her husband; she babbled over her childhood and spoke as though her mother were in the room. Dr. Franciscus drew Marc to one side.

"The child's too big for her, I may have to operate."

"No! I forbid it. It's never successful."

"I know what I'm doing. We could lose them both if this goes on much longer."

Marc hesitated. Judith looked terrible. Her skin was gray and covered with a film of perspiration, her eyes sunken and her lips chewed to shreds. She looked like Elizabeth the day before she died. Even as he watched her eyes flew open and she gave a shriek of agony, her body gave a tremendous heave and a trickle of fluid ran down the inside of her legs.

"Thank God for that," muttered the doctor. "Hold her down, it's nearly here."

It took Marc and Zilla's combined strength to keep Judith's shoulders on the pillows as the doctor worked busily at his task. Her distorted body continued to convulse and her eyes were wide with pain and terror.

"It's nearly finished," murmured Marc. "Hold on just a few moments."

She was frantic in her distress and tried to speak but a final spasm surged through her and her mouth opened in a scream.

"*No*! I can't stand it, I can't..."

Her body was still, the convulsions ceased. For a moment she floated free, her body her own again. She had survived. Tears of gratitude fell from her eyes and she looked down the bed. She had seen births on television and at school in the sixth form, she knew what she ought to see, but it wasn't this.

Between her legs there was a large, transparent, glutinous bag which the doctor and Zilla were frantically trying to break open. They were tearing at it with their fingers, scrabbling around inside it, their arms covered with sticky membrane. Judith pressed her knuckles to her mouth watching in horror as they hurried to release this monstrosity that she had nurtured for nearly nine months.

"Got him!" exclaimed the doctor and he withdrew his hands. Judith tensed, then gave a gasp of amazement as he held aloft a beautifully formed, dark-haired baby boy who immediately gave a lusty shout as he waved one newly released fist in the air.

"Magnificent!" pronounced the doctor five minutes later after the child had been washed and dried. "The best yet, Marc. Take a look."

"What does he weigh?" asked Judith weakly.

"Twelve pounds, three ounces, which is why you had so much trouble. Never mind, I expect it was worth it in the end?"

"Let her hold him," said Marc and he placed the child in her arms.

His dark eyes were already wide open, his neat ears flat, and his soft, dark hair lay close to his head like a cap. His limbs were firm and strong, his skin the same light coffee color as his half-brothers'. He was beautiful and Judith put a finger to his fist and watched as he curled his own fingers around it without taking his gaze away from her.

Unaware of how the others were watching her she found herself automatically lifting the child and putting him to her breast where he fastened greedily upon the nipple and suckled contentedly.

"What shall we call him?" asked Marc quietly.

"Laurence. It was my father's name."

"Then Laurence it shall be."

They all cleared up quickly and silently and then left Judith alone with her child.

From the moment that he was born Laurence became the center of Judith's world. She was fiercely protective of him, and watched with hawk-like eyes when Zilla bathed him before Judith had regained enough strength to do it herself. She hated to see other people handling him, and the baby himself was only truly content when he was being nursed by his mother.

His dark eyes, so unexpected in a tiny baby, followed her everywhere and for hours he would lie on her lap, his gaze never moving from her face.

As soon as she was strong enough Judith took over every task. She played with him, bathed him, soothed him and suckled him, and he responded by growing at an incredible rate and behaving so perfectly that the rest of the household scarcely knew he was there.

Marc was delighted at her response to the child. He kept the other children away from her, and marveled at her return to health. As she crooned to Laurence and sighed with pleasure while he was at her breast, Marc admired his son from a distance, and carefully refrained from being in the least possessive. He wanted his wife to think of the child as hers; the way things were going the bonding would become unbreakable.

For Judith, life had never been as good. She found her love for Laurence so great that it was almost painful. She would talk to him for hours at a time, telling of her own childhood and her determination for him to have the most perfect and carefree upbringing any child had experienced. The rest of the household might just as well not have existed. There was only Judith and Laurence, and they were both safe and happy in their private cocoon of mutual love.

Zilla was surprised but delighted at the way things had worked out. "She's a born mother," she confessed to Marc. "I honestly thought that you'd made a mistake this time, but I was wrong. Congratulations!"

"I'm never wrong about such things. It's a sixth sense, I know as soon as I see a woman whether she'll prove suitable or not."

"Let's hope it continues." Zilla laughed.

"Of course it will. Why should anything change?"

Piers Franciscus agreed with him. He expressed great satisfaction with the way Judith had taken to motherhood, and by the time Laurence was four months old both he and Judith had been given clean bills of health.

One warm August morning Judith awoke to find the house unusually peaceful, and then she realized why. Zilla had offered to have the boys and Kara for a few days of their holiday, giving Marc and Judith some time alone with Laurence. Judith knew that wasn't the only reason. It was nearly time for her to conceive another child, and she was pleased. Her joy in their first son was so great that the thought of another brought nothing but delight.

Marc smiled at her as he set off for the office. "Have a good day. Don't overdo things, I thought we might have a small celebration tonight."

"Celebration?" She pretended innocence but her cheeks felt warm.

"Because the boys are away!"

"Of course! Until tonight." She stood on tiptoe and kissed him while Laurence crooned contentedly in her arms, one hand waving near his father who took it and solemnly shook it. With a final smile Marc left, anxious for the end of the day and the evening that lay ahead.

Mrs. Watson wasn't due until ten and so Judith sat down on a kitchen chair and unbuttoned her blouse. Laurence fastened greedily upon her left breast—he still preferred her milk to anything else he was offered. She closed her eyes and began to daydream, letting the familiar pleasure wash over her. It was another peaceful, fulfilling day.

The sudden tearing agony in her breast took her completely by surprise. She screamed and snatched Laurence away from the nipple, ignoring his howls of outrage. Quickly she glanced down at herself. There, directly above her left nipple was a small, red, puncture mark. As she watched a tiny bead of blood welled up, and immediately Laurence struggled frantically to return to the breast.

Shocked and bewildered Judith dabbed at the blood with a tissue and then sat Laurence on the table. She opened his mouth carefully, and then she saw it. One white, pointed tooth in the center of his top gum. For a moment longer she stared, and then with a cry of disgust she pushed fiercely at Laurence when he tried to crawl along the table towards her. He blinked in surprise but continued his steady crawl, the gold flecks in his eyes gleaming brightly.

Judith watched him with loathing. All the time memories were flooding back. Memories of the dentist, and of Marc's smile of satisfaction when he told her of his death. She recalled Sam and the way the children had treated him. Even more vividly she remembered her wedding night, and realized exactly what lay ahead of her tonight when Marc returned home. She would be forced once again through the same degrading ritual which had resulted in the birth of Laurence, the deceptively attractive mutation who even now was holding out his chubby arms to her.

She wondered how she could ever have worshipped him. Why had she felt that he was so special? Had she really been prepared to devote her life to bringing him up? Apparently, for reasons that were beyond her comprehension, she had. But no longer. Laurence, without knowing it, had destroyed the bond his father had worked so hard to build up. From the moment she saw her son's pointed, white tooth Judith knew the truth. Laurence was no different from the other boys. He wasn't her wonderful baby, he was one of them, another mutation.

She edged away from the table without taking her eyes off him. He had stopped trying to reach her now and was sitting placidly in the middle of the table with his eyes locked on to hers. Judith felt sick as she realized what she had to do. If Laurence lived she herself would be destroyed, just like Elizabeth. There was no choice, Laurence had to die.

As she came to her decision the baby's eyes changed. They widened, their expression no longer gentle and trusting. He looked like a cautious animal, unsure of his surroundings. Judith tried to keep her mind blank as she advanced towards him. She held out her arms and slowly he raised his, only to try ducking beneath her hands as they closed around his waist. He was too slow, and now she had him held fast.

Laurence knew he was trapped and his top lip curled back, revealing yet again that horribly white tooth gleaming in the red gum. His tiny hands flashed out and made contact with her eyes; despite the pain she kept her grip on him. He began to scream with fury, an awesome, primitive sound such as she had never heard.

All the terrible things that had happened to her, all the humiliations and the pain of the past year welled up in her. With a cry of rage she lifted him above her head and then slammed him down with all her force on to the hard kitchen tiles beneath her feet. He made no sound; he lay there limply like a doll, and although his eyes were open they held no expression.

Judith began to tremble. She knew that she had to turn Laurence over, and could imagine vividly what the back of his head must look like. The impact had been tremendous, his head would have caved in like an egg shell. Tentatively she crouched next to the tiny body and put her hands beneath it to roll him over.

Just as she made contact he gave a gurgle of delight, and pulling himself onto all fours scampered away behind one of the table legs.

Judith gave a whimper of fear. She looked at the spot where he had been lying, but there was no blood. The tiles were immaculate. By some miracle Laurence had remained unhurt.

All at once she remembered Piers. Philip had destroyed Piers by throwing him down the stairs. Laurence's luck

couldn't possibly hold for a second time. She forced a smile
to her lips.

"Laurence! Come to Mummy, darling. It's time to get
you changed." He remained crouched behind the table leg,
and she walked slowly around the table to fetch him. Once
again his hands flashed out at her, but this time she was
prepared and he didn't succeed in making contact.

She held him in a grip of iron and carried him purposefully up the stairs. She had no thought in her head beyond
destroying Laurence. She could not let him live. He was her
own abberation, nurtured by her both in the womb and after.
She had a responsibility to every normal person in existence, and she intended to carry it through to the end.

At the top of the stairs she paused and then turned.
Laurence twisted his head and spat furiously at her, spittle
landed on her cheek and he crowed with pleasure as it ran
slowly down to her chin. I'll kill you if it's the last thing I
do, she swore silently to herself. The four-month-old Laurence
opened his mouth. "Kill," he said clearly.

"That's right, Laurence," she crooned to him. "I'm
going to kill you, and there's nothing you can do about it."
He gave a small smile, and the hatred rose in her throat until
it threatened to choke her.

Abruptly she pulled her arms close to her chest and then
propelled him forward with every ounce of strength she
possessed.

She watched him fall and it was as though she were
seeing a slow-motion replay on the television. His body flew
through the air like a rugby ball, then fell against the bottom
banister rail before bouncing on to the hall floor.

For what seemed an eternity Judith remained standing at
the top of the stairs. She wasn't going to be caught out
again, although it was obvious that no normal child could
have survived such a fall, but this wasn't a normal child and
so she waited. Eventually, when there was no sign of
movement, not even the smallest twitch of a limb, she knew
that she was safe. Laurence had been destroyed in the same
way as Piers.

Elated she descended quickly. This time he was lying face
down, and she was relieved. She hadn't wanted to see the

expression on his face. Desperately she wondered what she should do with him. Finally she settled on putting him back in his cot and leaving the house immediately. Mrs. Watson would discover him when she arrived, and then it was up to her what she did.

Quickly she scooped him up. He was limp and his eyes were closed. Almost running now she sped up to his bedroom and lay him on his back in the cot. She pulled a light blanket up to his chin and gave him one final look. His eyelids sprung open and his penetrating stare reached out to her. "Boo!" he shrieked, and screamed with laughter as Judith jumped away, her mouth opening and shutting but no sounds emerging.

She was becoming hysterical now. All caution was thrown aside. There was one burning ambition in her and she had to fulfill it before anyone arrived home to stop her. It took all of her courage, but she made herself return to the cot and lift Laurence up. He didn't try to scratch her this time, he was strangely passive, but she was too far gone in her terror to realize the significance of this.

She would drown him, she decided, as she pushed his door closed behind them. That's how people disposed of unwanted animals, they drowned them. Well, she would drown Laurence, and there was even a pool in the garden for her convenience.

Out in the back garden she stumbled towards the poolside. She resolved to hold him beneath the water for thirty minutes. No matter how different he might be from other children there was no way on earth he would survive such a lengthy immersion. Laurence continued to stare at her. "Wet," he shouted triumphantly.

"That's right, you horrible creature, you're going to get wet. Very wet indeed."

"Mummy," he murmured. Judith shook her head. "I'm not! I'm not! I was your incubator, nothing more. You're not my son, you're an abomination, and you're going to die." He put a hand to her cheek and patted it softly. "Pretty!"

"Will you *stop it*!" she shrieked.

They had reached the edge of the pool. Judith sat down

and let her feet dangle in the water while Laurence wriggled furiously in her arms. Slowly she lowered him in, then gripped his shoulders ferociously as soon as his head was completely immersed.

"Die damn you! Hurry up and die!" He had become motionless the moment she put him in but she now knew this didn't mean anything. She simply had to sit it out for the next thirty minutes. She leaned over the water to see if any bubbles were rising to the surface, then felt a sudden sharp thrust between her shoulder blades. With a cry of alarm she released Laurence and toppled in to the pool herself. Sputtering she surfaced to find the pool surrounded by her stepsons. They were all there—Paul, Patrick, Philip and Michael.

Judith caught hold of the edge of the pool and hauled herself out. No one attempted to stop her, they were all content to watch. She glanced back at the water and saw Laurence splashing happily in the middle of the pool. He beamed at her, and his tooth glinted in the sunlight.

"Why aren't you at school?" she demanded, deciding to attack first.

"Laurence called us," said Paul softly. "We just walked out of our classes and came straight here. Did you really think you could kill him? You were wasting your time, we're indestructible."

"You most certainly are not. Piers was killed."

"He hadn't got his tooth when he died. Once we get our tooth then we're protected. It's a sign that we've absorbed sufficient nourishment and are fully formed."

"What are you going to do?" she whispered.

"Do?" said Philip arrogantly. "Why we're going to kill you, of course. You would have died eventually in any case, but now it's got to be today. That's why we're all here. It will be quicker with the five of us."

"Five?"

"Mummy!" called Laurence doggy-paddling his way to the side where Patrick carefully pulled him out and sat him down in the sun.

"That's right. Laurence will help most of all, because he's still got so much to learn."

Judith started to walk towards the house. The five boys turned their heads toward her and step by step she was forced to retrace the route until she was back by the poolside. She moved away from the water, convinced they intended to drown her. Patrick laughed. "Don't worry, we won't push you in, that would be a waste."

"A terrible waste," the others chanted, and they all laughed.

"Look, there's no way you're going to get away with this. Don't you think people might get suspicious?"

Philip looked smug. "I shall write a note in your hand-writing, saying that you can't cope with us and have gone away to think things over. It happens all the time these days; mothers walk out on their children and are never heard of again. You'll be a statistic, nothing more." He laughed.

Judith was shivering from her dip in the water, the sun seemed incapable of warming her. "What if you're wrong? What if they start digging up the garden to look for me?"

"It won't matter," explained Paul politely. "You see, there won't be much for them to find. Are we all ready?" and he looked at the circle his brothers had made around Judith, Laurence sitting between Philip and Michael, his eyes gleaming more brightly than ever before.

Judith knew they were all looking at her, and she stared defiantly back at Philip, determined not to let him witness her fear. His eyes were on her but unseeing, his vision turned in on himself. She glanced around the circle. All their faces held identical expressions. Slowly their images blurred, she was unable to keep them in focus and there was a terrible lethargy creeping over her.

Her legs buckled and she fell to the ground. The boys moved closer, pulling Laurence with them and lifting him up so that he—like them—could continue to stare in to her face.

Judith didn't know what was happening. Strange images flashed through her brain. Incidents of years past re-played themselves before her eyes. Games of chess at her primary school chess club; long nature walks, armed always with a sketch pad and charcoal, walks she had taken with her mother when she was no more than seven or eight. The scenes flashed by faster and faster. Her head felt light, stuffed with cotton wool as though it would burst open like a feather pillow, but it didn't. The visions slowed. She felt a hand hitting her hard between her shoulder blades, a huge hand and she coughed and gave a cry.

"That's it," said Paul. "The beginning. There's nothing more."

Judith lay still. Her head was no longer ready to burst, instead it seemed to be contracting. She tried to lift it off the concrete but her neck muscles were turned to jelly. Frantically she tried to move an arm, and then a leg, but the result was the same. She tried to remember where she was, what was happening, but her brain refused to function.

Her eyes saw the five handsome faces staring down at her, but she did not know them.

"You're dying," said Paul precisely, anxious that she should understand. "You've no memory left, we've taken it all, that's why you don't remember us. You won't live much longer. Perhaps five minutes, certainly not ten. We've absorbed your life essence you see, and all we leave is the shell. You can't see yourself, which is lucky for you, but when you are dead then we'll get you back and let you have a look. That's only fair, we think." The other heads nodded in unison.

She felt no pain, merely a piercing ache that started in her head and traveled the entire length of her body. A dull, throbbing ache such as is caused when a deeply embedded splinter is being pulled out. She had never experienced such bone-shattering weariness. A weakness of mind and body that made the simple act of drawing breath an unbearable struggle. She had heard Paul, but his words made little sense. She began to drift away from the ache, to float pleasantly above the ground. It was peaceful and she relaxed.

The final pain when it came nearly tore her apart. It spread its agonizing tentacles through every inch of her body, and she twisted and turned in grotesque contortions as though the boys were passing an electric current through her. The pain was so excruciating that it blocked her throat. She couldn't even cry out, but lay opening and closing her mouth and flopping helplessly at the boys' feet as they scrutinized her final death throes.

"She looks like that fish I caught in the canal once," said Philip casually. Paul and Patrick laughed. "Nearly over," he continued, kicking the limp, shrunken figure with his right foot. Judith's outstretched hand gave a final, convulsive twitch and was still. The boys looked at each other.

"I didn't get much," complained Patrick. "Did you, Paul?"

"Not a lot. How about you, Michael? Or you, Philip?" Both boys shook their heads. Laurence gurgled and clapped his hands together, his brothers stared at him. "He must have taken most of it. I suppose that's fair, he had the most to learn."

As they talked among themselves Paul remembered his promise.

"Before we get rid of this," he said, pointing casually to the rapidly shrinking corpse, "I promised she could come back and have a look."

Philip's face gleamed in anticipation. "Great. Right, concentrate everyone." They screwed up their eyes and concentrated.

Judith felt as though she was waking up from a deep sleep, but it took her a few moments to open her eyes. When she did she immediately saw her own body lying at her feet. At least, it was wearing her clothes, but it had shrunk to half her size and was decreasing even as she watched. It was a revolting husk of a human being, like a skin shed by a snake and left to shrivel and rot.

She shook her head. It wasn't the first time she'd had difficulty in shaking off a particularly bad dream.

The boys watched her materialize with interest. They were delighted at their success, she was the first person apart from their mother upon whom they had tried their skills, and it was working perfectly. Judith's eyes looked imploringly at them, and she tried to speak but no sound carried to the boys.

"You're dead," said Philip happily. "Dead as a dodo. That's your body lying there; revolting isn't it? It's because we sucked everything out of you, there's only skin and bones left, it makes disposal so much easier.''

Their hold on her was tenuous and from time to time she was scarcely visible. Patrick pulled Laurence around to stare at his mother, and at once her outline was sharper, every feature clear.

''Of course! He's got the most, so we'll need him when we want you for a chat. You'll like that, won't you? Knowing what we're up to, watching Father and his next wife. That's what our mother likes best of all.'' Philip's jubilation was immense, and he had a wonderful idea to make this the most perfect day of his life so far. He whispered to his three brothers who all nodded.

After five minutes they were successful. Another figure appeared beside Judith. A gaunt, haunted face whose features she knew so well. The boys clapped in delight while the two women stared first at the children and then at each other. Their eyes were filled with the awesome knowledge that they were no more than playthings in the hands of the children to whom they themselves had given birth.

Elizabeth stretched out a hand towards the newcomer, but before she could reach her the boys snapped their eyes shut and she disappeared. Judith felt tears in her eyes. She had so needed the woman's comfort. She waited for her release, and Paul knew what she wanted.

''Come with us,'' he said cheerfully, ''you can be a spectator at your own burial!''

The children made their way across the lush, green grass and stopped at the rhubarb. They surveyed it thoughtfully.

''It did jolly well on Felicity, and I like rhubarb. Let's put her there as well,'' said Patrick. The others agreed and, as Judith watched, Paul and Philip dragged her remains over the lawn and left them in a crumpled heap while they went to fetch a spade.

It was all over in ten minutes, and Philip trampled on the earth to make sure it was firm again. He turned to Judith with a smile.

''There you are. Didn't we make a nice job of it? We're hungry now. It's time for us to have lunch, then we'll go back to school.''

Judith felt hungry, horribly hungry. She couldn't believe it. Surely it wasn't possible to be dead and hungry? But it was. They had taken her knowledge, her experience, everything that was of use to them, but left her with her appetites untouched. It was the final diabolical twist to their revenge.

"Roast lamb," he said thoughtfully, "with roast potatoes and mint sauce. Delicious! I can hardly wait. Laurence, let her go." Baby Laurence turned his head towards the house, and slowly Judith vanished. Smiling to himself Philip went indoors, his half-brother in his arms.

EPILOGUE

Marc left the car in the front drive and made his way towards the back garden. He could hear the children playing, and by the sound of their laughter they were having a good time. He frowned to himself. Today they were supposed to be at their aunt's. He and Judith should be spending the night alone, and anticipation had been high in him all day.

"Hello!" he called as he entered by the side gate. "What are you all doing here? Where's Judith?"

The children went quiet. Paul and Philip stopped their game of badminton and stared at each other. Patrick and Michael stayed in the pool, treading water and watching their father closely. Kara was sitting on the poolside seat; she didn't turn to look at Marc but kept her eyes on the water.

"What's the matter? Is your aunt ill? Has something happened to her?"

Laurence was sitting on his usual tartan rug in the middle of the lawn, looking plump and content. As the silence continued he glanced around at his half-brothers and then, without any warning, pushed himself up onto his feet. For a moment he hesitated, unsure of his balance, then his confidence increased and he began to trot towards his father, waving his arms in the air and shouting happily.

As Marc stared thunderstruck at the incredible sight of a four-month-old baby virtually running Laurence came to an abrupt halt in front of his father and raised his glorious brown eyes to Marc's. He stretched out his chubby arms. "Carry!" he commanded.

Automatically Marc obeyed, his eyes still searching for Judith, and he grew more anxious with every moment that passed. He raised his voice. "Paul! What the hell's been going on here? Have you all been struck dumb or something? I want an answer." None of the children spoke. Laurence wound his arms tightly around Marc's neck. "Ooobarb!" He laughed, and pointed down the garden. "Mummy gone ooobarb!" Chuckling cheerfully he buried his soft, baby face in his father's neck.

Marc felt the hairs at the back of his head prickle with a terrible foreboding. With the exception of Laurence the children were still motionless, standing like statues in the sun-drenched garden. He opened his mouth to speak again; to shout at them, demanding the truth but before he could utter a single word they began to move.

Slowly, remorselessly, they advanced towards him. They were all smiling their charming smiles and Marc knew, knew with complete certainty, that one day soon it would be his turn.

They no longer needed him. He had done his job too well.